'What should we have done without you, Miss Travers?'

'You make too much of my part...' Elizabeth said, but then her breath caught as he moved towards her, looking down at her with such intent that she knew what he meant to do even before he reached out for her. 'Cavendish...'

His lips stopped her words. For a moment she stood stiffly within his arms, but then something opened up inside her and she melted into him, her warmth flooding through in the kiss she returned without restraint. In that moment Elizabeth forgot prudence, forgot her mama's teachings and her notions of propriety. She would at that second in time have granted him anything he asked of her and considered the world well lost for love.

Dear Reader

In the late eighteenth and early nineteenth century there was a passion for gothic novels. When huge old houses were lit by candlelight and there were none of today's modern conveniences, it must have been gorgeously frightening for society ladies to read of young girls cruelly locked away and at the mercy of evil men. How much more terrifying would it be for a young girl stolen from the bosom of a loving family to be forced to take part in a satanic ritual? And think of how her family must have suffered when she could not be found! But in the age of Romance there were at least three brave men willing to walk through hellfire for the sake of the women they loved.

This trilogy deals with the abduction of Miss Sarah Hunter and the search for her by her brother Charles, the Earl of Cavendish and John Elworthy. It begins with Elizabeth Travers and the Earl of Cavendish, and continues with Charles Hunter and Lady Arabella Marshall, ending in the last book with Sarah's own story.

The element of darkness is balanced by the thrill of romance, and I hope you will love reading these books as much as I enjoyed writing them for you.

Best wishes

Anne

AN IMPROPER COMPANION

Anne Herries

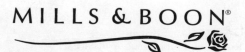

First published in Great Britain 2006
Large Print edition 2007
Harlequin Mills & Boon Limited,
Eton House, 18-24 Paradise Road, Richmond, Surrey TW9 1SR

© Anne Herries 2006

ISBN-13: 978 0 263 19388 6
ISBN-10:   0 263 19388 8

Set in Times Roman 15 on 17¾ pt.
42-0407-91567

Printed and bound in Great Britain
by Antony Rowe Ltd, Chippenham, Wiltshire

Anne Herries, winner of the Romantic Novelists' Association ROMANCE PRIZE 2004, lives in Cambridgeshire. She is fond of watching wildlife, and spoils the birds and squirrels that are frequent visitors to her garden. Anne loves to write about the beauty of nature, and sometimes puts a little into her books, although they are mostly about love and romance. She writes for her own enjoyment, and to give pleasure to her readers.

Recent novels by the same author:

THE ABDUCTED BRIDE
CAPTIVE OF THE HAREM
THE SHEIKH
A DAMNABLE ROGUE*
RANSOM BRIDE

Winner of the Romantic Novelists' Association ROMANCE PRIZE

and in the Regency series *The Steepwood Scandal*:

LORD RAVENSDEN'S MARRIAGE
COUNTERFEIT EARL

and in *The Elizabethan Season*:

LADY IN WAITING
THE ADVENTURER'S WIFE

and in *The Banewulf Dynasty*:

A PERFECT KNIGHT
A KNIGHT OF HONOUR
HER KNIGHT PROTECTOR

Prologue

'Charles!' The Earl of Cavendish stared at his friend in disbelief. He scarcely credited what he was being told. It was too shocking. 'You cannot truly believe that Sarah has been abducted?'

Charles Hunter raised his tortured gaze to meet Daniel's eyes. 'We found her shawl lying on the ground at the edge of the park, and it looked as if there might have been a scuffle—there were foot marks as well as those of carriage wheels.'

'But who—why?' Daniel looked at his friend in a puzzled manner. They had known each other all their lives and Sarah Hunter was almost like another sister to him. He was fond of her—had danced with her in the parlour of her home only a few days previously, helping to prepare her for her debut into society that summer. 'Surely…'

His voice fell away into shocked silence as he saw

the look of agony in Charles's face. 'I don't know, Daniel, I don't know,' Charles said, his voice breaking with emotion. 'Sarah is so young. She doesn't have a beau as far as I know. Besides, I should not have denied them the right to see each other if they had come to me. She must have known that—surely she knew? No, I do not believe she has run away from her family. I believe she has been stolen.'

Daniel was almost too stunned to answer. He was a man of the world and knew well that there were men evil enough to snatch young, pretty girls for their own foul uses. To think of Sarah, whom he thought little more than a child, in the power of such rogues was past bearing. It was no wonder that Charles looked so desperate and he could only imagine the agony that Sarah's mother must be enduring.

'You must not give up all hope,' he said, his hand on Charles's shoulder, his fingers gripping hard as the emotion turned in him. 'We shall find Sarah. I swear it, Charles. We shall not rest until she is found.'

'And what then?' Charles asked. 'What if she…?' He shook his head, unable to continue.

'We shall face that when we come to it,' Daniel said. 'Have faith, Charles. It may be that we shall find her safe…'

It was a nightmare! Surely she was having a bad dream? What was happening to her could not be real.

Her sight was blurred as she stared up at the creatures cavorting about her. She was lying on the ground on some kind of silken robe, but where was she? She seemed to be in a wood and it was dark save for the light of a full moon.

A figure was coming towards her. It loomed over her, looking huge to eyes clouded by the foul drugs they had given her and…it was a man and surely he was naked? What was happening? She must be dreaming! Yes, yes, it was simply a bad dream. She was in her own bed and quite safe. And yet through the fog that misted her senses, she dimly recalled being captured. She knew that she had been abducted, which meant that she was not dreaming and that she must wrench her mind from the cloud that bound it.

Giving a scream of terror, she forced herself to stand, her legs trembling with the effort. She had to get away from here or she was done for, she knew it instinctively although her mind was unable to function properly. She did not know how she had come here or who these people were. She only knew that she must run as fast as she could to escape them.

If they caught her, she would die…

Chapter One

Daniel Cavendish surveyed the room, his eyes dark and brooding as he watched the dancers enjoying themselves. Something was missing from his life and he did not know what it was—though he suspected that he still hankered after the adventure and danger of his army days. He had been forced to sell out when his father died, returning to take charge of the Cavendish estate. The past three years had been spent to good effect and his fortunes were now prospering—and yet he was restless. Sarah Hunter had been much on his mind of late, his failure to find her in all these months nagging at his conscience like a rat gnawing at the wainscot of a neglected manor house. Yet in the last few days information had come to them that had given him renewed hope.

'I think I shall go down to the country,' he said to the gentleman standing beside him. Where the Earl was tall, broad shouldered and dark haired, his friend was of a more slender build with soft fair hair that he now and then brushed back from his forehead. 'London has lost its attraction for me of late—and I want to see what I can discover of that other business.'

'Do you think that wise?' John Elworthy asked. 'Even if what we suspect is true, I do not see that there is much we can do about it. No lasting harm was caused to Maria, and as for Miss Hunter…' He shook his head sadly as another of their friends came up to them. 'Good evening, Robert. I did not think to see you here this evening.'

'I had nothing better to do,' Lord Young said and yawned behind his hand. Of the three he was the one most entitled to be classed as a dandy, his cravat so intricate and high that he could bend his head only with difficulty. 'It's dashed dull at the moment, don't you think?'

'Cavendish was saying as much,' John Elworthy told him. 'He has a mind to investigate that business with Maria…though, for myself, I think it may be dangerous to meddle in Forsythe's affairs.' Maria was the sister of his brother's wife, a young, pretty girl with a great deal of courage, who had recently beaten an attempt to abduct her.

'Nothing like a little danger to spice things up,' Lord Young said, a sparkle in his eyes. 'If you need any help,

I'm your man, Cavendish. I dare say Hilary would say as much if he were here. What do you plan to do?'

'Walk home with me, both of you,' the earl said. 'I do not wish to be overheard. I agree that this business is likely to involve some danger, but I think it must be attempted. Maria is a brave girl and the information she gave us helped me. I have begun to make fresh inquiries and I shall show you my agent's reports…'

'Don't mind if I do,' Lord Young replied. 'Coming, Elworthy? You may as well—there is nothing here to hold your attention.'

'True enough,' John agreed. 'Let us go then. I believe you are right, Cavendish. If we do nothing, Forsythe will be free to continue as he pleases. I do not know what I should have done if those rogues had succeeded in their foul intent.' The other gentlemen nodded agreement, for it was unthinkable.

They left Almack's together, deciding to walk back to Cavendish Place because it was a fine night, completely unaware that they were being followed at a discreet distance.

'My dear child,' Lady Wentworth said, feeling distressed as she looked at the girl's proud face and saw the underlying grief. 'You will surely not hire yourself out as a companion when I have told you that you may accompany me to Bath this autumn?

You know I love you as dearly as if you were my own daughter. Why will you not accept my offer to live with us at Worth Towers?'

'I cannot accept, ma'am,' Elizabeth Travers said, softening her denial with a smile. 'I am very fond of you and grateful for your kindness to Mama, Simon and me these past months since Papa's death. And after Mama's…' Her throat caught with tears that she refused to shed, for the loss of her mother was still raw and too painful to speak of. 'If you will have me, I shall stay with you whenever I am in need of a refuge, but I cannot be a burden to you. Lord Wentworth has kindly paid Simon's expenses so that he can stay on at Oxford until the end of the year, which was so generous that I shall be for ever in his debt. Besides, Lady Isadora is in need of a friend and I am delighted that she has sent for me.'

'But you do not know her,' Lady Wentworth protested. She was a small, plump lady with a kind heart and was genuinely fond of her late friend's daughter. 'And you could never be a burden to me, dear Elizabeth.'

'You are all kindness, ma'am,' Elizabeth said. 'But I have given my word and I believe you would not have me break it.'

'I suppose not, since it is given.' Lady Wentworth sighed. 'But you *will* promise to come to me should you be unhappy or in trouble?'

'Yes, indeed,' Elizabeth promised. She smiled at the lady who had been her mother's best friend for the past twenty years or more. 'I cannot think what Mama would have done without your help after Papa died, especially when we learned that he had lost the greater part of his estate to Sir Montague Forsythe in that infamous wager. Had you not supported us, allowing Mama to move into the dower house at Worth Park, I do not know what might have happened to us.' Tears stood in her eyes for the months that had passed since her father's death had been difficult and anxious, culminating in the illness and sudden demise of Lady Travers. 'I can never repay all you have done…'

'So foolish…' Lady Wentworth shook her head over the circumstance that had caused Sir Edwin Travers to hazard his estate on a horse race. Such tragic circumstances had resulted from that wager that it did not bear thinking of. 'Wentworth was inclined to discredit it, as you know. He could not believe that his old friend would do such a reckless thing, but he made inquiries and it seems that there were witnesses— and that your dear father may have been inebriated.'

'Yes, and that was very odd,' Elizabeth said, 'for Papa seldom drank to excess. Mama swore with her dying breath that he had been cheated, for she would not believe that he had been so careless of his family's well-being—and do you know, I think she was right.

I do not know how it came about, but Papa was not a careless man.'

'Indeed, that is Wentworth's opinion,' his lady said, 'but he was not able to shake the statement's of those witnesses—though, in truth, most were Sir Montague's cronies, but Mr Elworthy is an honest man. If it were not for his testimony, Wentworth would have contested the wager in court, but he respects Elworthy and says he would not lie.'

'Yes, I know.' Elizabeth frowned. It was only the testimony of Mr John Elworthy that had prevented her from asking their lawyer to fight Sir Montague Forsythe's claims against the estate, but Lord Wentworth had advised her against it, saying the little money they had left would otherwise be lost. Yet it had rankled with Elizabeth, for, like her mama, she had refused to believe that her father would do such a foolish thing as to bet everything they had on a horse race. 'I suppose we must accept it that Papa drank more than usual and threw everything away on a whim.'

'Sad as it is, that seems to be the case.' Lady Wentworth looked at her unhappily. 'Well, if you insist upon taking up this position, you will allow us to send you in our carriage, my dear. At least Lady Isadora will know that you have friends who care for you.'

'That is very kind and I shall not refuse,' Elizabeth said. She was glad of the offer; though she still had a little money at her disposal, it was not much above fifty pounds. She had given the better part of what they had to her brother Simon. It was Simon's fate she worried about more than her own: he had naturally expected to inherit their father's estate and would now have to make his own way in the world, which would not be easy for a young man of his volatile nature. She at least had been fortunate enough to be offered a position with a lady in Yorkshire—a lady of whom Elizabeth's mother had spoken warmly in the past.

'This Lady Isadora…' Lady Wentworth screwed up her brow in thought. 'Your mother's old friend, you said? What is her family, Elizabeth?'

'She is the late Earl of Cavendish's widow and the daughter of a marquis,' Elizabeth said with a slight frown. 'I have only met her once, when she called to see Mama on her way to stay with her husband's uncle—the Marquis of Brandon. She stayed with us one night and I remember that she was a kind, sweet-faced lady. She gave me a doll, and Simon five guineas.'

'A generous lady, then.' Lady Wentworth nodded approvingly. 'And what are her terms, my dear? You must not mind me asking, for I would not have your good nature taken advantage of and some people appear kinder than they truly are.'

'Lady Isadora asked me if I would prefer a dress allowance or a wage and I asked for an allowance.'

Elizabeth flushed. 'Mama would have been very shocked had she known I was to seek employment as a companion, and I think she would have preferred me to take the allowance.'

'If you would but let me…' Lady Wentworth sighed and gave up as she saw the girl's look. 'I shall say no more, dearest, but remember that you always have a home here.'

'Yes, of course. You are always so kind.' Elizabeth kissed her cheek and rose to take her leave. She still had some packing to do and there were other friends she should bid farewell that afternoon. 'I shall write to you as often as I can and let you know how I go on.'

Elizabeth was thoughtful as she walked towards the dower house that had been her home for the better part of the year. She was thankful for Lady Isadora's letter that had come just in time, because she had been on the point of approaching an agency to help her seek out the right kind of employment. She had secretly been examining the ladies' magazines that Lady Wentworth was so kind as to pass on for a suitable post these past weeks. Her situation had become more urgent since her mother's death. Lady Travers had been in possession of a small jointure, which remained hers despite the loss of the estate. However, it ceased on her death, leaving her children with almost nothing other than what she had managed to save. Even when her mother was alive, Elizabeth had believed she must look for employment and now she had no choice. Or at least none that she felt able to accept.

Elizabeth had known that her mother would find it painful to see her daughter take employment, but thought that she must have mentioned the possibility in her letters to Lady Isadora. Of course, they had not expected that Elizabeth would so soon be orphaned, for Lady Travers had not been particularly delicate, but she had taken a sudden virulent fever and perhaps had lacked the desire to live. Elizabeth had written to her mother's old friend to tell her the news and some weeks later received an offer to become Lady Isadora's companion.

Elizabeth had at first been afraid that she was being offered charity and had delayed answering for nearly a month, but Lady Isadora's second letter had made it clear that she was truly in need of a companion. She had been ill this past winter and was unable to walk far without assistance. She needed someone to run her errands and read to her, because some days she was confined to her bed. Her letter had touched Elizabeth's heart, and she realised that it was exactly the kind of position that would best suit her. Being so recently bereaved, she would not feel comfortable in a household where there was a constant stream of guests, and it appeared that Lady Isadora lived alone, rarely receiving visits from her family. It was exactly as Elizabeth had lived with her mother these past months—they had seldom gone into company after Sir Edwin's death.

Lady Wentworth had been all that was kind, but Elizabeth had felt that she was being smothered by her friend's good nature. Besides, to remain so near the estate that had been so cruelly taken from them was a source of continued grief. Had it not been for that wicked wager—which Elizabeth felt must somehow have been forced on her dear papa—he and Lady Travers might both be still be alive.

How could he have done such a foolish thing? Elizabeth had puzzled over it again and again, but she was no nearer to finding a solution. Simon had told her that he intended to get to the bottom of things, but she had begged him to be careful. He was nineteen years old, four years younger than Elizabeth, and inclined to be hot headed.

'Father was cheated,' her brother had told her angrily before he rode back to Oxford after her mother's funeral. 'I know it, Bethy, and one day I shall prove it and claim back my inheritance.'

'I do not deny that I think the circumstances strange,' Elizabeth said. 'But there were witnesses and—'

'Only one that was not in the palm of that rogue's hand,' Simon Travers said. 'I have written to Elworthy twice and asked to meet, but he has refused. If there were not some havey-cavey business, he would surely have agreed. Why should he not?'

Elizabeth had found it impossible to give him a reason for Mr Elworthy's behaviour, which seemed odd to her—as, indeed, were all the circumstances of the affair. She could not blame her brother for wishing to investigate further, as she might herself had she been in his shoes, but she did fear that he might land himself in some trouble. She could not bear it if Simon were to end up putting a pistol to his head as their father had done the day after the disastrous wager.

It had taken Lord Wentworth's word to persuade her that Papa had not been murdered. Even now, she still had a nightmare in which her father appeared to her and demanded justice for his wrongful demise.

Sighing, Elizabeth pushed the disturbing thoughts away from her. There was nothing to be gained from dwelling on the past—she could not bring back her beloved parents. She must make up her mind to do the best she could for her future employer and simply pray that Simon would stay out of trouble.

'But that is shameful of you, Mama,' the Earl of Cavendish said, a wicked sparkle in his blue eyes. He was glad that he had decided to come down, for it was exactly what he needed to sweep away his growing sense of restlessness. His mother was up to mischief and his good humour was restored, his quest to find Sarah banished temporarily from his mind. 'To lure the girl here under false pretences that way…' His gaze swept over her fashionable toilette, taking in her elegant gown and the lustre of eyes that were almost a mirror image of his own. 'I will own that it is almost two months since I last visited you, but…'

His mama gave a little cough and lay back against the piles of silken cushions on her elegant daybed. 'Have you no pity for your poor mother, Daniel? I have had a terrible chill and my doctor absolutely forbade me to leave my room for ten days. I was confined to bed for five. You cannot imagine how tedious that was, dearest—especially as your sister is increasing and cannot come to me. I was lonely. Besides…' her eyes twinkled with mischief '…in her last letter, my dear Serena told me that Elizabeth is very proud—a lady of character. She suspected that the girl intended to find some employment and of course it upset her dreadfully…poor Serena. It is all the fault of that scoundrel Sir Montague Forsythe, of course. He cheated her poor husband out of his estate and in desperation the foolish man put a pistol to his head.'

'Yes…' The earl's eyes narrowed thoughtfully. 'Had Elworthy not witnessed the scene I might have doubted

the wager ever took place—but he swears it was as
Forsythe says and I have never known John to lie.'

'No, indeed. When Serena told me that your friend
was the one reliable witness my heart sank, Daniel,
for I could not doubt him. He would never lie for anyone—and especially a man he despises.'

'That has been my experience, though he says he
was not one of their party, merely an observer.' The
earl's face was thoughtful, and there was something
in his eyes that might have led the men he had fought
with in Spain some years earlier to suspect that he was
not being as open as he might be on the subject of Sir
Montague Forsythe.

'Well, we must suppose it was an aberration,' Lady
Isadora said and sighed. 'But I have been determined
to do something for the family since I learned of their
trouble. I would have offered Serena a home here had
the Wentworths not done so before me—but I shall
do something for the boy and I am determined to find
Elizabeth a husband.'

'But did I not hear someone say that she is plain?'
The earl raised his brows. 'I know she did not take at
her first Season and there was never another. I do not
remember her for I was away serving with the army,
but I am sure someone told me—it may have been
you, Mama.'

'I did not see her when she had that Season,' Lady

Isadora said, wrinkling her brow. 'I recall her as a thin child, tall for her age, with a dark complexion and her hair in pigtails. Of course, she will have altered a great deal since then. I blame myself for not visiting the family more often. I always meant to, but somehow there was always something to prevent it. Your papa did not care for visiting and then I was busy with Melanie's wedding, and then your father was ill…' Lady Isadora sighed. She had been very fond of her husband, though it had not been a love match at the start. 'After he died, I did not wish to visit anyone for a long time. I might have gone when Sir Edwin died, but Melanie was expecting her first child and—'

'And now she is expecting her second,' the earl said with a rueful look. 'I dare say Rossleigh is delighted, though how he bears with her temper I do not know.'

Lady Isadora laughed wryly. 'Yes, well, I admit that your sister gets a trifle irritable when increasing, but it is a most uncomfortable time for ladies, Daniel.'

'Yes, I dare say,' the earl said and smiled at her. 'But we digress, Mama. You have lured Miss Travers here under false pretences. How do you know that she will not simply turn tail and go home again once she realises that you are not the invalid she imagines?'

'I am confident that she will not desert me when she realises that I need her.' Lady Isadora saw the challenge in his eyes. 'Well, I do need companionship now that Miss Ridley has left me, Daniel.'

'You know full well that she went reluctantly to nurse her ailing mother, and that she may wish to return if anything happens in that quarter —which it may well do, Mrs Ridley being past seventy.'

'Yes, and of course I shall take her back—how could I not?' Lady Isadora said. 'But sometimes I do long for young company, Daniel—and if my sweet Jane had not died of a fever when she was but a child, I should have been making plans to bring her out this year, you know.'

The earl nodded—he was aware that his mother had never quite recovered from the loss of her youngest child, and because of that made allowances for her. 'Supposing Miss Travers does not wish to be brought out, Mama? She is, after all, grieving for the loss of both her parents.'

'I do not mean to rush her up to town. I would not be so insensitive. However, once she has learned to know and like me, I shall suggest a visit to Brighton for my health. The sea air does me good, you know. I am not looking for a title for Elizabeth, dearest. I shall be quite content with a pleasant gentleman of modest fortune. It is merely that I know Serena would not have wanted her daughter to work for a living.'

'Well, you must do just as you wish,' the earl said,

giving his mother a warm smile. Although they did not live in each other's pockets there had always been a dccp affcction between them. 'But what is it that you wish me to do for you, Mama?'

'I shall entertain only a few of my neighbours for the next few weeks,' Lady Isadora said. 'We must be quiet at first until Elizabeth recovers her spirits, but…I wondered if you might bring a few of your friends to visit next month…'

'And whom had you in mind?' the earl asked, a militant sparkle in his eyes. 'I am not sure that any of my particular friends is likely to be interested in a plain spinster past the first blush of youth—especially if she has no fortune to recommend her.'

'But I intend to repair her fortune. Your father was generous to me, Daniel—and I have not touched the twenty thousand pounds my father left me. I thought I might settle ten thousand on her.'

'Indeed?' The earl raised his brows. 'That is generous, Mama. I dare say you may find someone willing to take a plain bride for such a sum—though I am not sure you would care for Winchester or Ravenshead.'

'Those fortune hunters?' Lady Isadora shook her head. 'No, indeed, they will not do for Elizabeth—but I rely on you to produce one or two others who might.'

'Mama…' Her son eyed her warily. 'Supposing

Miss Travers does not want to be married off to one of my friends?'

'Well, I am not saying she must, Daniel. Do not be so obstructive! I only wish her to have some acquaintance when we finally go into company.'

'You are a devious schemer,' the earl said, and laughed. She had managed to banish his fit of the blue devils. 'When does Miss Travers arrive?'

'She should be here by the end of the week—why?'

'I think that I shall stay and meet her,' the earl said. 'If I am expected to present the sacrificial lamb, then I should at least have some idea of what she looks like…'

Lady Isadora was careful not to allow her complacency to show. It suited her very well that her beloved son should remain at Cavendish Hall for a few days yet. Not that she would do anything to influence him, of course, but at the age of five and thirty it was time that the Earl of Cavendish began to think of taking a wife—and why not a girl of good breeding and character, even if she were a little plain? She had it on Serena's authority that Elizabeth would make a very good wife for any gentleman and, after all, Cavendish could keep his mistress if he chose. A girl of Elizabeth's breeding would very likely be pleased for him to visit her now and then, and actually prefer a country life once she had her children to love.

* * *

'You had plenty of warning that I would need two rooms for the night.' Elizabeth glared at the innkeeper He towered above her, a large, ruddy-faced man. His very size made him a challenge for she was forced to crane her neck to look up at him, and he might have knocked her to the ground with very little effort. However, his bull neck was flushed red and he stared at her uncomfortably, clearly in awe of the young woman who was very determinedly remonstrating with him.

'I'm sorry, miss, for I dunno how the mistake was made—and there's little I can do about it now, for the gentleman has taken the room.'

'Oh, well, I suppose there is no help for it. Have you a truckle bed for my maid to sleep in?' She saw the denial in his face. 'You do not expect us to sleep in the same bed?'

She saw that he did and sighed inwardly. Mary was a large girl and she snored. Elizabeth knew that for a fact, because she had fallen asleep in the carriage and after some half an hour or more she had been forced to wake the girl up.

She turned back Mary, who had lingered behind her, making faces at the young lad who was carrying tankards of ale through to a private parlour.

'Come along, Mary,' she said, just as the door of the private parlour opened and two gentlemen came out.

'It seems that the landlord has let one of our rooms to someone else, which means that you will have to sleep in my bed.'

'But I snore, miss,' Mary said looking as alarmed as Elizabeth felt. ''Tain't right you should have to share with me. Tell him as you want the rooms you sent for, miss.'

'I have already done so,' Elizabeth said. 'Unfortunately, there is nothing we can do. You must make up your mind to it, Mary.'

'But I kick, miss. Leastways, my sister allus said as I did when we were children.'

'Come along, Mary. I have told you, the room is let and we must make the best of things.'

'Excuse me, ma'am.' One of the two gentlemen from the parlour came towards her. 'I could not help overhearing your maid. I think I may have taken one of your rooms. Please forgive me for any inconvenience. I shall have the landlord move my things immediately.'

'There ain't no more rooms, Mr Elworthy,' the landlord objected. 'You'll have to sleep with the other gentleman or over the stables.'

'I shall be quite happy with the stables,' John Elworthy said and smiled at Elizabeth. 'I think that perhaps I have the best of the two rooms. If you would care to sit in the parlour for a few minutes, I am sure the landlord can make all right. Perhaps you wish to take supper?'

'I had thought the parlour would be ours,' Elizabeth said. She had stiffened at the mention of his name and did not wish to be obliged to him, for she could not help wondering if he were the same Mr Elworthy who had been a witness to her father's ruin. 'But I believe we shall do well enough in our rooms—if the landlord would be good enough to send us some supper up?'

'Yes, of course, miss. Just you wait in the parlour for a moment or two and my wife will fetch you as soon as maybe.'

'I would give the parlour up to you,' John Elworthy said and glanced awkwardly towards the stairs, up which the second gentleman had disappeared. 'However, Sir Montague has bespoken his supper there and I fear he would not accept a move to the taproom.'

'You are here with that man?' Elizabeth looked at him in horror. 'If he is using the parlour, then I shall not set foot in it. Indeed, I do not think I can stay here at all this night…'

She turned to leave, but Mr Elworthy caught her arm urgently. 'You know something of Sir Montague Forsythe?'

Elizabeth looked back at him, her face pale. 'He— and I think perhaps you in part, sir—were responsible for my father's ruin and his death.'

It was Mr Elworthy's turn to look shocked. 'Then you must be…'

'Yes, sir. I am Elizabeth Travers.' Her eyes were bright with a mixture of anger and accusation as she looked at him. 'I had not thought you such a close friend of Sir Montague, but since you are travelling together—'

'Indeed, Miss Travers, you wrong me.' John Elworthy hesitated, and then, 'Would you do me the honour of stepping into the parlour for one moment? I have something I would wish to say to you in private.'

Elizabeth was inclined to refuse, and yet he seemed a steady, pleasant man, not handsome by any means, but with an attractive manner. And of course this was the opportunity her brother had sought and been refused. She inclined her head and went in front of him into the parlour, leaving Mary to wait for her in the hallway.

'Well, sir—what have you to say to me?'

'Firstly, I wish to say that I was never more shocked in my life than when I heard what had happened to your father, Miss Travers. I knew him only slightly, but had not thought him a man to gamble so carelessly. Nor did I expect that he would—' He shook his head and looked grave. 'But I did see him in the company of Sir Montague and I happened to hear the wager he made on that horse race, for I was standing next to their party. I would say that Sir Edwin had been drinking unwisely and that he spoke recklessly.'

'You were standing next to Papa when he made the wager?'

'Yes, I was. I thought it foolish, but it was not my affair. I wish now that I had remonstrated with him, but of course I could not—a wager is, after all, a matter of honour between gentlemen and once accepted cannot be taken back.'

'But if Papa was drunk…'

'I agree that no true gentleman would have accepted such a wager—but I fear that Sir Montague is not of such nice scruples.'

'No, indeed, for we were given only two weeks to leave our home and we were not allowed any time to grieve.'

'That was wicked indeed.' Mr Elworthy looked distressed at the news of how harshly they had been treated. 'He should be ashamed of himself!'

'I had not thought you a friend to Sir Montague, sir? Lord Wentworth told me that your word was to be trusted.'

John Elworthy met the angry sparkle of her eyes. Miss Travers was a tall girl, attractive rather than pretty in his opinion, her figure shapely, her dark hair peeping beneath the brim of her bonnet. However, her eyes were lustrous and expressive and just now held a challenge that had to be answered. He could not tell her the truth, of course—which was that he had deliberately followed Sir Montague in order to have what seemed a chance meeting.

'We travelled here independently. We are polite to one another socially—our estates are no more than twenty miles apart—but I have never been more than an acquaintance, I assure you. I hope you will believe me?'

'Yes, I must do so since you tell me as a gentleman,' Elizabeth said. 'I have always believed there was some mystery in this matter of the wager, but—' She broke off as the parlour door opened and another gentleman came in. He was in his middle years, a tall, heavy-boned man with a ravaged complexion and a long nose. Knowing that he must be the man who had, she still believed, in some way cheated her father, she gave Mr Elworthy a speaking look and left the room immediately.

As she went out into the hall, the landlord came to tell her that her room was now ready, and Mary beckoned urgently from the top of the stairs. Elizabeth went straight up, her head held proudly as she fought the rush of anger that had come over her as her father's murderer entered the parlour. Nothing could alter the fact that he had caused her father's death by taking that infamous wager.

'We're side by side, miss,' Mary told her. 'I shall be able to hear you if you call me in the night.'

Elizabeth doubted that, for the girl slept like one of the dead, but she smiled and nodded. She had not wanted to bring Mary at all, but Lady Wentworth had insisted that she ought not to travel alone, because it would be necessary to stop at an inn for one night on the way.

'I do not think that likely,' Elizabeth told her. 'I intend to lock my door when I retire and I should advise you to do the same. I will require your help to unpack my things,' Elizabeth added. 'But I shall not need your services again this evening.'

After Mary had unpacked she left the room. Elizabeth took off her bonnet and travelling cape, laying them down on the stool at the foot of the bed. At that moment there was a knock at the door, and then the landlady's wife entered with a tray containing a dish of cold meat, pickles and some bread and butter together with a glass of ale, a jug of water beside it.

'You said as you wanted a light meal, miss?'

'Yes, thank you, that will do very well,' Elizabeth said. She might have wished for a cup of tea, but doubted that it would be worth drinking had she ordered it.

After the woman had left, she ate a little of the bread, with some butter. It was fresh and wholesome. Elizabeth had no appetite for the meat or pickle, and drank only a mouthful or two of the strong ale.

It was still light as she looked out of her window, and she felt restless, disinclined for sleep. Yet she felt it might not be prudent to go downstairs again, especially as Sir Montague was staying at the same inn. He probably had no idea of who she was—unless Mr Elworthy had told him after she left the room, of course—but she had no wish to meet him.

At least there was a decent supply of candles in her room, which meant she might read for a while before she slept. She would be glad to reach her journey's end, she thought, for it had been tedious with only Mary for company. How different it might have been if her dear mama had been alive.

Elizabeth pulled a wry face. It was time to start thinking of the future—even though there was little to cheer her in that if the truth were faced. She must be at the beck and call of her employer, and though she believed that would be an easy task in Lady Isadora's case, she might not always be in that lady's service.

Sometimes, Elizabeth wondered what her life might have been had she accepted one of the three proposals she had received when she was nineteen. She had not been universally popular during her Season, but she had attracted some admirers. However, she had not felt that she wished to marry any of them, and her mother had told her that she should wait, that the right man was bound to come along. They had spoken of giving her another Season, but somehow it had not happened. Her father had been unwell one year, and then he had seemed to be anxious about his estate, and things had drifted—until he had died and the estate was no longer theirs.

No, she would not have wanted to marry any of the gentlemen who had asked her, Elizabeth decided as she began to brush her hair. In the soft candlelight her skin looked creamy and her hair had a reddish tint. Her features were perhaps a little plainer than was required for true beauty, but her eyes were remarkable. However, she saw none of this, for she was not in the habit of noticing her own appearance, except to make sure that her hair was tidy and her gown clean and respectable. She had gone into company very seldom these past two years, and had long ago given up hope of marriage. The best that might come her way now was to be an aunt to her brother's children should he find himself able to take a wife.

Elizabeth read her book, which was a slender volume of poems that had come from her father's library, and was one of the few items that she had managed to bring away with her. She and her mother had been told they might take only personal possessions, and the book had been amongst her things for she often read at night. Lady Travers had taken a few pieces of silver, which had been personal gifts to her, but all else was denied them. Those silver items remained at Worth Towers, for Elizabeth believed they might be sold for a few guineas, and her brother would have need of money when he came down from Oxford if he were to have time to look about him for a suitable position.

Somehow she could not see Simon as a lowly clerk, but it would not be easy to find a post as an estate manager. Perhaps she would talk to him when he came down, try to discover what he would truly wish to do if he had the choice.

'Oh, Papa,' Elizabeth murmured as she got into bed. 'I do wish you had not made that wager…'

Elizabeth partook of a breakfast of bread and honey in her room the next morning. When she went downstairs she looked for Mr Elworthy, but saw nothing of him. On inquiry, she was told that both gentlemen had departed some minutes earlier. For a moment she regretted that she had not taken the chance to question him further about what he had seen, but supposed that he had told her all he could about her father's behaviour. It would simply have to remain a mystery, for she had woken with a new determination to put the past behind her.

Mary did not make the mistake of oversleeping, so they were able to leave the inn in good time. Elizabeth had asked the innkeeper's wife for a basket of provisions, and they ate a picnic in the carriage, stopping only once at a post house to change the horses, which meant that they approached Cavendish Hall at just before three that same afternoon.

Elizabeth craned to catch a glimpse of the house as the carriage drove up to the front entrance, feeling pleased as she saw that it was not a huge, ancient mansion, but a pleasant country home. She would guess that there were no more than ten or twelve bedrooms, and it had the look of a substantial building put up in the last century with long windows and a good slate roof. In fact, it was much like her father's house, and she immediately felt that she would be at ease here.

'You'll be all right 'ere, miss,' Mary gave her opinion as the door opened and an obliging footman helped them both down from the carriage. 'I reckon as it ain't much bigger than Worth House.'

'No, that is very true,' Elizabeth agreed. 'And very pretty. Look at those roses growing against that wall.'

'That'll be south facing, mark my words,' Mary said. 'If your room looks out this way it will be warm even in winter, miss.'

'I dare say the family has the front-facing rooms,' Elizabeth said. She glanced up at the windows and glimpsed a female figure clothed in a gown of pale peach for a moment, and then another woman, dressed more soberly in grey, came out of the house. She smiled as she approached them.

'Miss Travers?' the woman asked. 'I am Mrs Bates—Lady Isadora's housekeeper. You are in good time, miss. We wondered whether you might be late because of the state of the roads.'

'No, indeed, we made good speed,' Elizabeth said. 'I think some of the country roads were a little rutted, but the highways were well enough.'

The housekeeper nodded, leading the way inside. A young maid was waiting in the hall, and she came to take Mary away and show her where to go. Elizabeth wondered if she might be given a moment to tidy herself before meeting her employer, but instead Mrs Bates led her upstairs to a parlour on the first floor.

'Her ladyship is expecting you, Miss Travers. If you would care to greet her, your maid may unpack your things for you by the time you go up.'

'Yes, of course,' Elizabeth said. She stifled a sigh. She must accept that she was an employee now and not at liberty to do as she pleased. 'Thank you, Mrs Bates.'

The housekeeper opened the parlour door and announced her. She then stood back for Elizabeth to go past her, which she did with some trepidation. Her heart was beating wildly as she advanced into the room and glanced at the lady lying elegantly on a sofa near the fireplace, where a small fire was glowing despite the spring sunshine. Dressed in an elegant peach silk gown, she looked younger and more stylish than Elizabeth had imagined, and she was glad that she had chosen to wear one of her better gowns. Although grey because of her mourning, it was becoming and of good quality cloth.

'Ma'am...' Elizabeth said hesitantly. 'Lady Isadora...?'

'Elizabeth, my dear,' Lady Isadora said and eased herself into a sitting position. 'How kind of you to come to me so quickly.' She gave a little cough behind her hand. 'I have been very poorly, but I must confess I am feeling a little better today. Perhaps it is the prospect of your company that has made me feel more cheerful.'

'I was pleased to come,' Elizabeth said, advancing further into the room. She bobbed a slight curtsy and smiled. 'It was very kind of you to offer me the position as your companion.'

'Oh, no, I am happy to have your company,' Lady Isadora said holding out both her hands. 'My companion of many years has retired to take care of her mother, and my daughter is increasing, which means she cannot travel to see me—though my son has decided to visit me at last.' Her plaintive tone managed to convey the idea that it was a rare occurrence. 'He is out seeing to estate matters at the moment, but will be here for dinner, I dare say.'

Elizabeth took her outstretched hands, bending to kiss her cheek since it appeared to be expected. She was kissed warmly in return and then was asked to sit on the chair opposite Lady Isadora's sofa.

'You must be happy to have him here, ma'am?'

'Yes, of course,' Lady Isadora told her with a sigh. 'Cavendish is a good enough son to me, but it is not like having the company of a young lady. My youngest daughter would have been eighteen this year had she lived. It has been much on my mind of late. I would have been making plans to bring her out this summer.'

'Oh, I did not know of your loss,' Elizabeth sympathised instantly. 'I am so sorry. You must miss her dreadfully.'

'Yes, I do, of course,' Lady Isadora said. 'My eldest daughter is married, but I see her so infrequently…' Not quite the truth, for Melanie had spent a month with her earlier in the year.

'You have friends, ma'am?'

'Yes.' Lady Isadora waved her hand languidly. 'I have not entertained much recently because of my illness…' She coughed delicately. 'However, once I am feeling a little stronger—' She broke off, frowning as she heard footsteps in the hall. She had told Daniel to stay away from the parlour until the evening, but he had either forgotten or ignored her request. 'It seems we are about to have company…'

'Mama…' The earl came into the room and stood looking at his mother for a moment before turning his gaze on Elizabeth. His brows narrowed—she was not quite what he had expected. Not pretty by any means, but certainly not the plain-faced spinster he had been anticipating. He had been right to suspect his mother of some mischief. 'I beg your pardon, Miss Travers. We had not expected you this early.'

'If I am in the way…' Elizabeth sensed his reserve and stiffened. She had the feeling that he did not quite approve of her being here. She stood up as if prepared to leave the room.

'Oh, do not mind Daniel,' Lady Isadora said. 'Ring for tea, my love—that little bell on the table beside you. Unless you wish to go up and refresh yourself first?'

'Thank you, I should like to wash my hands before taking tea,' Elizabeth said. 'I shall return in fifteen minutes.' She lifted her brilliant eyes to meet the earl's. 'Will that be sufficient time for you to speak privately with Lady Isadora, sir?'

'Quite adequate,' he said and inclined his head, his expression giving little away. 'Besides, Mama will be impatient for your return. I am sure she wishes to talk to you about so many things…'

There was an odd expression in his eyes, almost as though he suspected her of something. Elizabeth inclined her head to him, smiled at her employer and walked from the room. Her head was up, her back very straight. She hesitated as to whether she should close the door behind her, and, as she lingered for a second, she heard the sound of the earl's laughter.

'Well, Mama, what are you up to?' he said in a mocking tone. 'Not quite the little country mouse you led me to believe. Not pretty, but not hopeless by any means. I think that perhaps you will have no need of my sacrificial lamb. I dare say you will find what you require without any help from me...'

'Daniel, do not be so provoking. Tell me, did you not think her a charming gel?'

Elizabeth's face went bright red as she heard the tinkling laugh from her hostess. She hurried across the hall and up the stairs, not wanting to hear another word of their conversation.

Chapter Two

A helpful footman sent Elizabeth in the right direction at the top of the stairs, and she found a young maid assisting Mary to unpack her things in a large, front-facing bedchamber. The sun was warming the room, giving it a welcoming atmosphere, and the two girls were laughing together, clearly getting on well. However, as Elizabeth entered, the rather pretty maid curtsied to her and smiled, telling her that she was called Amy and that Lady Isadora had asked her to wait on Elizabeth.

'I am to look after you when Mary goes home,' Amy said. 'I thought I would take the opportunity to see how you like things done, Miss Travers.'

'That is very kind of you,' Elizabeth said, 'but my needs are very few. I am used to dressing myself these days.'

Amy's eyes were approving as she took in the neat

bodice and skirt Elizabeth was wearing; its cut was good and it had more style than the gowns Lady Isadora's former companion had worn, but then Miss Travers was more of a guest than an employee from what Amy had heard below stairs.

'I shall press your gowns and you might like me to do your hair for you, miss—in the evenings when her ladyship entertains.'

'Yes, perhaps.' Elizabeth frowned—she had not expected to be assigned her own maid nor that her employer would give the kind of dinners that required her to need the services of a maid. However, she had brought all her best gowns with her so she would not disgrace her employer. 'Could you both come back a little later, if you please? I should like to be alone for a moment.'

'Yes, Miss Travers, of course. Come along, Mary. I will show you where we eat...'

Elizabeth washed her hands and made herself comfortable. She glanced at herself in the pretty dressing mirror, which was in the shape of a shield and in keeping with the rest of the furniture in the room. The furnishings were after the style of Mr Adam, she thought, and had obviously been replaced quite recently. It was an elegant, comfortable room and seemed to be one of the best guest bedchambers. That puzzled her a little, for she had not been sure what to expect.

Her cheeks grew warm again as she recalled the mockery in the Earl of Cavendish's voice as he had spoken to his mother about her. So they had expected her to be a country mouse, had they? Elizabeth felt a pang of chagrin—she did not take kindly to the idea that she was an object of pity. It was true that her circumstances were altered, but she was still the daughter of a gentleman and she did not need—would not accept—charity. She had thought that Lady Isadora would be a kind employer, but she had expected to earn her keep and the dress allowance her employer had offered.

But what had the earl been hinting at when he spoke of a sacrificial lamb? Perhaps she had misunderstood him? After some thought, she decided that he must surely have been speaking on another matter, which had nothing to do with her at all.

She must not jump to conclusions that might be false, Elizabeth decided as she left the room and went back down the stairs to the parlour on the first floor. She felt a little tentative lest the earl should still be with his mother, but when she tapped at the door and was invited to enter, she soon discovered that Lady Isadora was alone.

'Ah, there you are, my dear,' she said, smiling at Elizabeth. 'You have been very quick. I am sure it would take me much longer.'

'I did not wish to keep you waiting, Lady Isadora.'

'No, no, you must not be so formal when we are alone. Please call me by my name, Elizabeth.'

'That would not be fitting for I hardly know you and must show respect. May I call you ma'am?'

'Yes, of course, if you wish. But once you are settled here you may feel it easier to call me Isadora or Dora, as my friends do, Elizabeth. I know it must all seem very strange to you at first, but I live very simply here most of the time. Of course, it will be different when we visit Brighton in the summer—and perhaps Bath later in the year, for my health you know. I seldom go up to London—I find it too tiring.'

Elizabeth had imagined her employer to be a semi-invalid, but had begun to realise her mistake. Whatever her illness had been, it was obviously not serious enough to render her unfit for company.

'Mama found London very tiring also. I think that is why we did not often visit. Papa went up on business a few times a year…' Her words faltered. It was during one of his business trips that Sir Edwin had ruined himself and his family.

'Yes, that sorry business was all very sad,' Lady Isadora said, guessing what had brought that look of pain to her eyes, 'but you must try to put it behind you now, my dear. You are too young to waste your life in regret. You have come here to be my companion, and

I am truly in need of it at the moment, Elizabeth. We both have cause for grief, but we shall find ways to enjoy ourselves. Now that you are here I shall go visiting again…at least I shall in a few days, when I feel better.' She gave a delicate cough and dabbed her lips with a lavender-scented kerchief. 'But come and sit with me, Elizabeth. I was about to ask you if you would tell me about your-self before we were interrupted…'

Elizabeth blushed. 'Does Lord Cavendish often visit you, ma'am?'

'Hardly at all.' His mother dismissed her son's devotion with a wave of her hand. 'You need not bother your head about him, Elizabeth. Cavendish has his own life and will not interfere with us. We shall live very quietly, entertaining just a few of my old friends…'

Elizabeth was relieved—she was not to know that her employer was sometimes economical with the truth and inclined to paint the picture in her mind rather than reality.

'Mama and I have lived quietly this past year or so since…' Elizabeth lifted her head. 'And of course since she passed away I have been only in the company of Lord and Lady Wentworth.'

'Ah, yes, it was so kind of Lady Wentworth to spare you to me. I dare say she wished to keep you with her, did she not? Her letter to me was most complimentary, Elizabeth.'

'Oh, I did not know that she had written…' Elizabeth was surprised and a little annoyed that her friend had gone so far. 'Lady Wentworth was a good neighbour and friend to Mama these past twenty years. She wished me to make my home with her, but I could not accept charity. I had made up my mind to seek a position and your letter was most welcome. I hope that I shall be of some real service to you, ma'am.'

'Well, certainly you will. I am sorely in need of someone to keep me from falling into a fit of the sullens.' Lady Isadora smiled, hardly looking in need of any such assistance. 'It was my dear Jane's birthday just last week and I have felt a trifle off-colour ever since.'

'Yes, of course,' Elizabeth said, understanding perfectly that the occasion of her lost child's birthday must have affected her. 'Mama and I found Christmas very hard to bear—Papa loved entertaining all his friends and we always had wonderful celebrations at that time.'

'You understand how I feel as no one else can,' Lady Isadora said. 'But we must not be sad, dearest Elizabeth. We shall make plans to entertain our friends—for my friends will all approve of you and so they will become your friends too.'

'Yes, of course. I shall be happy to help you entertain them, ma'am. You must tell me what my duties are and I shall endeavour to please.'

'Duties…' Lady Isadora bit back the words that might have given her away; she thought of Elizabeth as a welcome guest, but did not want her to feel that she was being offered charity. 'Well, I like to embroider now and then and my silks are for ever tangled. Also I am constantly leaving things behind and need someone to fetch them for me—and when I am feeling lazy I like to lie on my sofa and listen to a pleasant voice reading from one of Cavendish's books. He has an extensive library, which you must feel free to use as you please—but most of all I need someone to talk to, Elizabeth.'

Elizabeth did not think that her duties sounded very onerous, but she would possibly find others for herself. She had noticed that some of the flowers in the various rooms were falling and had not been renewed for a day or so.

'I enjoy arranging flowers, if you would like me to do that for you,' she suggested tentatively.

'Oh, yes, that is another little task I find too tiring,' Lady Isadora lied. 'And the Vicar is always asking me for flowers for the church—you might like to assist him in various ways. He is such a pleasant young man—too young to be alone. His wife died in childbed last year, you know, and the baby with her. It was such a shame, for he doted on her.'

'That was a tragedy,' Elizabeth said. 'I am so sorry to hear of it.'

'Yes. I liked Amabel,' Lady Isadora said. 'She was such a busy woman, always helping others. She visited often and I gave her things for the poor—or the fête. We have a fête each year in August. The Reverend Bell is very keen to help the destitute of other countries as well as our own. A very dedicated young man…though somewhat too serious since his wife died.'

'He has suffered a great loss,' Elizabeth said. 'It must be a constant grief to him.'

'Yes, poor man.' Lady Isadora sighed. She had thought at first that her old friend's daughter might be an ideal replacement for Amabel—at least as a last resort if no eligible gentleman presented himself— but since meeting her she was inclined to think that it would not do. She would wish to look higher for Elizabeth. 'Well, I think that is quite enough to keep anyone busy, my dear.'

'Yes, I believe I can make myself useful here,' Elizabeth said, feeling pleased. In truth, it would not be so very different from the life she had led at home—or that she might have led at Lady Wentworth's house had she been able to accept her neighbour's kindness. However, she believed that her employer had fallen into the doldrums because of the anniversary that should have been such a happy one had Jane Cavendish lived. Her duties were light, but she thought that she could find others that would be of some use to her employer. It seemed that she would be quite at home here—providing only that the earl did not visit too often. She believed that she had sensed disapproval in him, and his mockery had pricked her pride. She would be happy to serve Lady Isadora, but hoped that she would not have to meet with the earl more than necessary.

They had been talking for some time when Elizabeth noticed the time, asking, 'At what hour do we dine, ma'am?'

'When alone I ask Chef to prepare an early dinner, but when Cavendish is here we dine at six, Elizabeth.' Lady Isadora looked at the mantel clock, a pretty gilded affair with cast-bronze cherubs and a silvered dial, made in France and a recent gift from her thoughtful son. 'I think perhaps we should go up for it is half past four and Monsieur Delfarge hates to be kept waiting.' She laughed delightedly—they had been talking for more than an hour and it seemed no more than a minute. 'How time flies when one is pleasantly engaged.'

'Yes, indeed.' Elizabeth nodded her agreement. 'You have a French chef here?'

'Oh, yes, Cavendish is meticulous about such things. I am well cared for—though too much alone.' Lady Isadora made a recover. 'This is his house, of course. He would not have me remove to the Dower House—he spends much of his time in London or at one of his other estates—but he likes things to be just so when he visits.'

Elizabeth nodded, feeling thoughtful. She had thought the earl a careless son, neglectful of his mother's feelings, but perhaps she had misjudged him.

She rose to accompany Lady Isadora from the room. 'Is there anything I may do for you, ma'am?'

'Oh, no, my dear. My maid will help me dress—but perhaps you will play for us this evening? I believe your mama told me that you play the pianoforte. Cavendish bought a rather fine instrument quite recently. I do not play much myself these days, but I should enjoy listening to you.'

'I find it a pleasant pastime,' Elizabeth said. 'I do not know if you will find me competent, but I shall do my best.'

'Oh, I am sure you will,' Lady Isadora said with a vague smile. 'I remember that Serena had a fine singing voice—do you sing, Elizabeth?'

'Yes, sometimes, though not of late.'

'Well, you shall play for us this evening, and perhaps sing another time,' Lady Isadora said, and on that note they parted, each to their own bedchamber to dress for dinner.

Alone in her room, Elizabeth took stock of her surroundings, knowing it would not take her more than an hour to dress. It was such a comfortable room, with everything that she could want, including an attractive writing desk and chair by the window where she might compose her letters, a stool, wing chair and several small tables and chests, also an impressive armoire for her clothes.

She had two good evening dresses, one of a pale, pearly grey silk, the other a dark blue heavy grosgrain, which she had worn only a few times. It was some time since she had purchased a gown for the evenings, and she had left her older ones behind, believing that two would be sufficient. She went over to the large armoire, thinking that her wardrobe would be lost in its vastness, but when she opened it, she stared in surprise—there were several gowns hanging there that she had never seen before. She took a pretty yellow silk evening gown out to look at it, and was holding it in front of herself to admire it when the door opened and Amy entered.

'Oh, yes, miss that would suit you well,' Amy said. 'I noticed that it was a little long when I put your things away earlier, but it would take no time at all to make a temporary hem and I could do it properly tomorrow.'

'But I have never seen this gown before,' Elizabeth told her. 'It does not belong to me.'

'Her ladyship told me that she had taken the liberty of buying you one or two things as a welcome gift,' the girl said with a smile. 'She said that she wasn't quite sure of your size, but had ordered them long enough so that we might alter them to fit when you arrived.'

'Oh, I see.' Elizabeth had expected that she would be able to choose her own clothes when she was offered a dress allowance. She was not yet ready to wear such bright colours, though there was no denying that the yellow silk was of good quality and in perfect taste. 'Thank you for explaining, Amy. I don't think I shall wear this yet—perhaps in a few weeks when I put off my mourning. I shall wear my own grey gown, thank you.'

'And very elegant it is too, miss,' Amy said approvingly as she took it out—she liked its simple cut, which she knew would look well on Elizabeth. 'Would you like me to dress your hair? I could style it a little differently, if you wished.'

'That is very kind of you,' Elizabeth said, 'but I think I will not make a change just yet—perhaps another time.'

'Yes, Miss Travers.' Amy made no further comment, though in her opinion the young lady could make more of her best features than she did.

Dressed in the pearl grey gown, Elizabeth fastened a small choker of pearls at her throat. They had been her mother's gift to her on her last birthday, and she knew they had been her father's wedding present to his bride. She touched them with her fingers—it made her emotional to wear them, but they would brighten the gown and give her ensemble the something extra she knew it needed.

When Amy left her, Elizabeth went back to the armoire and looked at the other gowns Lady Isadora had ordered for her. She discovered a pretty green-striped morning gown, a deep blue carriage gown, two afternoon gowns, one white and one peach, and another evening dress in white shot with silver. She could not fault her employer's taste—they were just such as she might have ordered for herself if she had been given another Season in town. However, she thought them a little too smart for a companion and would not have chosen them in her present circumstances. Since Lady Isadora had presented her with them, she decided she would wear them as soon as she felt able.

It wanted twenty minutes to six, but Elizabeth decided to go downstairs rather than remain alone in her room. Lady Isadora had mentioned her son's library and she was eager to see what she could find that might be suitable to read to her employer in the afternoons, and she might also find something she could bring back to her room to read before she slept.

She stopped to speak to one of the footmen, asking for the direction of the earl's library and was informed that it was on the ground floor at the rear of the house. She made her way unhurriedly towards it, entering with a feeling of pleasure as she saw that it was a large, long room lined on three sides with impressive mahogany shelves, the windows on the fourth side sufficiently large to let in a good light. There were several sofas and chairs with reading stands close by, and a leather-topped drum table at one end, a square pedestal table at the other. She walked along the length of the shelves, feeling puzzled as she realised that nothing was in order; there were all kinds of literature, estate records, poetry and serious works jumbled up together.

'It is in rather a mess, is it not?'

Elizabeth jumped as she heard the earl's voice and turned to look at him. 'I beg your pardon, sir. I did not hear you come in.'

He ignored her rather flustered address. 'My father was a great buyer of books, but he had no idea of how they should be stored. I have thought that I would make a start on cataloguing what we have one day, but as yet I have not begun.'

'I have seen several volumes that would seem to be first editions,' Elizabeth said, looking thoughtfully at the shelves. 'How would you wish the books to be arranged, sir—in categories or by author?'

The earl raised his brows, his piercing blue eyes

intent on her face. 'Are you offering to undertake the task, Miss Travers?'

'It would be a pleasure to at least make a start, though of course it could take many months or even years to complete,' Elizabeth said, turning her serious eyes on him. 'But only if I have your approval?'

'Well, you must not tire yourself,' the earl said, 'or my mother will have it that I am a wicked slave driver—but if you have a few moments to spare now and then…'

'It would be much easier for you if all the estate books were in one section, the serious works on another shelf, for they are perhaps the books you like to read, and then literature and poetry.'

'You have excellent judgement, Miss Travers. I see that I could do no better than to leave my library in your hands.'

'Oh…' She blushed with pleasure, for something in his look had made her heart flutter. 'If you are sure, it would be such a pleasure to me, sir. Of all things I love books, reading and touching them—and to catalogue such a wonderful collection would be such a treat.'

'Is it a wonderful collection? I had thought there were a few treasures, but most of it seems a hotch-potch of nonsense.'

'Oh, no, how could you?' Elizabeth caught the gleam in his eyes and realised that he was teasing her. 'But you know there are some rare volumes here, do you not?'

'Yes, I confess it is one of my interests, and if I were not dreadfully indolent I would have put them in order before this—but I have not been at home often since my return from the Peninsula, you see. And there has been much to see to at our various estates—my father had not been well for a while before his death.'

'And I dare say you did not like to make sweeping changes to your father's domain too soon?'

The earl gave her a thoughtful look, his eyes slightly narrowed. 'You are perceptive, Miss Travers. For one reason or another my father had allowed things to slide. I have improved things gradually, particularly here since this was my mother's home. She dislikes our estates in Hampshire and Devon, and of course I reside in London for much of the year.'

Elizabeth nodded. She had noticed the changes he had made—they brought a breath of fresh air to the house. 'I believe you have patronised Mr Adam, sir? I must say that I admire his work greatly.'

'His work gives a lightness not often found in the design of others—Mr Chippendale is a great furniture maker, but I believe I prefer Mr Adam's work.'

'That is my own feeling,' Elizabeth agreed. 'Lady Wentworth recently began the refurbishment of Worth Hall, you know. We discussed the merits of Mr Sheraton and Mr Adam at length—but in the end she decided that she would choose Mr Adam's work for the drawing room.'

'Ah…' The earl smiled. 'Then I shall know who to turn to when it comes to persuading Mama that she should have her own apartments refurbished.'

'Oh, no,' Elizabeth said, a faint colour in her cheeks. Was he mocking her? Perhaps she had spoken out of turn, forgetting that she was merely an employee? 'I could not possibly influence Lady Isadora. She has excellent taste.'

'Yes, she does,' he agreed. Hearing the longcase clock in the hall strike the hour, he inclined his head to her. 'We must not keep Mama waiting—or perhaps it would be more precise to say we must not upset Monsieur Delfarge. You must know that he is French and somewhat temperamental. I had to bribe him to come here, for he prefers London, but he obliged me and we must not do anything that would cause him to desert us. Poor Mama suffered with a terrible cook for years.'

'Oh, dear,' Elizabeth said and laughed, for he was clearly jesting now. 'I do understand. My mama had a dreadful cook for some years, too. Papa finally told her that if she did not dismiss her he would go to London and live at his club.'

'Then you understand why we are all at such pains to be punctual for meals.' The earl gave her his lazy smile, which unaccountably made Elizabeth's heart beat rather faster than usual. 'Tell me, Miss Travers, do you think you shall settle here?'

'Yes, I believe so, sir,' she replied. 'I was very grateful to Lady Isadora for offering me the position as her companion.'

'Ah, yes,' the earl said, and mischief lurked in the depth of his eyes. 'Did you have a good journey down?'

'Yes…' Elizabeth hesitated for a moment, and then, 'It was an odd coincidence…I met and spoke to Mr John Elworthy, who I believe is a friend of yours—and I also saw Sir Montague Forsythe at the inn we had chosen to break our journey. Mr Elworthy had been given one of our rooms, but he gave it up to me and slept in the stables when he learned of the mistake.'

Cavendish nodded. 'Yes, John would do that. He is one of the best—a perfect gentleman.'

'You know him well, sir?' Elizabeth looked at him, her fine brows raised.

'Certainly. His estate is some fifteen miles from here and we were at school together as lads.'

'Oh…' Elizabeth was thoughtful. 'Mr Elworthy was the only reliable witness to my father's wager, you know.'

'Yes, I do know. He has told me of what he saw and heard that day. John says that he wishes he had not heard Sir Edwin's words so clearly, otherwise he would have believed that your father was trapped into the wager—which would, of course, make it null and void.'

'It is what I have always believed. Papa would not normally have done anything that foolish. He was not a gambler nor did he drink to excess.'

The earl nodded and looked thoughtful. 'I dislike Sir Montague Forsythe for reasons which we shall not discuss, and there may come a time when his activities will be under intense scrutiny. I can say no more for the moment—but should his affairs be investigated, I will undertake to see what can be done about your father's affair.'

They had gained the top of the stairs. Elizabeth stopped to look at him, trying to read his expression and failing. 'Do you think my father could have been coerced into making that wager, sir?'

'I cannot tell what may have occurred,' the earl said. 'I only know for certain that I believe Sir Montague to be less than honest—and perhaps a dangerous man.'

'Dangerous?'

'Yes, I believe so, though I have no proof,' the earl said. 'But you must say nothing for the present, Miss Travers. I have only suspicions to go on, and there must be proof.'

'Yes, of course.' Elizabeth gave him a smile that lit up her eyes. In repose her features were not remarkable, some might even say plain—but when she

smiled her inner loveliness came through. 'I am glad
we have spoken of this, sir, for my brother has been
trying to arrange a meeting with Mr Elworthy. It was
in my mind to write to him to tell him that nothing
could be gained from such a meeting—and now I
shall add that I think he ought not to approach Sir
Montague either.'

'It would not be wise for him to do so, for without
proof he can do nothing.'

On that they ended their conversation, for they had
arrived at the drawing room in almost the same instant
as Lady Isadora.

'Ah, there you are, Elizabeth,' she said, smiling at
them both with an innocence that made her son at
least suspect her of mischief. 'I thought you must
have come down earlier, for I went to your room.'

'I am sorry—did you need me?'

'Not at all, my dear. I wondered if you had found
everything to your liking.'

'How could I not?' Elizabeth asked. 'Everything is
of the finest and I am very comfortable. I have also to
thank you for the gowns you provided, though I do not
think I shall wear bright colours just yet.'

'Shall you not?' Lady Isadora asked with a vague
smile. 'Well, they were just a small gift to thank you
for being so kind as to come to me—but your allowance shall be paid monthly and you may choose

whatever you wish when we go down to Brighton next month.'

'Oh, no…I mean, you have already been so generous.'

'I like pretty things, and I like to see those about me happy,' Lady Isadora said. She looked at her son. 'Have you been keeping Elizabeth company, dearest?'

'We happened to meet in the library,' Daniel told her. 'Miss Travers shares a love of books, Mama. She has very kindly offered to begin the task of sorting them into some order when she has the time.'

'I do hope you did not press her into it?' Lady Isadora frowned at him.

'Oh, indeed not,' Elizabeth said instantly. 'You must know that I like to be busy, ma'am. I am sure that I shall enjoying cataloguing and sorting the books, and there are many that I think we shall enjoy reading together.'

'Well, as long as you are happy,' Lady Isadora said. 'Shall we go in, my dears? I am perfectly certain dinner is ready…'

Elizabeth could not remember an evening she had enjoyed more for some months. After an excellent meal they had repaired to the drawing room, the earl refusing to drink his port in lonely isolation, and swearing that he would prefer to take tea with them. However, she noticed that he had been served with brandy in the drawing room.

Lady Isadora had declared that she was not in the mood for cards and begged Elizabeth to play for them on the pianoforte. She was happy to oblige and played two classical pieces before going on to a play and sing one of the popular ditties of the day. It was then that the earl came to stand beside her, looking through the music at her disposal before choosing something.

'We might sing this together if it pleases you,' he suggested. It was a duet for male and female, and told the story of lovers.

'I do not know this piece well,' Elizabeth said, 'but I am willing to try if you will forgive my mistakes.'

'We shall not scold her if she plays a wrong note, shall we, Mama?'

'Do not tease Elizabeth,' his mother told him, looking on complacently. The evening could not have gone better in her opinion.

The earl had a fine tenor voice and they blended well together. Elizabeth managed to find her way through the piece without too many mistakes and left the pianoforte at last just as the tea tray was brought in. The earl then excused himself, saying that he had work to do, and soon after the ladies made their way to bed. It was not until Elizabeth was undressing that she realised she had forgotten to bring herself a book to read.

She hesitated, but decided it would not do to go

wandering about her employer's house half-dressed at night. She would instead write a letter to her brother.

Sitting down at the desk provided for her use, she spent half an hour composing her letter. She told Simon about her meeting with Mr Elworthy, and went on to say that she had heard it on good authority that he was a perfect gentleman, suggesting that nothing could come of insisting on a meeting. She also hinted that she thought Sir Montague dangerous and advised her brother to stay well clear of him.

It had taken her a while to find the right words, for she knew her brother's fiery temper; it would not do to advise Simon too strongly or he would likely do just the opposite in a fit of rebellion. Laying down her pen, she sanded her letter and sealed it, then stood up to glance out of the window. As she did so, she saw a horseman riding away from the house. The night was quite dark and it was difficult to see, though she thought it was the earl himself.

Where could he be going at this hour? It was surely too late to ride out for pleasure and much too late to go visiting—unless, of course, he was visiting his mistress. Elizabeth squashed the suspicion—it was none of her business, and she ought not to be curious about things that did not concern her.

Retiring to bed, she slipped beneath the covers and closed her eyes, but her mind was busy and she did not sleep immediately. She was sure that she would enjoy her work for Lady Isadora, because she was willing to be pleased, and Elizabeth would find her duties light enough. However, she was not sure that she approved of the earl, though she could not put her finger on why she should have doubts concerning him. He was obviously generous to his mother, and though perhaps a little lazy—or indolent, as he called himself—seemed good-humoured. Why then did she suspect there was much more to Lord Cavendish than he cared for anyone to know?

'Does he suspect anything?' Daniel asked of his friend as they met that night at the Cock and Hare Inn, some three miles distant from Cavendish. 'He did not think it strange that you consented to dine with him, and to drink yourself almost insensible?'

'I was careful to keep my wits about me,' John Elworthy said, smiling oddly. 'And when he suggested a hand of cards to while away the time, I pretended to fall asleep, and sat snoring by the fire until he went up.'

'Did you learn anything that might help us?'

'Sir Montague is very close-mouthed,' Elworthy told him with a frown. 'But he did say something— just after Miss Travers left the room. He seemed surprised at the way she behaved for he did not know her, and when I told him who she was he looked strange.'

'You said she left abruptly when he entered?'

'Yes. We had been speaking of her father—she does not believe that Sir Edwin would willingly have gambled away his estate.'

'She has told me as much,' Daniel said. 'We know that Forsythe and his cronies prey upon the young idiots who venture to town with a pocketful of gold and hardly any sense in their heads. Although we may disapprove, we do not have the right to interfere other than to issue a warning if we get the chance. However, there is this other business...'

'Do you truly believe that Forsythe is involved in that?' John looked at him incredulously. 'The abduction of young girls for sale into houses of prostitution—it is a wicked thing, Daniel. I can hardly believe that a gentleman would do such a thing.'

'It would never have crossed my mind if we had not happened to be there that night—when Lady Elworthy's youngest sister was almost abducted...' Daniel looked angry. 'I dread to think what might have happened to Maria, John. And you know that she firmly believes Sir Montague had something to do with it.'

'Yes, I do know that she suspects him. We have talked several times for it is not a subject that she feels able to discuss with anyone else. She has not told her sister or my brother what happened, because she thinks people would believe she had done something to encourage the attack, though of course she did not. But as far as Sir Montague is concerned, she says that when she refused his offer of marriage he threatened that she would be sorry—and something the men said as they were trying to capture her made her believe he was at the back of it.' John frowned. 'Perhaps it was merely planned as an abduction, to force her into marriage. She is, after all, an heiress and Forsythe has already run through more than one fortune.'

Daniel was thoughtful. 'You know that Charles Hunter's young sister Sarah was abducted a year ago, of course.'

John nodded. 'It was a terrible thing, Daniel—and nothing has been heard of her since?'

'Nothing. Mrs Hunter was so distressed that she had a mental breakdown and has not come out of her room for the past six months—and Charles has vowed to kill whoever was responsible if he ever discovers who it was.'

John Elworthy nodded and looked solemn. Lady Elworthy's younger sister was young enough at seventeen, but Charles Hunter's sister had been no more than sixteen when she disappeared when out walking near her home. To imagine her fate if she had fallen into the wrong hands was unimaginably horrendous.

His eyes narrowed. 'I think I should have gone mad

with grief if we had not recovered Maria that night. I cannot imagine how Hunter must feel.'

'Angry, bewildered, frustrated,' Daniel said toying with the handle of his tankard as he struggled to control the fierce emotions raging within. 'He has been drinking too much of late. It was only my intervention that kept him from playing cards with Forsythe the other evening. Imagine what they would have done with him in a fit of recklessness! He might have been ruined as well as broken in spirit.'

'Poor fellow,' John said. 'But I still cannot believe that gentlemen would be involved in such wickedness, Daniel. One hears from time to time that a pretty maidservant has gone missing and wonders if the poor creature has been spirited off to a whorehouse—but the daughters of gentlefolk...'

'Young, innocent and virgin,' Daniel told his friend grimly. 'If men will pay for such things, there are those that will supply it—even to the extent of sending the girls abroad to eastern potentates.'

'No!' John looked sick. 'Do you think...?'

'I surmise nothing,' Daniel told him. 'I am determined to find proof somehow—and believe me, I shall one of these days. Sir Montague is being watched day and night. Wherever he goes, one of my spies follows. If he makes a wrong move, we shall have proof this time.'

'Sir Montague has an evil temper,' John said, his forehead creasing. 'Be careful, my friend. If he is what we believe him, and suspects that you are investigating his affairs, he would not hesitate to have you killed.'

'I am aware that he is dangerous,' Daniel said. 'Some think him just an opportunist, and feel no pity for the flats he fleeces—but I believe there is much more to him. I have wondered if perhaps Sir Edwin stumbled on something he should not have seen.'

'You think that he may have been drugged, forced into making that wager somehow? But why? I do not see how…'

'He may have been forced to drink too much—or take some foul drug. Where the wager comes in I do not know, unless Sir Montague saw some profit in it for himself. And if he wished to dispose of Sir Edwin—what better way to cover murder than to ruin him in public and make it seem that he had taken his own life in a fit of despair? But that is mere speculation and I keep an open mind,' Daniel said. 'But you said he looked strange when he saw Miss Travers—did he say anything?'

'Only that the fool had it coming,' John said. 'And that his daughter might think herself lucky…' He frowned. 'Do you think he meant some harm to her?'

'It is possible, but we must not speculate too much for the moment. We must listen and watch, and when the time is right we shall act,' Daniel said. 'At least Miss Travers is safe enough with Lady Isadora—but I have vowed to help Charles Hunter find his sister, and to discover what I may about Forsythe's affairs. What I need is proof.'

Daniel stared moodily into his tankard. He had hardly touched his ale; when he thought of the possible fate of Sarah Hunter, he was sick to his stomach with anger. She had been but a child, sweet and pretty and trusting. Several times he had been on the point of forcing a duel on Sir Montague, but he had fought his natural desire for revenge, knowing that one man alone could not be responsible if something evil was afoot. He must wait, watch and listen until the time was right.

Elizabeth rose early as was her usual habit, washed and dressed in a plain grey skirt and a pretty white blouse with a high neck, which she fastened with a gold brooch. She looked elegant despite the plainness of her dress, her hair swept back from her face into a knot in the nape of her neck.

She knew that the household would hardly be stirring, but she wanted to begin her duties. It was not likely that Lady Isadora would have need of her before eleven, for she did not come down until noon. That meant Elizabeth would have some free hours in the mornings, which she might spend in one of several ways. She could walk down to the church with flowers, tend the vases in the house—or begin work on the library.

She had decided to make a start in the library, for she thought it would be best to consult the gardeners before raiding the garden for flowers. She knew from experience that it was unwise to pick blooms without first consulting the man who tended them, who could often be fiercely protective of his flowerbeds.

As she went downstairs she met one of the maids, a young girl dusting in the hall, who looked startled when Elizabeth smiled at her and asked if she might borrow one of her feather dusters.

'Have I missed summat, miss?' the girl asked, looking puzzled.

'Oh, no, I am sure you have not,' Elizabeth said. 'I am to work in the earl's library and I wish to begin by dusting some of the books.'

'Are you sure, miss? Only none of us is allowed to touch 'is lordship's books.'

'I promise you that I have permission,' Elizabeth said, hiding her amusement as the girl reluctantly handed over one of her feather dusters. She made her way to the library, feeling a tingle of excitement as she entered the long room.

She looked round her with satisfaction, thinking

about where she wished to make a start, for it would be best to plan her work rather than rush into it and find that she must begin again. Noticing that there was a shelf with rather fewer books on it than the others had, Elizabeth decided to investigate. It was at the far end of the room, and it was only as she reached the shelf that she realised that someone was lying on the sofa, which faced it. She halted, her heart catching as she saw it was the earl, and he looked as if he might have been drinking the previous evening. There was an empty decanter of brandy on a small wine table beside the sofa and his glass had fallen from his hand. He looked vulnerable, younger in his sleep, and, as she bent to retrieve his glass from the floor, he murmured a woman's name and moaned as if in some distress. He opened his eyes and looked at her just as she was straightening up, his face on a level with hers.

'Good God,' he said in a voice of what she took to be revulsion. 'What the hell are you doing here?'

'Forgive me,' Elizabeth said, embarrassed. 'I did not know you were here, sir. I was about to make a start on dusting some of the books before putting them into order.'

The earl sat up, groaning as he felt the pain in his head. He remembered his foul mood on returning home the previous night, the frustration he had felt at being unable to get any nearer to finding Charles

Hunter's sister. He had foolishly started drinking brandy, and this was his just punishment.

'I shall go,' Elizabeth said as he gave her what she thought was a look of dislike. 'I am sorry…'

'Why? It is I who have reason to be sorry,' Daniel said, uttering a muffled curse. 'I had forgotten where I was as I woke. Please do not go. I thought myself in my bedchamber and it startled me when I saw you bending over me.'

'Oh…' Elizabeth was relieved—he had seemed so angry at seeing her. 'I see. It was to retrieve the glass only, but…it would be rather startling had I come to your bedchamber at this hour, sir.'

Daniel caught the hint of mischief in her voice and looked at her sharply. Her eyes were bright with laughter and he realised that underneath her slightly prim manner lurked a wicked sense of humour.

'Just a little,' he said wryly, 'but it has happened, Miss Travers. Let me assure you that you would not be the first, especially when I was in Spain with the army.'

'I dare say you have been much plagued by eager ladies, sir?'

'As it happens I have,' Daniel growled, a little piqued by her manner. 'You would not believe how often a young lady feels faint when I am near.'

'If you look at them so severely, I should not be at all surprised, sir.' Elizabeth's eyes sparkled, and for the first time Daniel realised that she was something out of the ordinary.

'You have a ready wit, Miss Travers,' he acknowledged, 'but you must excuse me if I do not respond in kind—I am not at my best this morning. I must go upstairs and make myself ready before Mama sees…' He glanced at the beautiful gilt mantel clock. 'Good grief! What are you doing up at this indecent hour?'

'I always rise early,' Elizabeth said. 'And I thought it a good time to begin the task I have promised to undertake for you. I dare say Lady Isadora will not need me for some hours yet.'

'I should think not.' He pulled a face at her. 'It is but ten minutes past the hour of seven. I like to rise early when I have not spent the night hours indulging in too much brandy—but I seldom leave the house before eight.'

Elizabeth laughed huskily. 'Oh, dear, I am so sorry. It is a custom I formed when young. I used to ride with my brother before our governess was ready to begin the day's lessons, and I fear the habit has stayed with me.'

Daniel nodded thoughtfully. 'So you ride, then? I shall inspect my stables and discover if I have a suitable mount for you.'

'Oh, no, that is too kind,' Elizabeth said. 'I have not often ridden since Papa… Our horses were deemed part of the estate, you see, and Lord Wentworth had nothing in his stable that I cared to ride…'

'Not a good judge of horseflesh?' Elizabeth shook her head and he gave a snort of laughter. 'I shall be on my mettle, shan't I?'

'Oh, I did not mean…' She looked flustered and his eyes gleamed in triumph for she had lost her air of unconscious command, which, with a head that felt as if it contained a thousand working hammers, he had found daunting. Now he was back in charge, which was his usual status with ladies.

'No, of course not. Nevertheless, I shall expect you to ride with me tomorrow morning at eight, Miss Travers. You will not refuse me, otherwise I shall know that you think my cattle not worthy of your skill.'

'I think you like to mock me, sir.' Elizabeth gave him a reproving look.

'My mother says I suffer from an excess of levity,' Daniel said, though the gleam faded to be replaced by a disturbing expression that sent a little chill down her spine. 'But this is a cruel world, Miss Travers. If a man may not find something to make him laugh sometimes, it would hardly bear the living.'

He nodded to her and walked from the room, leaving her to stare after him and wonder what had brought that look of near despair to his eyes.

It seemed to her that the Earl of Cavendish was a man of many parts, and she was not sure which was the real man.

Chapter Three

After two hours of uninterrupted work, during which she had become rather dirty, Elizabeth went back to her room to change her clothes. She ought to have worn an apron, and would do so in future, she decided, for many of the books had not been touched for years. She had begun on the shelf that had only a few books and was pleased to discover that they were estate journals, which Lord Cavendish had obviously placed there himself in an effort to make his work easier. She had cleaned them carefully and then put them back on the shelf at the bottom—she thought it might be best to have the older volumes at the top and work downwards. It would then be quite simple to reach up for something when some research into the past was needed. She was pleased with her efforts, though as yet she had not attempted to begin the cataloguing. She would get the estate journals into good order first, before she began on the larger project.

She had just finished changing her clothes when a tap came at the door. She answered it to discover an elderly woman, whom she believed to be Lady Isadora's personal maid.

'Miss Travers,' the woman said. 'Her ladyship asks if you would be kind enough to visit her in her room this morning.'

'Yes, of course,' Elizabeth said. 'Am I right in thinking it is the room at the far end of the landing?'

'Yes, miss, that's right,' the woman smiled at her. 'I am Jean Phipps, and I've been with her ladyship since before she was married.'

'Then you must know her very well,' Elizabeth said. 'May I come to you if there is anything I need to know concerning Lady Isadora's preferences?'

'Yes, miss, of course. I shall be only too pleased to help you if I can—but her ladyship is well looked after. It is young company she needs, if you ask me. It would have been Miss Jane's eighteenth birthday this year and she has been brooding over it. With Miss Melanie being mistress of her own home, and a mother herself, it has left her ladyship at a loss.'

'Yes, I can understand that,' Elizabeth said. 'Well, I am here now and I shall endeavour to take her mind from her unhappy thoughts.'

'Oh, she seemed much more cheerful this morning,' Jean Phipps said. 'I do not doubt that she will throw off the megrims now that you are here and start to entertain once more.'

Elizabeth nodded to her. They had walked together to Lady Isadora's rooms, and Miss Phipps indicated that she should go in, which she did, though her companion turned away. As she went into the little sitting room, her ladyship called to her to come through to the room directly behind it. She was sitting at an elegant little desk in her boudoir, a pen in her hand. She rested it on an exquisite French boulle tray, which was made with patterns of intricate silver and gold inlaid into tortoiseshell, and smiled at Elizabeth.

'I trust it is not too early for you, my dear?'

'Oh, no, I have been working in the library,' Elizabeth said. 'I have made a start with the estate records, which should help Lord Cavendish to find what he needs more easily.'

'You have been working?' Lady Isadora looked surprised and then slightly put out. 'My son is a slave driver. I did not ask you to come here to work yourself to death, Elizabeth dearest.'

'No, no, I shall not,' Elizabeth told her with a smile. 'You must know that I have been accustomed to being busy, and I enjoyed myself. Books are so fascinating, are they not?'

'Are they?' Lady Isadora looked so doubtful that Elizabeth laughed.

'Yes, I assure you that they are for me—and you have such a treasure house here at Cavendish.'

'Do we?' Lady Isadora wrinkled her brow. 'I know Cavendish spent a lot of time visiting sales of old books and was quite excited when he found something special, but it was not an interest we shared—though I believe Daniel has similar tastes.' She nodded her head. 'Well, I shall not stop you if it pleases you, Elizabeth—as long as you do not tire yourself.'

'I shall not, ma'am, and I shall not desert you for the task. It is my habit to rise early and I may easily spend an hour or so in the library in the mornings before breakfast—though Lord Cavendish has asked me to ride with him tomorrow at eight.'

'The fresh air and exercise will be good for you,' Lady Isadora said, looking pleased. 'Now, my dear, do you think you could find your way to the vicarage? I should like you to take a note for me. I wish to ask the Reverend Bell to dine with us tomorrow evening. I can send one of the servants, of course, but I thought you might like to become acquainted with the vicar and perhaps discuss the flowers for the church.'

'Yes, I should very much like to do that,' Elizabeth said, 'but is there anything I may do for you before I go?'

'Oh, no, I shall not come down for another two

hours or so,' Lady Isadora said, waving her hand vaguely. 'Please feel free to consider the mornings your own, Elizabeth.'

Elizabeth thanked her, for it was much as she had expected. She took the note Lady Isadora had given her and went out. As she walked along the landing she met Amy, who told her that she had taken a pot of tea and some bread, butter and honey to her room.

'I wasn't sure if you would want breakfast downstairs, miss. Her ladyship has just a pot of chocolate and some biscuits in bed at about half past nine...'

'As you have no doubt discovered, I am always up much earlier. But I do not wish to cause more work for the household—something in my room at about this time would be agreeable, unless you are setting the breakfast room for his lordship? I could just as easily take mine downstairs.'

'Yes, miss. While his lordship is here we set breakfast at about nine o'clock, when he comes in from his ride.'

'Then shall we say that I will breakfast downstairs when there are guests or his lordship is in residence, and in my room at other times?'

'Yes, miss.' Amy looked pleased. 'That's thoughtful of you, though it would be no trouble to do whatever you want.'

'I shall have my breakfast before I leave,' Elizabeth

said. 'But then I intend to walk to the vicarage—could you tell me the easiest way to get there?'

'Yes, of course, miss. It is close to the church, and that is just across the meadow behind the house. That's the quickest way when it's dry as it is now. Though in the winter it is best to follow the road to the village, but that is the long way round and you would do better to go in the carriage.'

Elizabeth thanked her. They parted and she went to her room, drinking a cup of tea and eating two of the delicious freshly baked soft rolls with butter and honey.

Within half an hour she was wearing her pelisse and bonnet and heading for the meadow, which was at the back of the house. It was a pleasant morning, the sun peeping out from behind a few fluffy clouds, and the grass perfectly dry beneath her sensible black boots. She could hear a lark singing and looked up to see it perched in the branches of an oak tree at the edge of the meadow. She had a feeling of content, of being at home, for she had often performed such chores for her mother, and it was almost as if the grief of the past months had never been.

As she reached the church, she saw a tall, thin, black-gowned man leaving, and guessed that he was probably the person she had come to see. He was wearing a flat, wide-brimmed hat, which he doffed as she addressed him, to reveal hair that was sandy red.

'Reverend Bell?' Elizabeth asked. 'I have come from Lady Isadora with a note.'

'Ah, yes,' he said holding his hat to his breast. He had serious grey eyes and a gentle face. 'You will be Miss Travers, I make no doubt. Her ladyship has spoken of you to me. I am pleased to meet you.' He put his hat back on and offered to shake hands with her, a faint colour in his cheeks. 'It was good of you to walk all the way down here.'

'It is not so very far. At home the church was much further from the house, but I often walked there on fine days,' Elizabeth said. 'Besides, I wanted to meet you, sir. Lady Isadora tells me you are in need of flowers for the church.'

'I should be grateful if we could have some for next Sunday,' he said. 'We are having a special service for one of my oldest parishioners who has lately recovered from a severe illness, and it is a service of thanksgiving, you see. I like to see flowers in the church as often as it can be managed and sometimes one of my parishioners will bring a few—but I should like more. And then we are to have a flower festival next month, and I was hoping that Lady Isadora would contribute substantially. We shall attract visitors if there is a good display and it raises money for good causes—as do the fêtes and bazaars we hold several times a year.'

'Yes, I see,' Elizabeth said. He was clearly very dedicated to his parish and to the good causes he supported. 'Well, now that I am here, I shall be pleased to help you in any way I can. I shall certainly ask the gardeners about a supply of flowers for the church, though I must be ruled by what they can spare, of course— but when it comes to the bazaars, I shall help as often as I may. I have some free time in the mornings.'

'If you are sincere in wishing to be of help I should be most grateful,' he told her. 'We have various stalls and any contributions are welcome, either your own work—or items from the attics at Cavendish that are no longer required. And on the day, if you could be spared to help on one of the stalls, it would be much appreciated.'

'Well, we shall see,' Elizabeth told him. 'I cannot say what might be spared from the attics, but I shall certainly tell Lady Isadora of your needs.' She smiled at him, little knowing the effect she was having on a man still only in his middle twenties who had been lonely for the past several months. 'And may I tell her that you will give us your company tomorrow evening? I believe there are some others invited.'

'Yes, of course,' he said, beaming at her. 'I should not dream of refusing her ladyship. Besides, there is always a good dinner to be had at Cavendish; though one should not consider such things, it makes a pleasant change.'

Elizabeth guessed that he was not used to fine cooking in his present circumstances, and felt some sympathy for him. A young man in his situation needed a wife, and he had been unlucky to lose his so early in his marriage, and the child too.

'Oh, I believe well-prepared food is something we may all hope for,' she said. 'Though I suppose when you think of the starving we should not grumble if we are fed sufficient.'

'You speak very truly, Miss Travers. It is a delight to me to hear a young lady of quality speak so thoughtfully, for so many think only of their own pleasures. Not that I wish to judge them, of course— but sometimes one sees such frivolity…' He shook his head. 'One would not wish to deny others pleasure— but there are so many in need, you see.'

'Yes, of course, I do see,' Elizabeth told him. 'I believe in helping others less fortunate than ourselves—but surely we all deserve a little pleasure in our lives, sir?'

'You are right to censure me,' Reverend Bell said. 'I should not be critical of others because they have so much—but I cannot always help myself when I know of the great need in the world.'

'But you want to do too much,' Elizabeth told him

with a gentle smile. 'Do you not think that we must be satisfied to do what good we can? You are only one man and the cares of your parish are heavy enough. You cannot right the wrongs of the world. Only God may do that, I think.'

'How well you understand me,' he said, struck by her words. 'You are very right, I do take too much upon myself at times. I must learn humility, Miss Travers.'

'I think you are very well as you are, sir,' she said, for she liked him. His earnest desire to help others, and his willingness to listen, were traits that must be admired in any man. 'It is good to strive in the cause of others, but we must accept our limitations and not despair that we cannot cure all ills. Do you not agree?'

'Yes, indeed. What a sensible, caring young lady you are,' he said approvingly. 'I am glad to have had this opportunity to talk to you, Miss Travers, and I shall look forward to furthering our acquaintance.'

'As I shall,' Elizabeth assured him. 'And now I must go—it will soon be time for nuncheon and I must not keep Lady Isadora waiting.'

'No, no, of course not. Good day to you, Miss Travers. I shall see you tomorrow evening, I hope?'

'Yes, certainly,' Elizabeth said. 'It will be an opportunity for me to meet others of Lady Isadora's friends.'

She took her leave of him, setting off across the meadow at a good pace. As she did so, she saw a young lady heading towards the church and heard her call to the reverend, but she did not look back for the time was slipping away and she did not wish to be late for nuncheon.

Lady Isadora came down for nuncheon, which was served at some twenty minutes past the hour of noon. It was a light meal of cold meat, thin bread and butter and some pickles, followed if one wished for it by a lemon-flavoured custard. However, the earl, who had gone out on estate business and was not expected to return until the evening, did not join them.

After lunch they repaired to the small parlour at the back of the house. From its long windows there was a pleasant view of the gardens, and beyond them the meadow and the church spire in the distance.

'Now we can be comfortable,' Lady Isadora said, smiling at her. 'Shall we do a little embroidery, I wonder? Or shall you read to me while I stitch?'

'Have you your embroidery with you, ma'am?'

'It is in that worktable. Pull out the compartment at the bottom and you will discover a hanging I have been working on for the church. At least, I began it, but I must confess that Miss Ridley—Helen—has done most of it for me. But do pull it out, Elizabeth dear, and let us see what remains to be done.'

Elizabeth did as she was bid, and discovered that

Lady Isadora and her former companion had been working on what was clearly intended to be an altar cloth. It was an ambitious project and the work was very fine, but it would need an ambitious needle-woman to complete such a task.

'It is rather lovely,' Elizabeth said. 'The silks are a little tangled, but I can soon sort them for you—though it would be done sooner if we worked on it together.'

'I do not think I care to embroider today,' Lady Isadora decided. 'What have you brought to read this afternoon?'

'I have here a book of poems, Shakespeare's *The Taming of the Shrew*—or Fanny Burney's novel…'

'I enjoyed Mrs Burney's *Evelina,* but I do not care for some of her later work. I think I should enjoy a little of Shakespeare's play,' Lady Isadora said. 'If you could bear to read that?'

'It is most amusing,' Elizabeth agreed. 'I love the struggle between Petruccio and Kate.'

'Yes, indeed,' Lady Isadora said and lay back against the silken cushions on her sofa. 'Please begin when you feel ready, my dear.'

Elizabeth opened the book and began to read. She had a pleasant voice, and put expression into her reading. In actual fact she acted out each part, and after a few minutes Lady Isadora sat up, laughing, her face animated and eager.

'Oh, my dear!' she exclaimed. 'I declare it is the equal of being at the theatre to hear you. Helen only read the words, but you put so much expression into them. But I am interrupting you. Please do continue. I had forgotten how wonderful it was to hear William Shakespeare's words spoken with feeling.'

Elizabeth continued to read for almost an hour, after which Lady Isadora rang for tea, for as she said Elizabeth's throat must be dry.

'It has been such a joy to me,' she told her young companion. 'I shall look forward to continuing tomorrow—but I must not tire you. Now we shall relax and talk, my dear. Tell me, what did you think of the Reverend Bell?'

'He seems both pleasant and dedicated to his calling,' Elizabeth said. 'I liked him—and I have promised to help where I can. I felt a little sad for him, knowing that he had lost his wife and child. A man in his position needs a wife—do you not think so?'

'Yes, perhaps,' Lady Isadora said, frowning a little. 'I think Miss Giles might like to fill that position, though perhaps she is a little too silly for his taste.'

'Miss Giles?'

'You will meet Julia tomorrow evening. Her parents are neighbours—Sir Henry and Lady Giles. They have an estate no more than six miles to the south of Cavendish. They are, in fact, our nearest neighbours.'

'I see,' Elizabeth said. 'Their estate cannot then be far from the village?'

'No, it is not more than three miles, I dare say. Why do you ask, my dear?'

'Oh, merely curiosity,' Elizabeth told her. 'Do you see the family often?'

'Lady Giles calls now and then, but she prefers London or Bath to the country. They are planning on a Season for Julia this year…'

'I see,' Elizabeth said. 'No doubt Miss Giles is looking forward to the trip.'

'Yes, I expect so. I find London too tiring myself, but I shall enjoy a few weeks at Brighton in the summer— and of course we may go to Bath in the autumn.'

'I am sure the sea air will do you good, ma'am,' Elizabeth said. 'I have never—'

What she was about to say was lost, for through the French windows she saw a sight that put everything else from her mind. Two men were walking across the lawns towards the parlour, one supporting the other, their footsteps uneven and awkward. Jumping to her feet, Elizabeth went to open the French door, for she could see that something was wrong. One of them was either hurt or ill and she sensed that help was imperative.

'Miss Travers,' the earl called to her. 'Thank you for seeing our need. I fear that Mr Elworthy has been shot through the shoulder. I think the wound is not serious, but we must get him to bed and the doctor must attend him immediately.'

'What is wrong?' Lady Isadora had followed Elizabeth out to the terrace, and now gave a cry of alarm. 'Daniel—what happened? You haven't done anything foolish, I hope?'

'John was shot at from behind as he rode here to visit me,' Daniel said. 'I dare say it was a careless poacher. Fortunately, I returned sooner than I had planned and discovered him lying in the road. He has lost a lot of blood and is barely conscious.'

'Please ring for the servants, ma'am,' Elizabeth said to Lady Isadora. She went to the other side of Mr Elworthy and put her arm about his waist, taking some of the weight on to herself and earning a surprised look of gratitude from the earl. 'Come, sir. We must get you upstairs as easily as we can for your wound has bled and needs attention.' Glancing over her shoulder at her employer, she added, 'Please send Amy up to me with linen and salves, for this wound must be bound until the doctor arrives.'

'Yes…of course.' Lady Isadora rang the bell hastily. Elizabeth had an unconscious air of command about her, seeming to be completely in control of the situation, whereas she felt that she might faint if Mr Elworthy continued to drip blood on to her parlour floor. 'Please, do whatever you feel necessary, my dear.'

Elizabeth did not respond. She was concentrating all her efforts on assisting the earl to get Mr Elworthy into the hall, where she saw a young, broad-shouldered footman lingering. He looked at them uncertainly.

'Please,' she said. 'You have more strength than I, sir—help his lordship carry Mr Elworthy up the stairs. I shall go ahead and prepare the bed.' She passed her share of the burden to the young man and ran on ahead. At the top of the stairs she met the house-keeper about to come down, and asked which bed-chamber was available for an invalid.

'This way, Miss Travers. The room has been cleaned only this morning, and is suitable for a gen-tleman,' the woman replied, understanding the problem immediately.

Elizabeth followed her inside the guest bedcham-ber and together they pulled back the covers so that when the gentlemen entered—the strong, young footman now carrying Mr Elworthy in his arms—they were able to lay him straight onto the clean linen. The injured man gave a sigh and his eyelids fluttered open for a moment, his eyes looking into hers.

Elizabeth bent over him, stroking back a lock of hair from his sweating brow. 'You are safe now, sir,' she told him in a gentle voice. 'I shall bind your wound for you and then you will feel easier until the doctor comes.' She turned as Amy came in, carrying some linen and salves, followed by another young girl bearing a jug of water. 'Ah, good,' Elizabeth said. 'Did either of you think to bring some scissors?'

'Yes, miss,' Amy said, 'for we shall need them to cut the bandages.'

'First we must cut away his coat,' Elizabeth said. 'It is a pity to ruin such elegance but it would be too painful and lead to the loss of too much blood to try to remove it. His shirt too must be cut up the arm, Amy.' She turned to the young footman. 'Would you be so kind as to lift Mr Elworthy—gently, please.'

'I shall do that,' the earl said. 'Thank you, Forrest. Perhaps you would go downstairs and instruct the grooms to look for our horses? I left mine about half a mile to the east of Cavendish and I dare say you may find Mr Elworthy's horse somewhere in the vicinity. And make sure that the doctor has been sent for, please.'

'Yes, sir,' the footman replied and went out at once.

Daniel and Amy supported the patient between them as Elizabeth carefully cut his coat sleeve and then across the back until it could be eased away from his uninjured shoulder without causing him too much pain. She worked swiftly, competently, to ease the blood-soaked shirt away from his torn flesh and looked at the damage beneath. Dipping a cloth into the water, she washed carefully around the edge of the wound, before applying a small pad of linen and some of the healing salve to the mangled flesh. Between them, she and Amy then bound him tightly with a strip of clean linen, Daniel supporting him until they had finished.

'There, we have finished for the moment,' Elizabeth said.

'I believe he has fainted,' Daniel told her as he laid his friend back against the pile of feather pillows Amy had arranged. 'Which may be just as well for the moment. That was well done, Miss Travers. I thank you on John's behalf for your excellent care. You may have been instrumental in saving his life—in these parts it takes time to bring a doctor to his patient. You managed the whole—and us—with great skill.'

'Oh…' Elizabeth blushed. She had not given a thought to the fact that she was merely an employee, acting exactly as she would have had she been at home. 'Forgive me if I was too imperious, sir. No doubt the doctor will be scornful of my poor attempts, but I felt that instant attention was necessary if Mr Elworthy was not to lose significant amounts of blood. And Mama had a dislike of blood, you know, so that it was I who helped Simon when he cut himself on a scythe, as he did, quite badly, as a youth.'

'That explains your competence in an emergency,' the earl said. 'I confess I was never more glad of help in my life, for at one time I thought I should never get him home. I might have done better to fetch help, but I did not wish to leave him there in case…'

Elizabeth looked at him, but nothing more was forthcoming. Clearly he had not wanted to leave his friend in case the assassin came back to finish his evil work, but for some reason he did not wish to say as much.

'It was fortunate that you returned earlier than intended, sir. Mr Elworthy might otherwise have bled to death before he was found.'

'Yes, that was my own thought,' Daniel said, a harsh line to his mouth. 'You have been kind, Miss Travers. Mr Elworthy will be grateful—the more so as he feels in part responsible for your father's ruin.'

'But he should not,' Elizabeth said at once. 'He told the truth as he saw it and an honest man could not do otherwise.'

'You are generous,' he said, 'but you have done all you can here for the moment, Miss Travers. I shall stay with John until the doctor arrives.'

'Yes, of course. I must go to Lady Isadora, for she will be anxious.'

Elizabeth left immediately, unaware that his eyes were upon her until she had gone from his sight, Amy following on behind her.

'Was there anything else, miss?' Amy asked before they parted company.

'Nothing for the moment,' Elizabeth told her. 'I

shall speak to Lady Isadora and then go up to change. I think I shall wear my blue gown this evening, Amy.'

'I have altered the hems of your yellow silk, miss and the green walking gown, if you should wish to wear them.'

'I shall keep them for an occasion,' Elizabeth told her. 'But thank you for your industry, Amy. I shall be able to wear them when I wish.'

'Yes, miss. That yellow will suit you a treat,' Amy offered before turning away.

Elizabeth smiled as she went downstairs. It would be dishonest of her to pretend that she was not tempted by some of the new gowns in her armoire, but it was not yet six months since her beloved mama had died and she would not show disrespect.

Lady Isadora was standing before the window, looking out, as Elizabeth entered. She turned, giving her an anxious glance.

'Why does it always take so long for the doctor to come?' she asked, clearly agitated. 'Poor Mr Elworthy! I do hope he will not bleed too much before Dr Roberts gets here.'

'I thought you might be anxious,' Elizabeth said. 'You may ease your mind, ma'am. Amy and I have bound his wound and he will be well enough until the doctor decides what must be done. I do not know if the ball is lodged deeply, though I think it may have gone clean through—which will be the best of all, for it means the doctor does not have to cut for it.'

'Oh, I feel quite ill to think of it,' Lady Isadora said and tottered to the nearest chair. 'It was such a shock to see poor John like that. I thank God that you were here, dear Elizabeth, for I do not think I could have helped him as you did.'

'I dare say your housekeeper would have managed,' Elizabeth said. 'It may seem a little improper to you that I acted as I did, ma'am, but I thought only of what ought to be done for his comfort.'

'Improper? I thought it heroic,' her employer said. 'You must not imagine that I would censure you for such a kindness, my dear. Kindness to me as well as to Mr Elworthy.'

'Then I am happy to have been of service,' Elizabeth told her. 'Shall we go up? The afternoon has fled I do not know where, and we do not wish to keep your chef waiting.'

'You are perfectly right,' Lady Isadora said and smiled. 'You are such a sensible girl, Elizabeth. Your mama told me that she valued you highly, which was what made me offer you a…place here with me.' She had been about to say 'home' but corrected herself in time. 'I can see that you will be indispensable to me, Elizabeth. I do hope that you will be happy with us.'

'Yes, of course. How could I not be?' Elizabeth

asked. 'You have been kindness itself. I already feel quite at home here.'

'That is exactly what I hoped for,' Lady Isadora said, looking pleased as they went up the stairs together. 'It is so pleasant to have young people about one, Elizabeth. I am feeling so much better since you came.'

Elizabeth thanked her and they parted company. As she went into her bedchamber, she saw that Amy had laid out her blue evening gown on the bed. Elizabeth went behind the painted Chinese screen to take off her clothes and refresh herself before slipping on the fresh gown. The bodice fastened down the front, and she was wrestling with the tiny pearl buttons as she came out from behind the screen to discover the earl standing by the dressing chest. He had picked up a Bristol blue glass scent bottle and was holding it to his nose, sniffing delicately.

'Sir! I did not hear you enter.' Elizabeth was shocked—it was not proper for a gentleman to enter the room of an unmarried lady. She could quite easily have walked out from behind the screen in her petticoats or, worse, in nothing at all!

'Forgive me. I knocked before I came in, though I am aware that this is perhaps a trifle unconventional…but I thought to leave a note if you were not here.'

'Yes, indeed, it is a little out of the ordinary,' Elizabeth said, frowning at him. Did he imagine her to be fast simply because she had shown no qualms in dealing with Mr Elworthy's injuries? 'Did you wish to speak with me privately?'

'Yes, that was exactly it,' Daniel said. He did not truly understand what had brought him to her room when he might have spoken with her later but he had felt an urgent—and inexplicable—need to see her. 'I would ask for your discretion in this matter, Miss Travers. I intend to tell Mama that a poacher shot Mr Elworthy by accident. She is of a nervous disposition at times, as you may have noticed.'

'But you do not believe that is the case?' Elizabeth nodded as she saw the answer in his eyes. There was more here than met the eye, and though it was not her business to inquire his reasons, she might guess them. 'I understand that you do not wish to cause Lady Isadora needless worry. Perhaps you are wondering whether or not the shot might have been intended for you? Do you perhaps have an enemy, sir?'

'I believe the assassin knew his target,' Daniel said. 'Whoever did this may have believed that John knew more about a certain matter than he does, because he is my close friend. It is a matter I am investigating, and that leads me to think that I must take certain precautions. I must therefore cancel our ride tomorrow morning, Miss Travers. I shall ride instead to York, where I hope my business may be completed.'

'Yes, of course. You must do as you think fit, sir.'

'You are very understanding, Miss Travers.' Daniel felt an odd desire to touch her or hold her, but restrained himself, knowing that she would be shocked. 'I think Mama has done better in asking you to become her companion than she might have dreamed.'

'That is kind of you, sir. You will forgive me if I suggest that you should leave now?'

'Yes, of course.' He lingered a moment more, feeling unaccountably reluctant to go. For a moment he was caught up with the desire to kiss her, simply to discover what she might do. Would she retain her calm demeanour or melt into his arms? The idea of her melting against him was unexpectedly pleasant, bringing a swift surge of desire that surprised him. She was not in the least the kind of woman he usually sought out for such things! He smiled oddly at his own thoughts because he was being ridiculous. He could hardly seduce his mother's companion—a lady he hardly knew. 'Forgive me. I should have waited and spoken to you later this evening.'

'You are forgiven, my lord,' Elizabeth said. 'But if you care for my reputation…' She walked to the door and opened it for him.

Daniel inclined his head as he walked past her, and then stopped to glance back at her. 'Your perfume intrigues me, Miss Travers. What is the essence?'

'I believe there is lily of the valley and a woody essence,' Elizabeth said, a little surprised. 'It is called Wood Nymph, or some such fanciful nonsense, I believe. Papa bought it for me in London as a birthday gift just before he died.'

'It suits you very well,' Daniel said. He smiled ruefully. 'If you have not decided that I am to be avoided at all costs, may we ride together another day?'

'Yes, of course,' Elizabeth said, a smile on her lips. 'You are a gentleman, sir. I believe you meant no harm this evening—though perhaps you were a little thoughtless?'

'Let others think as they will,' Daniel said, a mocking light in his eyes. 'We know the truth, do we not?' He inclined his head to her and walked from the room. She closed the door and leaned against it, her heart beating rather swiftly.

Did she know the truth? Elizabeth could not be sure of what she had felt as she walked out from behind the screen to find the earl toying with her perfume flask. For a moment she had thought his visit of a very different nature and her heart had leaped at the idea that he had wanted to make love to her—but that was ridiculous!

Elizabeth laughed as she dismissed her foolish thoughts. The Earl of Cavendish would not be interested in a spinster of almost four and twenty years!

He had told her that ladies threw themselves at him, and she knew that he must be considered one of the best matrimonial catches of any season. Why should he look at her when he could take his pick?

Of course he would not! She was not even sure that she would wish him to, though he had caused her heart to race wildly as he asked what kind of perfume she used.

Elizabeth laughed softly as she sat down at her dressing chest and began to brush her hair. She glanced round as the door opened, her heart jerking, but this time it was Amy.

'Do you need any help, miss?'

Elizabeth hesitated, and then handed her the hairbrush. 'Perhaps you would like to do my hair for me? It is a long time since I bothered to do more than dress it in a simple knot.'

Amy looked pleased. 'You have lovely thick hair, miss,' she said, 'and it always looks nice, but I could make it a little softer about your face.'

'I shall leave it to you,' Elizabeth said. 'Tell me, has the doctor arrived yet?'

'He came a few moments ago. I brought him up to Mr Elworthy's room and…saw his lordship. I told him the doctor had come and he went to ask him how the patient was.'

'That is good,' Elizabeth said. She suspected that

Amy might have seen the earl coming from the direction of her room, but decided to say nothing about it. Amy was clearly being discreet and she could only hope that the girl would keep any thoughts she had on the subject to herself. 'We must hope that he has taken no lasting harm.'

'I dare say he will be better in a few days, providing he does not take a fever. I think you stopped the bleeding, miss, and that of course was the danger.'

'We did it together,' Elizabeth told her. 'You did very well, Amy. I thought that you could keep a cool head in an emergency, which is why I asked for you.'

'Thank you, miss.' Amy looked pleased. 'I've two older brothers at home and they were for ever in some scrape when they were young—and I helped Ma give birth to my little sister.'

'Then that is why you were not afraid of a little blood,' Elizabeth said. 'I was very glad to have you with me.'

'There, miss, what do you think now?'

Elizabeth looked at herself in the mirror, and then Amy held a silver-backed hand mirror for her to see the back of her head. Her hair was much as she usually wore it, but fuller and softer.

'It is very becoming. I am very lucky to have you to look after me.'

'Oh, no, miss,' Amy said, a faint flush in her cheeks. 'The privilege is mine.'

Elizabeth thanked her and went downstairs. The nights were lighter now and it was a pleasant evening. She went out into the garden for a few minutes, enjoying a walk beneath an arch of trailing rose bushes, which she thought would be glorious once they began to flower. Some of them had little clusters of buds no bigger than the nail on her little finger, but soon they would blossom. Beyond the rose tunnel was an arbour with a wooden bench and massed beds of perennials interspersed with more roses.

As she walked back, she stopped to admire some of the last spring flowers. There were some irises and tulips still in flower and she wondered if the gardeners had any in the kitchen gardens, for they would make a beautiful display in the church. One of the tulips was a deep red colour with a purplish stripe at its heart. She bent to examine it more closely, hearing a sound or rustling in the shrubbery to her right. She straightened up, glancing over her shoulder, but even as she did so she heard her name called and saw the earl coming towards her. She went to meet him at once, her heart beating a little too fast.

'Good news,' he said as she went up to him. 'The doctor has called and he says that the wound is clean—the ball went right through the flesh and should have done no lasting harm. John is conscious, and he sends you his heartfelt thanks for helping him. Dr Roberts was also very complimentary.'

'It was nothing,' Elizabeth said with a faint blush. The look in his eyes made her feel quite warm! 'You and Amy did as much as I, my lord.'

'No such thing. It was you who instructed and we who obeyed,' Daniel said, a flicker of amusement on his lips. 'Did I see you daring to pick one of the tulips? Mama told me you intended to dress the church with flowers this weekend.'

'I should not dare to pick flowers from the show beds,' Elizabeth said, an answering gleam in her eyes, for she knew he intended mischief. 'That would be a crime of the first magnitude, you know. I shall speak to the gardener in the morning and ask if he will be so good as to cut some blooms for me where they can best be spared.'

'Shall you indeed? I had not thought you were to be intimidated by a mere gardener, Miss Travers?'

'The man who orders the care of these gardens cannot be dismissed as a mere anything,' she reproved him with severity. 'He is as much an artist as your chef, my lord.'

'I think I agree with you,' Daniel said, a look of speculation in his face, 'but do you think you could bring yourself to call me Cavendish, Miss Travers? Or sir, if you must—but I do not care to be "my lorded" every second, it reminds me of toadying mamas with ugly daughters they wish to bring to my attention.'

'Sir!' Elizabeth cried and then gave a gurgle of laughter as she saw the wickedness in his eyes. 'I believe I agree with your mama. You do suffer from an excess of levity at times.'

'It is a fault,' he admitted, with false contrition. 'I must learn to curb it if I wish to earn your good opinion, must I not?'

'Indeed not,' Elizabeth said. 'I am sure I have no power to compel you to anything, sir.'

'Better,' he said, brows lifting. 'Not Cavendish yet, but I dare say we may get there one day.'

'When we are better acquainted, perhaps,' Elizabeth said. 'I think we should go in now. We must not keep your mama waiting.'

'No, indeed,' he agreed. 'I wanted to tell you that John was a little easier. He has asked if you would visit him, but the doctor gave him something to make him sleep so it will not be until the morning—that is, if you do not object to visiting him in his bedchamber?'

'It is a sickroom,' Elizabeth told him, her clear eyes looking up into his. 'Do you not think that makes a difference?'

'Ah…' A little smile touched his mouth. 'Yes, I see—and of course that was not the case when I came to yours. Have you forgiven me yet? Or do you suspect me of having some ulterior motive? Did I perhaps come in the hope of seducing Mama's companion—a helpless female who would then be cast defenceless into the streets once I had had my wicked way?' The challenge in his eyes was so provoking that for a moment she was startled out of her usual control. Was he trying to seduce her or merely teasing her?

'My… Sir!' Elizabeth's eyes sparked at him. 'I acquitted you of such a charge and you know it. Nor am I by any means a helpless female—if I suspected any gentleman of such a thing I should box his ears!' She gave him a wrathful look as he laughed. 'I think you like to provoke. You have been deliberately provoking on more than one occasion I believe?'

'Yes, you are very right,' he agreed, thinking how very attractive she was when animated. 'But you see, had I not, we should not now be on the way to becoming good friends. Convention is a dreary thing, do you not agree? People smile and nod and say nothing of any importance, and consider themselves acquaintances, but that is not friendship.'

Elizabeth was forced to laugh and admit that it was true. She had revised her first opinion of him, and was beginning to enjoy his company very much. 'I think that it is always good to break down the barriers that prevent one from being oneself, sir. If it is possible to speak without reserve to another person, then there is a chance of true friendship.'

'How wise you are for one so young,' he remarked. 'I have seldom met with such a level-headed young woman, Miss Travers. It is refreshing to meet a lady who knows her own mind.'

'I believe that perhaps I am a little too forceful at times,' Elizabeth said, a faint flush in her cheeks. 'Simon was used to say that I was a bossy boots when we were younger. It is a fault, I believe.'

'No? How could it be?' Daniel's eyes quizzed her. He was delighted by her—in his experience ladies seldom admitted their own faults—but then, he was fast discovering that she was like no other woman of his acquaintance. 'I shall not allow it to be a fault, Miss Travers. I find it refreshing to be ordered by a general in petticoats…'

'Oh, you wretch!' Elizabeth cried, startled into laughter. The sound of it was warm and husky, and wholly enchanting. 'No, no, I shall not talk to you any more, sir. You are a wicked, provoking man.'

'Indeed, I admit it,' he said and smiled at her in a way that caused her heart to flutter most oddly. 'I am a wretch to tease you so and I beg you will forgive me.'

'I think that smile has won you forgiveness too often, my lord,' she said and looked at him severely.

'I believe we should go in at once before this conversation reaches the level of the schoolroom.'

'Now I am rebuked, am I not?' he said, giving her a chastened look, but the odd thing was she suspected that, rather than being remorseful, he was very pleased with himself.

Chapter Four

Elizabeth slept well that night, but she was still dressed and in the library by seven-thirty the next morning. Since her ride with the earl had been cancelled, she had decided that she would spend the hour or so before breakfast in dusting and arranging books. She was steadily working her way along the shelves, removing only those that related to the estate, which she then cleaned and placed on the shelves allocated for them. She now had all the journals for the past fifteen years on the middle shelf; there was one for each year and she knew that they went back for some years prior to that date. Possibly the present earl's father had written all the journals. Having glanced inside one, she knew that they contained details of a personal nature relating to the fortunes of the family rather than the accounts, which were more likely to be found in the agent's office elsewhere on the estate.

As she was transferring a pile of books from the shelves to the table, a paper fell out of one without her noticing. It was some minutes before she saw it lying on the floor and bent down to pick it up. She saw that it was addressed rather oddly but did not read it, merely placing it between the pages of one of the journals. Quite clearly the late Lord Cavendish had had a habit of placing things inside his books.

When the mantel clock struck the hour of nine, Elizabeth went upstairs to her room, taking off the apron, which had protected her gown and washing her hands. She had just finished tidying herself when Amy brought in her breakfast tray.

'Do you know where I may find the head gardener this morning?' she asked. 'And can you please tell me his name?'

'It's Able Browning, miss,' Amy told her. 'And if you send for him he would attend you in the parlour.'

'Oh, no, I would prefer to go to him,' Elizabeth said.

'Then I dare say you may find him in the kitchen gardens,' Amy told her. 'Cook asked for more fresh vegetables this morning—for the dinner this evening.'

'Oh, yes, I had almost forgotten that we had guests,' Elizabeth said. 'He will be busy, but I shall not keep him long from his work.'

'He is a bit of a curmudgeon,' Amy said and grinned.

'But he likes a few words of praise—if you know what I mean, miss? Always going on about not having enough space for all he is expected to provide for the house, and how no one appreciates what he does.'

'Indeed? Yes, I see,' Elizabeth said, looking thoughtful. 'And he certainly deserves praise, for the gardens here are a credit to him.'

Amy smiled and went away, leaving Elizabeth to eat her meal alone. Some twenty minutes later, she slipped a light shawl about her shoulders and went in search of Mr Able Browning.

That large and worthy gentleman was in the sheltered, walled kitchen garden, supervising the selection of some early spring greens, and she saw that a basket of onions and well-preserved root vegetables was being prepared. Everything was laid out beautifully and looked to be of the finest quality.

'Mr Browning?' she said, approaching him with a smile. 'How lovely those roots look. You must have good storage for them. I have not seen such excellence at this season before.'

'Ah, well, it be all in the preparation and knowing how to keep 'em,' he said, touching his cap to her. 'You'll be Miss Travers as has come to stay with her ladyship, I reckon?'

'Yes, that is correct,' she said. 'I have come to discuss how we may help the Reverend Bell. He needs flowers for the church this weekend and next month. There is to be a flower festival, you see, and people will come for miles to see them. He asked if we could help, and I wondered what could be spared, Mr Browning. Naturally, we need fresh flowers for the house quite often—but if there is sufficient we might manage a few flowers for the church now and then, do you not think so?'

'We grow flowers special for the house,' he said a little grudgingly. 'It be a balance of flowers and veg, you see, miss—and there's only so much ground allocated for it. It be a puzzle how to keep a steady supply through the year. I don't like it when we've nothing to offer and they have to buy in rubbish up at the house. Market goods be poor quality and not what we're used to, miss.'

'No, I am sure you are right. Of course, it can be a problem if you have insufficient space,' Elizabeth said, 'though his lordship might let you take a little more land under cultivation if you have not sufficient for our needs.'

'Oh, aye, well, there's a bit going spare behind the stables,' Mr Browning said. 'I've had a mind to ask for a while now, miss, but his lordship is a busy man.'

'I am sure he would spare time for you if the problem was made known to him,' Elizabeth said. 'I shall do that when he returns—he is away for a few days. If the flowers for the church are a difficulty…'

'Well, I reckon as there might be a few in my glass-house, and mebbe a handful of iris, if you was wishful of decking out the church of a Saturday morning, miss. Don't you go picking them yourself, like—and never from the front gardens, miss.'

'I should not dream of doing so,' Elizabeth told him. 'If you were to send me whatever you can spare to the house on a Saturday morning, I shall be very grateful.' She looked up at him, her eyes wide and clear. 'I expect you have some flowers for us for this evening?'

'Yes, miss—if you would care to come and see. The glasshouse is where I grow my best blooms. It's the only way to get a decent supply year round, you see, and her ladyship likes her flowers.'

'Yes, I am sure she does,' Elizabeth said, following him to the ornate greenhouse, which had a lovely high-pitched glass roof and long windows. She noticed the rise in temperature as they went inside and realised that a small boiler at the far end heated it. 'Oh, how nice this is,' she exclaimed looking about her with interest, for there were all kinds of plants in tubs, many of them of a subtropical nature. 'Those palms are wonderful, Mr Browning. How do you manage to get them to look so healthy? Papa had a small con-servatory at home, but his plants were never so fine.'

'Ah, it's up here, miss,' he said, tapping the side of his head. 'Plants are like a beautiful woman, they wants nurturing. Give 'em what they needs and they blooms, neglect 'em and they withers away.' He glanced at her sideways as if to see if she were offended, but Elizabeth was examining some gorgeous white lilies growing in a pot and he could not see the faint blush in her cheeks.

'These are wonderful,' she said. 'I have not seen any as fine, Mr Browning.' She looked at him, her manner calm and unruffled. 'I suppose you would not consider bringing the lilies to the house just for this evening? We could use that large Chinese jardinière in the dining room to hide their pot—and of course they would come back here in the morning.'

'I could bring them for the evening and fetch them back when you're done for the night.'

'That would be so much trouble for you.'

'Ah—but it's what I does, miss. Them lilies will stand a few hours in the house, but they might have a fit of the sullens if left there overnight.'

'Oh, that would be a pity,' Elizabeth said, giving him a winning smile. 'But it is a shame that they are so seldom seen, sir. Few people will have seen anything as fine as these. They deserve to be seen and admired, do you not think so?'

'Ah, there is that,' he said, nodding wisely. 'Well, I reckon as there be no harm in them going to the house for a little visit now and then.'

'How generous you are, for I know they must have been so difficult to grow to that excellence,' Elizabeth said. 'It has been very interesting to see your plants, Mr Browning, and I look forward to receiving flowers for the church whenever you can spare them.'

Elizabeth left him then, well pleased with her morning's work. There were a wonderful variety of flowers in the greenhouses and it was obvious that Mr Able Browning knew his work. Clearly, he did not part easily from his treasures, but with a little persuasion he could be brought to deliver a regular supply of blooms for the house and church.

Remembering that she had promised to visit Mr Elworthy in his room, Elizabeth tidied her hair and gown before going along the hall to the wing where the unmarried gentlemen guests were housed. She knocked at Mr Elworthy's door and was invited to enter, finding him sitting in a wing chair, fully dressed apart from his coat. His left arm was in a sling to help ease his shoulder, and a small wine table had been placed at his side with a carafe of water. He had a newssheet on his lap; he had been reading it, for he wore a small gold pince-nez on the end of his nose, which he removed.

'Miss Travers,' he said with a pleased smile. 'How kind of you to visit me. I am feeling much better, as you see; if I continue this way, I may be able to come down as early as tomorrow.'

'I am relieved to see you looking so well, sir. We were a little afraid that you might take a fever.'

'I am a little weak still—from the loss of blood, I dare say—but otherwise quite well. I believe I have you to thank for it that I did not lose more blood.'

'I dare say Lord Cavendish might have done the thing had I not taken charge,' Elizabeth said with a faint flush. 'I fear I thought only of your well-being, sir, and not of propriety.'

'And I am dashed glad of it,' he told her. 'No doubt Daniel would have patched me up. He is the best of fellows in a tight spot, you know. We have been friends for ever and served with Old Hookey together in Spain—the Iron Duke—I mean, of course, Wellington.'

'Of course.' Elizabeth smiled, aware that the nicknames given to the Duke of Wellington by his men were affectionate. 'His lordship told me that you were friends. I dare say you have more idea of what has taken him to York than I, sir. I believe he will not be gone more than a day or two.'

'I think he will return as soon as possible,' John Elworthy said, an odd expression in his eyes. 'But I must tell you that I am grateful for your prompt action, Miss Travers—and I hope that you will forgive me for any part I played in your father's downfall?'

'That is forgotten as far as you are concerned, Mr Elworthy. I think Papa must have fallen into some kind of trap, but I do not blame you for it.'

'Thank you, that is generous. I believe that your father may well have been led astray, Miss Travers, though I saw no sign of it—but I suspect now that there was some mischief. It is my hope that the villains in this may be brought to justice sooner than you think. And you may be sure that they will be punished for their crimes.'

'I would hope for justice, sir, nothing more. I have no desire for revenge.'

'You are as wise as you are generous, Miss Travers.' His smile was warm, full of admiration, which brought a blush to her cheeks.

'I believe I should leave you in peace now, sir,' she told him. 'We have guests for dinner this evening, and I have several small tasks to perform before her ladyship comes down.'

'I must not delay you,' he said. 'Thank you for coming to see me.'

'It was a pleasure to see you looking so much better,' Elizabeth said. 'Please excuse me now.'

'Of course.'

Elizabeth went out, leaving the gentleman to stare at the door after she had gone and reflect on the quality of her fine eyes, and the quiet dignity that gave her such an air of distinction. She might hold the position of companion to Lady Isadora at the moment, but she was fit for much higher things.

Daniel frowned as he approached the city of York. He had a difficult problem to solve and needed all his wits about him, and yet his thoughts kept returning to the few stolen moments he had spent with Elizabeth in her bedchamber. She had looked so refreshingly cool as she came from behind her dressing screen, buttoning crisp white cuffs that were a little prudish and suggested something that was far from the truth. Elizabeth presented a very calm manner to the world, but her eyes told a different story. For a moment, as they had looked at one another, he had seen a woman of passion, a woman who set a fire within him.

A smile touched his mouth; he could not understand the strong attraction he was feeling towards a woman who was nothing like the beautiful flirts he had indulged in the past. Elizabeth was quiet, of determined character, and could not be called a beauty— and yet she had drawn him to her room like a moth to the flame. What was it about her that made him want to share his thoughts and his fears with her?

He could not decide and made an effort to put her from his thoughts. He must attend to the business in hand—he had started something by investigating Sir Montague Forsythe's affairs, and it could not now be left unfinished. The sooner it was done, the sooner he could return home and…

Daniel smiled wryly. What then? Was he truly thinking of seducing his mother's companion? A lady of character… Suddenly, he laughed out loud for he knew that he was well and truly caught in a web of his own making.

Lady Isadora came down for nuncheon and Elizabeth told her about the discussion she had had with Mr Browning earlier. She smiled, seeming very much amused.

'You did very well,' she said. 'My husband told me I should be firmer with him—as he said, the flowers belong to us—but I never could bring myself to demand that he send his beloved plants to us. He is so devoted to them, and spends so much of his spare time pampering them that I think his poor wife hardly sees him.'

Elizabeth smiled. She hesitated and then repeated what he had said to her about his rare blooms being like a beautiful woman. Lady Isadora laughed, delighted with the anecdote.

'Oh, my dear,' she said, dabbing at the corner of her eye with a lace kerchief as tears of mirth escaped. 'It is so nice having someone I can talk to like this, someone with a sense of humour. Poor Miss Ridley would have been too shocked to repeat such an anecdote, but then, I dare say he would never have shown her his lilies. You are much honoured, Elizabeth.'

'Yes, and I fully appreciated the honour, ma'am,' Elizabeth said, a naughty twinkle in her eyes. 'But I believe Mr Browning might be brought to realise that such beauty should be admired by a greater audience. With a little judicial praise from the right quarter he might be prepared to lend us some of those wonderful plants from the glasshouse for the house now and then, and some of the hardier ones might be the star of the church flower festival.'

'Oh, Elizabeth,' her ladyship cried. 'If you can achieve that, it is more than I ever could.' And, she added silently, you, my dear, might be the perfect match for Daniel if he has the sense to see it. 'Daniel told me that you have a nice sense of humour, Elizabeth.'

'Oh…' Lady Isadora was intrigued to see a faint flush in her companion's cheeks. 'I think Lord Cavendish likes to tease, ma'am.' She recalled their meeting in the garden, her heart fluttering as she remembered the rather odd look he had given her. She had been aware of something between them—a strong pull of physical attraction that made her think his intentions towards her were perhaps not what they ought to be. She realised that she must take great care when in his company, for he had more influence on her emotions than was right and proper.

'Yes, you are right. I have scolded him for it many times, for he seems to take nothing seriously.'

'You think not?' Elizabeth frowned and looked thoughtful. 'I must bow to your superior knowledge, ma'am—but do you not think that his levity sometimes hides the fact that he takes things very seriously? It has seemed to me that his lordship has much on his mind—is, in fact, quite worried about something just now.'

'Yes, perhaps.' Lady Isadora wrinkled her brow. 'It is odd that you should see it so swiftly,' she said. 'I have sometimes thought that his teasing is a mask to hide a hidden hurt—some grief that he cannot or will not share.'

'Grief… Yes, that may be so,' Elizabeth said. She had thought that it might be more than that, wondering if the earl was perhaps caught up in some dangerous game that he did not wish his mama to know about.

The subject was dropped in favour of the evening's entertainment. They discussed the arrangements for dinner, and then Elizabeth read to Lady Isadora for half an hour before she retired to her room to rest before changing for dinner. Left to herself, Elizabeth went to check what flowers had been sent up for the evening. She discovered that the magnificent lilies had been placed in an urn on a pedestal at one end of the dining room, where they could be seen to advantage. They were highly scented and their perfume lingered softly in the air of the long room.

A large bucket of flowers awaited her in the little room used especially for the purpose of arranging them. She had done the flowers for Lady Isadora's private rooms earlier, but asked for the others to be left in the cool until now for they would be all the fresher once arranged in their vases.

She carried the finished arrangements into the drawing room and the hall, and discovered to her delight that some of the graceful palms she had admired earlier had been placed near the long windows in the drawing room. Well pleased with the effect of the greenery, she went up to her bedchamber to change for the evening.

'It was most provoking of Daniel not to stay for this evening,' Lady Isadora said to Elizabeth when they went downstairs to receive their guests. 'I had expected him to be here and it has made my table a little uneven for there are not enough gentlemen.'

'It is a pity he had business elsewhere,' Elizabeth agreed, 'but it cannot be helped, ma'am. Had it been a day or so later Mr Elworthy might have felt well enough to come down for dinner.'

'I did inquire,' Lady Isadora said, 'but he is feeling a little tired and wishes to rest for a day or so longer. I believe the doctor visited him this afternoon and changed the dressing, which proved quite painful.'

'Yes, I believe it might,' Elizabeth agreed. 'However, he has been extremely lucky to escape so lightly. We must hope he continues to improve and does not take a fever.'

'Oh, yes…' Lady Isadora said a little vaguely. 'I believe it will be better if—' The rest of her sentence was lost for the guests had begun to arrive and for the next twenty minutes or so she was busy introducing Elizabeth to her neighbours.

'Sir Henry and Lady Giles, may I introduce you to my dear Elizabeth. Serena, her mother, was a lifelong friend, and I am fortunate that Elizabeth has consented to bear me company.' She smiled as they shook hands and then looked at Julia Giles, who was standing a little behind her parents. 'Elizabeth has been looking forward to meeting you, my dear. You must come and visit her sometimes if you wish.'

Julia was a bright, pretty girl with dark hair and brown eyes. She had a pert nose and a confident air about her, and Elizabeth liked her immediately.

'Please do come whenever you have time,' she said. 'I am sure you must always be welcome here.'

'Well, yes, I have been visiting for ever,' Julia said.

'But we shall not have so very much time now, for we are to visit London quite soon.'

'Yes, so I have heard,' Elizabeth said. 'You must be excited, Miss Giles.'

'I am and yet…' A small sigh escaped Julia. 'I am sure it will be great fun and I shall meet lots of people, but—' She broke off, a faint colour in her cheeks as the butler announced more guests.

'Sir Walter and Lady Brackly. Lady Pamela Mole and the Reverend Mr Bell…Mr and Mrs Henderson…Miss Henderson and Miss Rosemary Henderson…Lady Roxborough.'

Elizabeth was engaged in a fluster of introductions as several people arrived altogether and she was introduced to each in turn. However, she did not miss the fact that Julia's gaze had gone immediately to one particular person and that her manner had become less certain, as if she feared his criticism.

She felt almost sure in her own mind that Julia Giles was the young woman she had seen walking in the direction of the Vicarage as she left it the previous morning—and was perhaps the reason for his frowning look this evening. Could it be that she was the one he had meant when he had spoken of frivolous persons thinking only of vanity and selfish enjoyment? If so, she thought it a little unfair of him; Julia was young and entitled to her Season and some pretty clothes.

It was not long before he sought Elizabeth, coming straight towards her like a retriever dog tracking the scent of his prey. His eyes gleamed at the sight of her and he nodded his approval.

'You look charming, Miss Travers,' he told her. 'May I compliment you on your choice of gown? You have such excellent taste in all that is proper.' He threw a speaking glance towards Julia Giles, who was wearing a lovely gown of leaf green silk with several flounces on the hem and pretty puffed sleeves that showed off her slender arms to advantage. She was also wearing a simple diamond pendent and two bracelets of gold set with diamonds and pearls. 'You do not need to dress in an extravagant manner to outshine others.'

'I am in mourning for my mother,' Elizabeth said. 'I do not dislike pretty colours at the appropriate time, sir. I admire Miss Giles's gown this evening, for the style and that shade of green becomes her well.'

He considered this for a moment, and then nodded. 'Yes, I dare say it is very pretty—though a little frivolous, would you not agree?'

'If I wore that gown, you might censure me, sir,' Elizabeth said. 'It would look foolish on a woman of my years, but on a young girl it is quite charming.'

'Yes, I suppose one must forgive the young their foolish notions,' he agreed, looking much struck. 'You have an elegant turn of mind, Miss Travers, and such a generous nature. You make me ashamed that I have been too harsh.'

'I am persuaded that you did not mean to be harsh,' Elizabeth said smiling at him in a way that caused him to think her a pearl amongst women. 'I dare say you see so much poverty and want on your rounds that you cannot but dislike a show of extravagance—but you must try to understand that even if Miss Giles gave up her bracelets she could not alleviate the need in the world.'

'How true that is,' he observed. 'Sad but very true, I fear.' He frowned as he saw a gentleman heading towards them. 'Oh, dear, I fear you have taken General Montigrew's eye. I must warn you that he is a man of coarse manners, Miss Travers. He has buried three wives and looks for a fourth to care for his children. Please do not let him monopolise you all evening, for he will if he gets the chance.'

Elizabeth was a little startled, for his manner was almost that of a jealous dog with his bone. She glanced at the gentleman bearing down on her, a determined gleam in his eyes. He was a very large man, bewhiskered and ruddy cheeked, but still quite handsome in his way.

'Lady Isadora wants you, sir,' he addressed the vicar in a bluff manner, but with a hint of command in his voice, winking as the Reverend Bell went off looking less than happy. 'Can't have that fellow boring you to death all evening, m'dear. Lady Isadora sent me to rescue you. Dashed if you ain't too fine a woman to waste your time on a dull chap like that, Miss Travers. Out of the best stables, ain't you, m'dear? I'm nothing if not a good judge of horseflesh—and ladies, if you will pardon the comparison. But there ain't much to choose between women and horses in my experience. Good blood and breeding is what makes or breaks 'em, and I can tell a bolter from a true stayer with my eyes shut.'

'I believe I should feel flattered,' Elizabeth told him, a naughty sparkle in her eyes. 'A compliment not easily given, I imagine.'

He eyed her suspiciously for a moment and then gave a loud laugh. 'My, but you're a game filly, m'dear. Damned if you ain't roasting me!'

'Oh, no, sir. I should not dare,' Elizabeth said, but her eyes belied her prim manner, and unknown to her she made her third conquest of the day. 'I know when a horse suits me, but I would not pit my knowledge of such things against such a connoisseur as you, General.'

'Well, damned if you ain't sent me to the right-abouts,' he told her, highly amused. 'I had been expecting a milk-and-water miss, but it ain't no such thing. You've got spunk and a nice sense of humour, m'dear—and if there are two thing I admire in a woman…' He glanced across the room at another guest. 'Lady Roxborough is here tonight, I see. Her husband was a great rogue and some say she is no better—though for myself I like her, and of course she is accepted everywhere—good connections, m'dear.'

Elizabeth looked at the woman he had spoken of and received a nod in return. They had spoken earlier for a few moments, and she had thought the older woman both lively and outspoken. Perhaps that was what the general liked about her?

'Yes, I've heard some tales about Lady Roxborough that would make your ears tingle, m'dear. Not that I should dream of telling a young lady—'

He was interrupted by the announcement of dinner. Lady Isadora beckoned to her and Elizabeth threw her companion a teasing smile that made him stare after her as she left him to join her employer.

'You were to have been taken in by Daniel this evening,' Lady Isadora told her in a soft voice. 'But I have rearranged the table and now you will sit between Sir Henry and Lady Pamela. You will find she is a little deaf, my dear, but just smile and nod and she will be happy. And now, Sir Henry will take you in, Elizabeth.'

Elizabeth smiled at the gentleman, who presented

his arm. He was a mild, pleasant gentleman and she felt very comfortable with him.

'Lady Isadora tells me you enjoy reading, Miss Travers,' he said as he drew a chair for her at table. 'Tell me, what do you like to read? My Julia loves silly novels, but I dare say you have worthier tastes?'

'Oh, I enjoy a novel sometimes,' Elizabeth told him. 'But I love poetry and histories, and plays.'

'Ah yes,' Sir Henry said. 'Lady Isadora says that you read very entertainingly. My wife is giving a literary evening in town and she hopes to capture some of the best minds of our society. It is a pity that you could not be there, Miss Travers.'

'Yes, I should have enjoyed such an evening,' Elizabeth said. 'But you know that Lord Cavendish has a fine library here and I am able to indulge myself by reading whatever I choose.'

Elizabeth found that the evening passed very pleasantly. She managed a rather one-sided conversation with Lady Pamela, who talked incessantly about her pug dog called George.

'Named him for Mole, you know,' she announced in voice that carried across the room. 'But he's a better companion than my husband ever was, don't you know. Had him neutered as a pup. He don't stray, don't gamble and don't swear. His breath is like a sewer and he breaks wind frequently—but so did

Mole and I put up with him for forty years. Gone now, of course.'

Her tone was one of satisfaction, and Elizabeth was hard put to it to hide her smile, for it was clear that the lady was not one to mince her words.

'Word of advice, young woman. Look for money, position and a weak constitution when it comes to marriage and you'll live to enjoy the fruits of your labour.'

'Thank you, ma'am. I shall remember your advice.'

'I dare say a young woman like you thinks of love and romance,' her ladyship said, not having heard a word Elizabeth had spoken. 'But marry an old man and bed a young one, that's what I did—and I don't regret it!'

Elizabeth nodded and murmured something appropriate. Suddenly, she longed for someone to share her amusement with and wished that Lord Cavendish were sitting across the table from her so that she might catch his eye. However, it was Lady Roxborough that returned her gaze, looking decidedly amused. Elizabeth smiled, sharing the jest for a moment. She discovered that she liked Lady Roxborough, despite her rather rakish reputation.

After dinner the ladies retired to the drawing room. Julia Giles came to sit beside Elizabeth, engaging her in a conversation about clothes and fashions until she was called upon to play on the pianoforte. Elizabeth took her turn, singing a pretty little song before giving up her place to Julia.

Julia's hands ran expertly over the keys and Elizabeth acknowledged a superior talent. As Julia began to sing a pleasant melody, she was aware that the girl had a fine voice that might have graced any stage had she not been born into a family that would disapprove of such an outcome. She applauded enthusiastically as Julia's song came to an end, just as the gentlemen rejoined them.

'Ah, there you are, Miss Travers,' Reverend Bell said, gleefully occupying the vacant seat on the little sofa beside her. 'I was wondering if you had done any more about flowers for the church?'

'Yes, I believe so,' Elizabeth told him. 'I shall bring some flowers to the church tomorrow morning—and I hope we shall be able to make a worthwhile contribution to your festival next month, sir.'

'That is wonderful…' the reverend began, but was interrupted as General Montigrew came up to them.

'There you are, m'dear,' he said. 'I came to ask if Cavendish can mount you from his stables—if not, I am sure I have a nice little mare that would suit you a treat.'

'I believe Lord Cavendish has already decided on a mount for me,' Elizabeth told him. 'But it was very kind of you to think of it, sir.'

'Do you hunt, m'dear? I run a good set of hounds, though I believe Cavendish ain't a hunting man himself. You could always join us when we meet.'

'How thoughtful,' Elizabeth said. 'But Papa was not a hunting man and I have never followed the hounds.'

'Well, that is my good fortune. I can initiate you into the pleasures of it, m'dear.'

'Thank you, but we must see how things go on,' Elizabeth said. 'I am here to be a companion to Lady Isadora and I already have so many engagements and tasks to keep me busy.' She did not wish to join the hunt, but would not offend him for the world. 'And now, if you will excuse me, gentlemen. Lady Isadora needs me.'

Elizabeth escaped with a sigh of relief, and for the next half an hour or so was kept by her employer's side, talking to the ladies who sat close to her.

'I am so sorry, my dear,' Lady Isadora said as they went upstairs together after the guests had left. 'It was rather a boring evening for you. Reverend Bell is a very worthy gentleman, and the General is well meaning—but they did try to monopolise you, Elizabeth. If Daniel had been here, it might have been different.'

'Please do not worry,' Elizabeth said with a smile. 'Both gentlemen are very pleasant in their different ways—but I fear they do not like each other too well.'

'They usually rub along quite well,' Lady Isadora

said, 'but I did notice a little friction between them this evening.' She suspected that the cause of the black looks that had passed between the two gentlemen was her companion, but the notion did not please her and she said nothing of it to Elizabeth. Before the girl arrived, she had spoken of the visit to her friends, for she would have welcomed either of the two gentlemen as a prospective husband for her friend's unfortunate daughter. However, she had discovered very quickly that Elizabeth was not the poor creature she had half-expected, and she now believed that a rather different outcome would please her more.

Elizabeth also kept her thoughts to herself on the subject. She had formed her own opinions of General Montigrew and the Reverend Bell, also of Julia Giles, her parents and Lady Pamela, for they were the guests who had made the most impression on her. However, it was not of any of them that she was thinking as she undressed, went to bed and to sleep. Indeed, she did not sleep at once; her mind kept returning to the look in a certain person's eyes—the moment when she had been sure that he wanted to kiss her.

Oh, how foolish she was, Elizabeth thought. She was quite sure that even if it amused the earl to flirt with her to pass a little time, he would never think of her with love—and she was determined to accept nothing less from any man.

'Bother, bother, bother!' She sighed and turned over, restlessly seeking sleep, but when she did sleep her dreams were not at all the kind of thing that any proper young lady would admit to, for she was lying in his arms, being kissed in a way that was not at all decent! Really, she was being very foolish and she would do much better to keep a distance between them in future, instead of eagerly expecting his return.

Daniel glanced around the inn at which he had agreed to meet certain gentlemen. It was not the kind of place he usually frequented—it smelled of stale ale and unwashed bodies—but it was exactly the place he needed for what he was about to do that evening.

The attempted assassination of his best friend had made him realise just how dangerous were the men he was after. He could not be certain if they had suspected John Elworthy of playing a double game or if he had been shot in mistake for him, but either way it had brought Daniel up short. Until the moment that he found his friend, lying wounded on the ground, and bleeding profusely, he had, like John, found it hard to believe that Sir Montague Forsythe could truly have been behind the plot to kidnap Lady Elworthy's young sister, even though Maria had told them of her own beliefs. Now, he had begun to wonder just what he had stumbled into, and what kind of men he was dealing with.

That they were dangerous was not in doubt, which meant that he must take steps to protect his own back, and those he cared for. He had not considered giving up his quest for one moment. It was imperative that these evil men be brought to justice, and he would risk his own life to see that they were exposed. However, he did not wish to be the cause of harm to others. John, Lady Isadora and…Elizabeth must be adequately protected.

A grim smile touched his mouth as he thought of the young woman who had come into his life so recently. He had not expected her to be so…interesting. There had never been a shortage of ladies in Daniel's life. Indeed, he might have married years ago had he been inclined, but his youthful hopes had been dashed by a girl he had thought himself deeply in love with when he was but nineteen. Marina had been twenty, a year older, stunningly beautiful and a little wild. He had still been at Oxford when he met her, living on the allowance his father made him, which was generous but not the fortune Marina had been looking for at that time. She had married a duke nearly twice her age and seemed quite content with her bargain, giving her husband two healthy sons in exchange for a fortune in diamonds, emeralds and other baubles.

Her mocking refusal of his own proposal had been

painful. Because of it Daniel had begged his father to buy him a pair of colours, and spent the next few years learning to fight and to become a man. He was, at the age of five and thirty, very different from the youth who had fallen in love with a beautiful face. He had distinguished himself in the army, making a handsome portion from prize money, which he had then invested rather cleverly, and was now equally as wealthy as Marina's duke.

But his recollections were interrupted as he saw the large, ugly man enter the taproom, looking about him cautiously as he made his way towards the bar.

'A tankard of your ale, good landlord,' he said, and then, when he had it in his hand, approached Daniel's table. 'May I sit here, good sir?'

'Yes, surely,' Daniel said and smiled, for it had been agreed thus and he had already guessed that this was his contact. 'You are welcome to share my table and the fire, for the evening is chilly, is it not?'

'Aye, sir, it is, though the better nights are to come.' He sat down and looked at Daniel, his eyes bright and knowing. 'And what may I do for you, sir, if I may be so bold as to ask?'

'I believe you have several men at your disposal, sir?'

'Aye, I have that, my lord,' the stranger said, making up his mind that he was with gentry, though Daniel was plainly dressed and might pass as any other traveller. 'They be for hire to the right man at the right price. I don't murder and I don't rob, but there ain't much else out of bounds as I see it.'

'You have been reported to me as an honest man, Jesiah Tobbold—for that is your name, isn't it?'

'Ah, for the purposes of our business. You might call me Tobbold, sir, and I should answer right enough.'

'Good. Listen carefully, Tobbold. I have need of more good men—fellows that can be trusted in a tight spot.'

'Aye, I thought as much. Go on, sir. I be listening.'

'The men we are dealing with will, I believe, not have your principles. They do not stop at murder or robbery. A friend of mine was recently shot and left for dead. Had I not found him he might have died—and there is the kidnap of a young woman, perhaps more than one. Of the cheating of young idiots at the card tables I shall say little for there is no law to protect them from their folly.'

'These men are friends of yours, sir?'

'No, indeed, though I must claim them as acquaintances for the time being. I wish to discover the truth about their activities and bring them to justice. I have men watching them already, but they cannot be everywhere. I need more cover than I have at present. I have realised that there is more at stake than I had at first thought.'

'I'll put a few of my best men on it, sir. They won't suspect a thing—but there was more, I believe?'

'Yes, I am afraid for the safety of certain people I care for. I know that I may be a target, but I am aware of it and shall be on my guard—they, however, are vulnerable and may be used to bring me to my knees. I am willing to take risks with my own life, but not with theirs.'

'Understood, sir,' Tobbold said. 'If you would be so kind as to furnish me with names and locations, I shall endeavour to bring this business to a satisfactory conclusion.'

'Thank you,' Daniel said with a grim smile. 'What these men have done is a hanging matter—but we need proof.'

Tobbold looked at him hard. 'And if the proof is there but not admissible in a court of law, sir?'

Daniel frowned. 'We shall cross that bridge when we come to it.'

'But you want to be careful who you deal with, sir,' Tobbold warned. 'I stops short of murder, see—but there are other ways to see as these men come to their well-deserved fate.' Daniel raised his eyebrows, but Tobbold merely smiled. 'As you says, me lord—we'll cross that bridge when we comes to it…'

Elizabeth woke with a start. She lay for a moment in the darkness, wondering what she had heard, but everything was quiet and she thought that she must be mistaken. She had imagined the sound of breaking glass coming from somewhere downstairs, but very faintly, as if it might have been at the back of the house, perhaps. She lit a branch of candles at her bedside, but, looking at the little silver pendant watch that her father had bought her on her twentieth birthday, she saw that it was not quite six o'clock. Too early to rise, and yet now that she was awake she did not truly wish to lie in bed.

Sighing, she left her bed and dressed in a plain grey skirt and bodice and went downstairs, carrying her candle, for it was hardly light. As she reached the hall, she halted as she saw the young footman who had helped Mr Elworthy to bed a few days earlier. He put a finger to his lips and she felt a little chill down her spine.

'What is it?' she asked in a whisper. 'Did you hear something too?'

'I think there is someone in his lordship's library,' he said. 'You stay here, miss, while I go and investigate.'

'I shall come with you,' she said. 'I have no fear of intruders if you are with me, Forrest.'

'Stay well behind me, then,' he warned. 'Remember what happened to the gentleman upstairs, miss.'

'Yes, of course. I am not afraid,' she said, and clutched her heavy candlestick a little tighter. She would use it as a weapon if need be, though it would not be of much help against a pistol. 'Lead on, Forrest.'

She kept a few steps behind him as he walked softly down the hall, throwing open the library door and charging in with no sign of fear. Elizabeth followed behind, her heart racing. The light of her candle immediately revealed the shattered glass on the floor, which was evidence that someone had indeed broken in, but after a muffled curse, the footman completed a tour of the room and soon discovered that no one was there. And then Elizabeth saw that one of the windows was opened wide, as if someone had scrambled through it. She pointed it out and Forrest looked at her, a bewildered expression on his face.

'Now what was he up to, miss?' he asked. 'For he broke in, that much is sure—but why? Can you see if anything is missing?'

Elizabeth had started to light more candles. The massive brass candlesticks, which were placed about the room to facilitate the easy reading of books on dark afternoons, were still on their mahogany stands, as were the smaller silver ones on the mantelpiece. She glanced around her, looking for something that might be missing, and then her eye fell on the books she herself had placed on the table to be catalogued.

'I think there were six journals and now there are only five,' she said, feeling puzzled. She looked at the leather-bound books, which were family records and dated back to almost twenty years earlier. 'How strange. I think the records for 1791 are missing. Now, who would want to steal them—and at this hour of the morning?'

'It must be some village lout out for mischief after a night drinking bad ale,' Forrest said. 'It were a prank, miss. You go back to your room and I'll soon have this cleared. I don't think you should come here until I've got the glass replaced and made a search of the house—in case he is still here.'

'You mean in case it was not a prank,' Elizabeth said and frowned. 'I am vexed that this should have happened. Had I not left those books lying there, it would not have been such an easy task.'

'If it was just some old records, it shouldn't matter to his lordship,' Forrest said. 'Good thing it weren't one of the books he values, miss.'

'Yes, I suppose you are right,' Elizabeth said, but she was doubtful. Records dating back to twenty years earlier might contain all kinds of information that Lord Cavendish needed, and she was extremely disturbed that they should have been stolen. She shivered, leaving the room as the footman had advised. It was an uncomfortable feeling to know that someone had broken into the house so easily.

Walking back to her room, Elizabeth was thoughtful. She was convinced that Lord Cavendish was mixed up in something dangerous, but she could not for the life of her see why anyone should want to steal his records. Had they stolen silver or valuable books she could have understood it—but why a journal that contained only details of the earl's family?

Not for the first time, she wished that he would return from his visit to York. He might not have prevented what had happened that morning, but she would feel much easier once she had told him what had occurred in his absence.

Chapter Five

Elizabeth asked if she might borrow the pony and trap to drive herself to the church a little later that morning. It would have been too far to walk, carrying the bucket of cut flowers that Mr Browning had sent up to the house for her use. She was particularly pleased with the irises and the lilies, which, though not as fine as those he had loaned them for the house party, were still sufficiently beautiful to make a wonderful show in the church.

Elizabeth saved four of them for a vase for Lady Isadora's boudoir and took the rest to the church, where she spent an enjoyable half an hour arranging them in suitable vases. She was just leaving when the Reverend Bell came up to her.

'My sincere apologies for not being here to greet you, Miss Travers,' he said. 'I was called out early this morning to the bedside of a dying woman. Mary

Cotton was nearly ninety, a great age. However, she had always been sprightly and her loss is a grief to all who knew her for she was a kindly soul.'

'That is a shame,' Elizabeth said. 'I dare say your presence gave her comfort at the end.'

'She said that it did, for she was a true believer.' Pausing for a moment, he said, 'I am glad that I caught you before you left—I wanted to say how much I enjoyed last evening.' He glanced around the church. 'What a truly remarkable display, Miss Travers. I do not know when I have seen the church look better. I must thank you for your efforts on our behalf.'

'Thank you, but I believe that Mr Browning deserves your gratitude. It is he who grew these flowers. I have only placed them in water.'

'But to great advantage,' he said. 'Miss Julia Giles sometimes brings flowers for the church, but she does not have your artistry or your excellent taste.'

'Oh, I think I have achieved nothing special,' Elizabeth said. 'And now I must leave; I have kept the pony standing long enough.' She smiled at him. 'May I take you up, sir? I could drop you off somewhere if you have a journey to make.'

'No, no, there is nothing for the moment. I must go into the house and break my fast, but I wished to see you first.'

Elizabeth nodded and they parted company. She

drove back to the house at a fast trot and was just in time to see the earl draw up outside the front entrance in his curricle. He threw the reins to his groom, jumped down and came to her as she prepared to hand the trap to a stable lad.

'Miss Travers,' he said. 'I did not know that you drove yourself. You are full of surprises.'

'Oh, I am accustomed to driving the governess's cart at home,' Elizabeth said. She was feeling a little light-headed, no doubt from jumping down a little too fast. 'Simon and I both learned when we were small, and I often took it when I wished to visit the village. I have been doing the flowers for the church this morning, and they would have been too heavy to carry alone. Rather than take Amy from her work, I decided to drive myself.'

'You are telling me that Browning actually gave you more than a handful of his precious blooms? You must have impressed him greatly.' The earl raised his brows, a quizzing look in his eyes. She looked re-markably well, the fresh air having brought colour to her cheeks. 'Tell me, do you intend to manage us all, Miss Travers?'

'Now, sir, this will not do,' Elizabeth said reprov-ingly. 'You must know that Lady Isadora asked me to help with the flowers for the church.'

'Indeed, I am sure that she did.' Daniel smiled, recovering from an urgent need to sweep her up and carry her off to his bed. 'Pray inform me—how is John?'

'He was much better when the doctor looked in on him yesterday. I believe he told Forrest that he had had a good night and would come down later today.'

'I am glad to hear it,' Daniel said as they turned towards the house. 'Did you enjoy meeting our neighbours last evening, Miss Travers?' There was a hint of mischief in his face and Elizabeth was suddenly reminded of her conversation with Lady Pamela.

'Oh, I did so wish you had been there,' she said impulsively. In that moment their minds were perfectly in tune and she glanced up at him, mischief sparkling in her face. Daniel caught his breath, for she little knew the effect she was having on him at that moment. He had seldom felt such an urgent need to bed any woman, and some of his mistresses had been very beautiful—far more beautiful than the woman who was causing him such physical discomfort at this moment. 'It was most amusing. Lady Pamela was telling me about her pug dog, which it seems she named for her departed husband.'

'Ah, yes, Lady Pamela. She is one of my favourite people,' Daniel said, a hint of amusement in his eyes. 'Some may find her a little difficult, but I like her way of speaking her mind.'

'She certainly does that, sir.'

'Yes, indeed,' he said, his eyes intent on her face. 'It would seem that we have much in common, Miss Travers.'

'Perhaps…' Elizabeth recalled the incident earlier that morning and frowned. 'I fear I have something less amusing to tell you, sir. I have said nothing of it to your mama and I warned Forrest not to speak of it below stairs.'

'You intrigue me, Miss Travers.' His gaze was narrowed, intent, for it was clearly something of importance she had to tell him. 'Pray continue if you will.'

'I was woken just before six this morning by a sound, which I thought might have been breaking glass. It is my custom to sleep with the window open, you see, and the sound came from outside. At first I thought I must have been mistaken, but, feeling restless, I dressed and came downstairs. I then discovered that Forrest had also heard something, which he believed might have come from the library. He went ahead of me just in case, but though we found broken glass, no one was there. Whoever it was must have entered and left again very quickly.'

'An intruder had broken into the library?' Daniel frowned, his ardour dampened as he suddenly became deadly serious. 'That is very strange. I know some of the books to be valuable, but I would have thought there were other items of greater value elsewhere.'

'Yes, I dare say,' Elizabeth agreed, 'but I do not think the motive was to steal valuable items. I cannot be sure, of course, but I believe one of the family journals has been taken, though I think nothing else. It seems that the intruder did not have enough time to go elsewhere. Forrest was already downstairs and he says he would have seen anyone coming from the library.'

'You think a journal was stolen—for what year?'

'I believe it was a record of the year from 1791 to 1792,' Elizabeth told him, wrinkling her brow. 'It seems so foolish to break in to steal it, for I dare say the book contained nothing but family papers. I cannot imagine what anyone would hope to find in such a journal.'

'Nor I,' Daniel admitted. 'Unless…' He shook his head. 'I cannot imagine of what use my father's records would be to anyone but myself.'

'That is what I thought,' Elizabeth said. 'Of course, your father did have a habit of slipping letters and documents between the pages…'

'Did he?' Daniel was surprised. 'I had no idea. You have discovered something that is new to me, Miss Travers.'

'A paper dropped from the books when I was moving and dusting them the previous day,' Elizabeth said. 'I replaced it in one of the volumes that I have stored on the middle shelf, though I was not quite certain where it had come from. After that, I was careful not to let anything fall out, and I noticed that there were several lists lodged between pages, as well as a letter or two.'

'What kind of letters?' Daniel was intrigued.

'I really do not know,' Elizabeth said. 'I did not read them. The one that dropped on the floor began oddly, but I did not read its contents.'

'What do you mean, oddly?'

'I glanced at it as I retrieved it,' Elizabeth said. 'I think it read something like "To Whom it may concern…"'

'Indeed?' Daniel looked thoughtful. 'That sounds like a confession or a will…interesting. And you placed it in a book on the middle shelf?'

'Yes. I believe it was for the year 1805 to 1806, if my memory serves me rightly, but it may not have come from there because I had been dusting for some time before I noticed it on the floor. I did not actually see it fall.'

'Ah…' Daniel nodded. 'Now I am truly intrigued, Miss Travers. Do you think that our mystery intruder could have been looking for that letter?'

'It is possible that it fell from between the pages of the book he stole, sir. If he suspected that it should be there, he might not have stopped to look. I did not examine the date, because it was private, but I would say it was an old letter for the ink was faded.'

'Then perhaps luck was on our side and we shall find it where you placed it,' Daniel said and smiled at her approvingly. She was as intelligent as she was desirable—a lethal combination in any woman, and particularly so in this one. In the few hours he had spent in her company she had got beneath his skin—at the moment he was not sure what he ought to do about it. 'You are observant, Miss Travers.'

'It is my habit to be so. I only hope that it will help you solve the puzzle of the intruder, sir.'

'Is it still sir? I had hoped for Cavendish by now.' His keen eyes dwelled on her face, trying to read her mind and failing. Did she like him, did she trust him—would she respond to his lovemaking or be horrified? And if she melted into his arms as she had in his recent dreams, what then? How could he think of his own concerns when he still had not succeeded in finding Sarah Hunter?

'You are impatient, sir,' Elizabeth said. 'We have not yet been acquainted for long enough to be upon such terms, I think—and I *am* your mother's companion, after all.'

'Yes, of course, or so she claims,' Daniel said, 'though I believe she thinks of you as a friend.'

'Indeed, I hope to become her friend, and yours, sir, in time, but I would not wish to presume.'

'I thought we had established that we were friends

before I left?' He raised his brows at her, for he sensed a new reserve in her manner. She had not been thus when they talked in the garden.

'You must excuse me,' Elizabeth said, knowing what he asked with that look, but feeling unable to answer his unspoken question. 'Lady Isadora will be needing me soon.'

As she disappeared into the house, leaving the earl to stare after her, Elizabeth was asking herself why she had been so formal with him. When he came to her at the start her heart had behaved very strangely, and she had felt such a leap of joy that it had frightened her. It was ridiculous that she should feel such pleasure in his return. He had been away from home only a couple of days. She would be foolish indeed to become reliant on the sound of his voice, and the smile that made her heart race so wildly. The earl was an attractive man who might choose the ladies in his life as he pleased, and she was his mother's companion. For a moment she had been in danger of forgetting, and so had thought it prudent to remind both him and herself.

If she were to make a new life for herself here, she must be careful to keep the earl at a distance, for if she let him under her skin he might break her heart. But, a tiny voice asked in her head, was it not already too late? Was he not already too deeply in her heart and her mind?

No, no, she must not be foolish! This was all nonsense and it would not do for Miss Elizabeth Travers, who prided herself on her strong will. She would put such foolish thoughts away from her, for she was probably making something out of nothing.

'How are you, sir?' Elizabeth saw Mr Elworthy leaving his room as she prepared to go down for nuncheon later that morning. 'You look much better than you did.'

'I am feeling pretty well,' John told her with a smile. 'I think I am fortunate not to have taken a fever, as is so often the outcome in these cases. I may be a little weak still, but the pain is not so bad as it was for a start.'

'I am glad to see you so much recovered,' Elizabeth said. 'But are you quite sure you wish to leave your room so soon? It might be best if you were to rest for a day or so longer.'

'You are so thoughtful,' John replied, looking at her with affection. Daniel, coming out into the hall at that moment and looking up at them as they paused together at the head of the stairs, was struck by his friend's expression. 'But I think—Daniel! So you are back then…'

'I was about to visit you,' Daniel said. 'Are you well enough to be down, man?'

'I shall not overdo things. But I did not wish to make more work for your household.'

'Good grief, what nonsense,' the earl said. 'It will give them something to do. There is little enough when it is just Mama here.'

'Well, do not fret over it,' John said. 'It is such a nice day that I thought I might walk a little in the gardens after nuncheon—perhaps Miss Travers would accompany me?'

'I should be happy to do so after tea,' Elizabeth said. 'I do not know what Lady Isadora would have me do this afternoon—but we are reading *The Taming of the Shrew* together, you know.'

'You mean you are reading it and Mama is pretending to listen while she dozes,' Daniel said with a wry smile. His eyes dwelled on Elizabeth; she had been relaxed in John's company, but he sensed that she now had a barrier in place—a barrier that was meant to shut him out. Which was provoking of the wench when he was trying to get to know her better!

'Indeed, I do not doze while Elizabeth is reading,' his mama said, from the top of the stairs. 'You should join us, Daniel. You might learn something.'

'Unfortunately, I have business this afternoon,' Daniel said, 'but I am sure that John would enjoy the reading.'

'Yes, indeed,' he said. 'Very much. If I may sit quietly in your parlour, Lady Isadora? I promise to be no trouble to you.'

'How could you be a trouble?' she asked and gave

her son a hard look. 'We shall be glad of your company, sir. Elizabeth reads so well that I am sure you will not be bored.'

'Oh, no, I should never be bored in your company, ma'am—or Miss Travers's, I am sure.'

'Well, we shall be glad to have you,' she said again. 'Daniel, I cannot think what business takes you away from us so soon. You have just this moment returned.'

'My apologies, Mama,' Daniel said. 'But this time it is urgent estate matters. One of our tenants has a problem with his roof and I must decide what repairs need to be done.'

'Oh, very well,' she said with a wave of her hand. 'We shall excuse you—but I want your promise that you will escort us to Brighton in two weeks' time.'

'So soon, Mama?' Daniel raised his brows, for he had not expected it. 'Would you not find it more convenient to visit Harrogate as you usually do at this season? It might be a little cool at the sea just now.'

'Harrogate is full of old men and women with the agues,' Lady Isadora said. 'If it is too soon for Brighton, we shall go to Bath.'

'I take it you are recovered from your illness?' Daniel said, a wicked glint in his eyes. 'I had thought you still an invalid, Mama.'

Lady Isadora gave a little cough behind her hand as she advanced down the stairs, giving her son an awful look. 'It is for my health that I need to take the waters,' she said. 'Perhaps we shall stay here until the end of next month. It should be warm enough for Brighton by then, for we shall be into June.'

'A much better idea, Mama,' Daniel said. 'I shall post up to London tomorrow. I have business there—forgive me, but it is important—and then I shall bring a party of friends to stay with you for a week or two so that you will not lack for company.'

'Oh, very well,' his mama said, accepting that he intended to have his way. Clearly he did not want her to leave the estate for the time being, though she could not think why. He was always telling her that she ought to visit these places. 'But I shall want your escort when we go to Brighton, Cavendish.' She never called him by his title unless displeased and Daniel knew himself rebuked.

'Indeed, Mama, I should not think of letting you go unescorted.' Daniel looked satisfied, as well he might, having made arrangements for the estate to be protected day and night. It would not be so easy once his mother and Elizabeth left Cavendish—and he thought that he would do his best to keep John here for the time being also. It was easier to protect those dearest to him if they were under the same roof. He turned his thoughtful gaze on John Elworthy. 'You look pale, my friend. I hope you are not thinking of leaving us for a while?'

'Well, no…that is, if I am not a burden to Lady Isadora?'

'Of course not, you silly boy,' Lady Isadora said looking at him warmly. 'We shall both be delighted to have your company—shall we not, Elizabeth?'

'Yes, of course, ma'am,' Elizabeth agreed. Her eyes had hardly left the earl's face as he was speaking to his mother and she was puzzled. Why did he not wish Lady Isadora to leave the estate? Unless it was for a special reason. 'Besides, I think that Mr Elworthy should rest for some days, at least until he has recovered from the severe loss of blood. I see no harm in him coming down for a while, but he must certainly not think of making a journey just yet.'

'There, John, now you have been told,' Daniel said, a gleam in his eyes. Oh, what a joy she was! Used to his mother's habit of coy persuasion or sullen pouts to get her own way, he found Elizabeth's direct manner refreshing. She said what she thought and made nothing of it! One could almost have been dealing with a man—except that he had never been in the least inclined to throw any man upon the sheets and ravish him. 'Miss Travers speaks for your own good, you know. I think you must listen to her.'

'Yes, of course. I am only too happy to remain,' John said, quite content to take everything at surface value and unaware of the undercurrents circling between Elizabeth and Daniel as their eyes met and fought their secret battle. 'I have nothing at all to return home for, you know.'

'Then it is settled,' Daniel said and gave his friend a meaningful look. His look for Elizabeth was deceivingly innocent, giving nothing away. 'I must go to London, but I shall return as soon as I may—and hope to bring some friends with me.'

The subject was dropped. Lady Isadora led the way into the dining room. The sideboard had been set with silver chafing dishes, which contained a variety of hot and cold meats, and for the next hour or so they ate and drank. The table conversation ranged from the flowers Elizabeth had taken to the church to the latest reported exploits of the Prince Regent—who had once again been shockingly lampooned in the newssheets! And, having enjoyed herself, it was with regret that Elizabeth watched the earl rise from the table and excuse himself to the company.

'Daniel is a conscientious landlord,' his mother remarked after he had left. 'I know that I have reason to be grateful for his industry. My husband did not leave his affairs in good order and Daniel has had hard work of it to make things right—but I sometimes wish he was not continually so busy.'

'My father liked to be busy,' Elizabeth said. 'Mama always maintained it was best to let him do as he pleased, otherwise he would be like a bear with a sore head and cause more trouble than it was worth. I dare say Lord Cavendish likes to have his own way now and then.'

John Elworthy almost choked on his wine, but managed to suppress his mirth, sensing the humour that lay beneath Elizabeth's remark. 'I fear we men are a shocking trial to you ladies,' he said, a twinkle in his eye.

'Oh, no,' Lady Isadora said, quite unaware that she was being teased. 'It is nothing of the kind—I have always thought you very nice in your manners. It is only Daniel who can be so very provoking.'

'I dare say he has much to do,' Elizabeth said to soothe her. Much as she might agree that the earl was indeed provoking, somehow she did not like to hear him disparaged in his absence. 'Running a large estate such as this can be difficult—and I believe Lord Cavendish has more than one.'

'This is the smallest of them all,' Lady Isadora said. 'And by far the most comfortable house. The others are ramshackle barns and should be pulled down in my opinion—but my late husband would not have it. I believe Daniel has some such plans for the house in Devonshire.'

They rose from table and went into a sunny front parlour. After Lady Isadora was settled comfortably on her daybed, Elizabeth opened the book of plays and took up where she had left off. She read for a while, and then they came to the part where Kate was married and so well pleased with her state that she made the speech telling wives to be mindful of their husbands.

'Why, there's a wench! Come on and kiss me, Kate,' Elizabeth said in the voice she was using for Petruchio. She then read the lines between Lucentio and Vincentio, but before she could read out Petruchio's last lines, a voice spoke from the doorway.

'Come, Kate, we'll to bed. We three are married, but you two are sped.'

Elizabeth glanced round, her heart catching as she saw that the earl was looking directly at her. She could not mistake the look in his eyes, for with the words he had spoken it was a clear invitation. He was certainly flirting with her—perhaps as a prelude to seduction. 'Well done, sir,' she said, a faint flush in her cheeks for the realisation had brought with it pictures that she found wildly erotic and were not suitable for a lady's sitting room. 'You have a good memory.'

'Nay, for I remember only that line,' Daniel said, advancing into the room. He gave her a look of contrition, for he saw he had thrown her into confusion and this was not the place or time for dalliance. 'Forgive me. I should not have interrupted your excellent reading.'

'Well, you have,' his mother said a little crossly. 'But it is the end of the play and it does not matter. I thought you had business elsewhere?'

'Indeed, I had, but it took less time than I had thought,' Daniel said. 'I should like to steal John from you now—unless you wish to rest before dinner, my friend?'

'That was an excellent reading, Miss Travers,' John said, getting to his feet. 'I was thinking of having a rest before dinner—but I can spare a little time for you, Daniel.'

Lady Isadora frowned as the two men went off together. 'It was very unkind in Daniel to put you off your stride, Elizabeth.'

'Oh, no, he did not,' Elizabeth lied, for there had been something in the earl's eyes that had made her mouth run dry. Had she not been sitting down she might have felt her knees buckle. It was clear to her now that he was amusing himself at her expense, though whether out of a provoking humour or a genuine desire to get her into his bed she could not be sure. Either way it was too bad of him! 'What shall we read tomorrow—or do you not read for entertainment on Sunday?'

'My father disliked it,' Lady Isadora said. 'When I was a child we were allowed only our Bibles, you know—but perhaps we ought to do a little work on the altar cloth. I began it such a long time ago and I am afraid I am very lazy about such things.'

is not wise—but perhaps whoever stole the book was looking for this and believed…'

'That his name might be in a letter of this kind?'

'Yes, that is what came to mind,' Elizabeth admitted and wrinkled her brow in thought. 'But…why now? Forgive me, but I think this must have been written many years ago. I see now that it is not dated, but it was in the records of nearly twenty years ago and the ink is faded. Besides, your father has been dead some time.'

Daniel nodded. 'Why steal it now? That is what you are asking, isn't it? I have no idea of what my father saw or knew, though the inference is plain enough. Some mischief was done to a decent girl, mischief he suspected prior to the offence, but did nothing to stop. Why was that, do you imagine?'

'Perhaps the men were acquaintances or friends?'

'Yes, I think that may have been the case. I know that he stopped going to town at about the time this letter was probably written. He had been in the habit of visiting London alone, for Mama has never liked it. She has always preferred Harrogate or Bath, more recently Brighton. I believe my father may have got into bad company at one time, for his estates suffered and he was forced to live modestly for the last few years of his life.'

'But that does not answer…unless…' She looked at him as an idea occurred. 'Are you involved in some dangerous game, sir? You warned me of Sir Montague Forsythe…does this in some way concern him?'

'I had not planned to tell you anything,' Daniel said with a frown, 'but I thought you had begun to suspect something was afoot. And perhaps for your own safety you should know. I am investigating the affairs of a certain gentleman and if what I suspect is true…'

'I know that he somehow cheated Papa, and was responsible for his death, if only because he had led my father to ruin—but are you saying that he might be involved in worse?'

'Much worse,' Daniel told her. 'I may not reveal the whole to you. It is better that you do not know, for you would be much distressed—but I now suspect that my father may have known something of the business years ago. And that means Forsythe and his cronies are greater villains than even I suspected.'

'The abduction of young girls for the white slave trade,' Elizabeth said, her face pale. 'You may imagine that I would be shocked, sir, but my father spoke out against the foul trade more than once. He never discussed it with me, of course, but I know that he had had some experience of it in our wider family—a distant cousin's daughter, I believe. He wrote to *The Times* on more than one occasion as I recall. And then we had a young maidservant who was lured away to London and disappeared. Her family never heard of her again. My father was most concerned about it, and I know he tried to have her disappearance investigated…'

Daniel looked at her as she stopped speaking, horror in her eyes. 'Yes, it would explain why Sir Montague set out to ruin your father, would it not? If your father had discovered something that might point the finger of blame at him and his friends.'

Elizabeth put a hand to her throat. 'If that is the case, Papa may have been murdered. I have never believed that he would kill himself and leave us to pick up the pieces. That is the coward's way, sir, and my father was never afraid to face what life offered. Even if he had been foolish enough to lose everything, he would have done his best for us.'

'No, I am sure he was not a coward, for he could not otherwise have fathered a daughter such as you. It seems he may have known too much and had to be silenced,' Daniel said and frowned. 'But the murder of a gentleman is no easy thing to cover—unless he appears to have ruined himself and takes his own life. Perhaps with some forceful assistance.'

'Poor Papa,' Elizabeth said. Her head was spinning and for a moment she felt faint. She gave a little cry, clutching at the nearest object to steady herself. Daniel moved towards her, catching her in his arms, holding her. She could feel his strength, the support of his arms comforting her. She longed to melt into his body, to let him take her as he would, but then she recalled herself. This was not the behaviour of a properly brought up young lady! The world might be well lost for a few moments of pleasure—but what then? She made a little movement and he released her instantly. 'Thank you, but it was only a slight faintness. I suspected foul play in my father's death—but I did not understand why. Now I begin to see that there were reasons for what happened.'

'We have no proof,' Daniel reminded her, frowning. The feel of her in his arms had aroused feelings that he had not experienced before: a fierce need to protect and cherish her, to keep her safe from all harm. 'This letter is useless as it stands. If only the writer had made it more clear…named the men who had shamed that poor girl all those years ago.'

'Perhaps he did at a later time,' Elizabeth suggested. 'It may be that there is something in those journals…'

'And that he spoke of the proof to someone…' Daniel frowned. 'But this is only conjecture.'

'If the journal has been stolen, we shall never know the truth,' Elizabeth said. 'But I cannot be sure where this page fell from. It may be that something still remains.'

'It would still not be sufficient, even if we could find it, for it is but one man's word against another's—but it would be a big help.' Daniel looked thoughtful. 'I have an agent in London I must see about this business. He should have a report for me, but…'

'If I could find something in the meantime, it might be of help to you?'

'Yes, it must be of use,' he told her. 'I have made arrangements to have the house watched day and night, Miss Travers. There should be no more intruders.' It was even more imperative now!

'I imagined you had some such plan,' Elizabeth said, 'for you clearly did not wish your mama to leave the estate for a few weeks.'

'Once she goes to Brighton it will be more difficult to protect her,' he admitted. 'I hope to have this business finished before then.'

'Then you think you have something more substantial than a letter written many years ago?'

'I know that my father briefly belonged to the Hellfire Club,' Daniel said. 'My agent has traced others who were also members at one time. It is to speak with one of those gentleman that I make my journey tomorrow. He may be able to supply me with further information.'

'I understand,' she said, for she had heard something of the club, which was rumoured to have Satanic rituals. 'I must admit that I have a keen interest in the outcome of your investigation, sir, and I wish you well of it. I hope that you will let me know the outcome?'

'I shall certainly tell you as much as I can,' Daniel said. 'And now I must not delay you longer—I am sure you have things to do before dinner.' It was best that he let her go—if she stayed his good intentions might be lost once more.

'Yes, of course,' Elizabeth said. She had nothing in particular to do, but guessed that he wished to end the conversation for reasons of his own. Leaving him in the library, she considered what she had learned. He was indeed caught in a dangerous game—and it appeared likely that her father had been destroyed by the same evil men that Lord Cavendish was trying to bring down.

She experienced a knot of apprehension in her stomach, for she did not like to think of him in danger. He was a provoking, dangerously attractive man who she believed had some thought of seducing her for amusement's sake—but she would not have harm come to him. No, that would be the cause of some pain to her. However, nothing she could say would change his purpose. Indeed, she admired him for what he was doing, though she prayed that he would not suffer a similar fate to her father—or indeed his friend, who had been shot so wickedly on his way to visit Daniel.

Elizabeth was at her window when Daniel drove away the next morning. She saw him speak to a groom and then take up his seat on the board of the sporting curricle. He flicked his long whip above the heads of his team of splendid grey horses and set off at a spanking pace.

Sighing, she turned away from the window. She had spent a restless night thinking of him and his mission, and the knowledge that he might be in some danger hung on her heavily. He had told his mother that he would be away a few days, but she doubted whether he would return before the week's end. However, it was not for her to repine over his absence. He might decide to stay in town for some weeks, especially if his business proved fruitful. Besides, she must not become too accustomed to his presence in the house for her own sake. To let herself care too deeply about a man who was unlikely to return her sentiments would just not do! She must remember that he might take his pick of eager ladies and was not likely to settle for his mother's companion. Toying with her might amuse him for a while, but his mind would pass to other things once he was in London.

Lady Isadora was up earlier than her usual custom to attend church that morning, and they drove to the church together in a comfortable carriage. It was a pleasant sermon, for the Reverend Bell was celebrating the recovery of a parishioner and refrained from lecturing them on the evils of selfishness or greed. There were beautifully embroidered cushions for them to kneel on, and the pews had comfortable hollows where they had been worn away over the centuries by generations of devout worshippers.

After they left the church, they lingered for a while, talking to friends and enjoying the mild spring sunshine. Elizabeth found herself talking to Julia Giles, who was looking very pretty in a blue-and-white striped silk gown with short puffed sleeves, a wool shawl draped over her bare arms.

'Do you not think that Mr Bell has a wonderful speaking voice?' Julia asked, looking at his tall figure as he stood shaking hands with his congregation one by one. 'He is such a fine man, would you not agree?'

'Yes, very worthy,' Elizabeth said. 'He seems to care for the needy almost too much.'

'He is everything that a truly good man should be.' Julia sighed, a look of longing on her pretty face. 'He speaks very highly of you, Miss Travers.'

'Does he?' Elizabeth was a little surprised. 'He hardly knows me. We have met but twice, and he can have formed no true opinion.'

'Oh, but he says you are everything a woman should aspire to be—and that I would benefit from your company.'

'No! That was too bad of him,' Elizabeth said. 'How

provoking for you. I assure you, Miss Giles, it is not so. You have no need to learn anything from me.'

'There, you have proved what he says for you are too modest. The flowers in church today were magnificent and put my poor efforts to shame.'

'I merely placed them in water,' Elizabeth said. 'Mr Browning—our head gardener—grew them and it is their perfection that makes them look so well.'

'We have never had such beautiful flowers before.'

'They were perfect specimens—particularly the lilies,' Elizabeth agreed. 'Do you like flowers, Miss Giles?'

'I love them,' Julia said. 'But please, do call me Julia.'

'Then you must call me Elizabeth in return.' She smiled at the younger girl. 'I know that you are very busy preparing for your visit to London, but if you should like it I might arrange for you to see Mr Browning's glasshouses. He has some wonderful plants, many of which flower in their season.'

'Oh, I should like that very much,' Julia said. 'May I come tomorrow morning? If it is fine I shall walk, but if there is rain in the air Papa will send me in the carriage.'

'Yes, please do come,' Elizabeth told her. 'Stay for nuncheon and tea if you wish. I am sure Lady Isadora would enjoy your company.'

'Oh yes, I like Lady Dora,' Julia said, dimpling

mischievously. 'She is so relaxing, is she not? I should have liked to come today, but Papa has a guest coming this evening—and I shall be required to be there for dinner. I would rather not for I do not like the gentleman, but…' She frowned, the light leaving her eyes.

'Yes, well, you must do as your father thinks best,' Elizabeth said. 'If your father's guest is a friend, it would not be right for you to be absent or late, Julia.'

'Yes, I know, but…' a little shudder went through Julia '…it is just the way that he looks at me. He is so much older and yet I think…but, no, Papa would not allow it.'

Elizabeth had no time to ask more questions as Julia's mother was beckoning to her. They parted company and Elizabeth joined Lady Isadora, who was about to climb into their carriage.

'I am glad to see you making friends with Julia,' she said as Elizabeth followed her. 'She is a nice girl, if a little silly. Time will alter that, of course. She is still very young for her age. It is good of you to take an interest in her, Elizabeth.'

'I like her,' Elizabeth said. 'I believe she is a gentle, willing girl and if she is a little excited about her Season in London, who shall blame her?'

'Who, indeed?' Lady Isadora smiled at her.

'I have invited her to come to us tomorrow. She was admiring the flowers in the church and I said that Mr

Browning might show her his prime blooms in the glasshouses. She may stay for nuncheon and tea if that is suitable, ma'am?'

'Yes, of course,' Lady Isadora said. 'You know that I love young company, and it will be pleasant—especially if Mr Elworthy feels able to join us again.'

'I understand he was feeling a little tired this morning,' Elizabeth told her. 'Which is a result of his staying up late with Lord Cavendish last evening, but I dare say he will be recovered by tomorrow.'

The two ladies returned to the house in harmony with each other. Mr Elworthy had sent his apologies and asked them to excuse him from coming down, and so they spent the rest of the day quietly. Elizabeth got out the altar cloth and managed to complete one panel, though Lady Isadora made little contribution apart from encouraging her and suggesting certain colours that blended well together.

However, progress was made and Elizabeth felt that she was establishing a place for herself in the Cavendish household. She sat writing a letter to her brother that evening, telling him that she had met Mr John Elworthy and that he would gain nothing from insisting on an interview.

Mr Elworthy is quite willing to see you if you wish, Simon, but you must not expect too much. Just be patient, dearest, and things may work out better than you hoped. I can tell you nothing more for the moment, but I have hopes of justice in the future.

She went on to tell him how well she was settling in, sanded her letter and sealed it. She would place it on the hall table in the morning for posting with the other letters. Sighing, she sought her bed. She was annoyed with herself for letting her thoughts dwell too often on a man who she was perfectly sure had not given her a second thought.

'I have never seen such wonderful plants,' Julia exclaimed as she looked in awe at some of the unusual ferns and flowering species. 'Papa has a glasshouse, of course, but our gardener does not produce anything half as fine.'

'That is good of you to say, miss,' Able Browning said, looking pleased with himself. 'Them orchids be temperamental creatures and takes some coaxing. I pampers 'em, see, and that's why they blooms like they does.'

'They are exquisite,' Julia said. 'Do you not think so, Elizabeth?'

'I have told Mr Browning that I think him a magician to produce such a wonderful variety. And it seems that there is always some new treasure to find.'

'Well, they likes to shine on their own for a bit,' Able said. 'Them lilies was the prima donnas when you came the first time, Miss Travers—but now them little orchids there is having their turn. I moves 'em round when they starts to fade, and they rests until it be time for them to take the leading light again.'

Julia laughed, a light trilling sound like a little bird. 'Oh, how wonderful,' she said. 'I am so glad that you allowed me to visit your treasures, sir.'

'Well, miss, you be pretty yourself, and pretty things should do well together I always says. Here, this be for you, miss. Take it home, but don't kill it with kindness—not too much water, like—and bring her back if she takes sick and I'll sort her out for you.'

He presented Julia with a little pot of tiny pink flowers sprouting out of a prickly cactus plant. Her cheeks blushed prettily and she took it from him with a shy smile.

'Thank you, Mr Browning. That is very kind of you and I shall take great care of my cactus.'

Elizabeth hid her smile, for Julia was undoubtedly a hit with the gardener. 'We had best go back now,' she said. 'Lady Isadora will be expecting us for lunch.'

'Yes, of course.' Julia said and glanced at the gardener. 'Thank you so much for my present. I should like to come again one day if I may, sir.'

They left together, Julia carrying her cactus gently. Elizabeth was happy with the way things had gone, for the younger girl had shown good manners and been genuinely pleased with what she saw.

'Mr Browning must have approved of you,' she said as they walked towards the house. 'He does not part with his treasures lightly, Julia.'

'It was so generous of him,' the girl said. 'He was so kind and funny…I did not feel at all afraid of him.'

Something in her voice made Elizabeth look at her. 'Are you sometimes afraid of men, Julia?'

'I do not like some of Papa's friends,' Julia said, a shadow in her eyes. 'Mr Palmer frightens me when he looks at me. His eyes…' A little shudder ran through her. 'I feel uncomfortable. Almost as if…'

'As if what?' Elizabeth asked. 'Do not be afraid to tell me, Julia. I shall not censure you.'

'He looks at me as if he can see me with no clothes on,' Julia said and blushed bright pink. 'I go hot and my stomach clenches inside. I am afraid to be near him, because he touches me…oh, not in an intimate way, but the touch of his hand makes me want to run away and hide.'

'Does your father know how you feel?'

'I could not tell him,' Julia said. 'I have tried to explain to Mama, but she says I must be careful not to show my dislike too openly. I think Papa has some business with Mr Palmer…' She shook her head. 'I must not be foolish. I am sure he means me no harm, for he is always paying me compliments.'

'You should be careful of him,' Elizabeth said. 'If

your instincts tell you that he is not a nice man, you are probably right. Be polite as your mama tells you, but be careful not to be alone with him.'

'Well, he has gone now,' Julia said, 'and I dare say I shall not see him again for a while—though he may be in London, of course.'

'When do you go up exactly?'

'At the end of next week,' Julia said. 'I am looking forward to it—at least I was…'

'Has something happened to change your mind?'

'Oh…' Julia looked awkward. 'It is just that I should not like to marry anyone like Mr Palmer.'

'Your father has not said that you should?'

'Oh, no. Papa is too kind to force me into something I should dislike. It was just that Mama said he is a little worried about his business dealings with Mr Palmer and I thought—' She broke off and shook her head as if it was too much for her.

'I see,' Elizabeth said. 'I dare say there is nothing for you to fear, Julia. I am sure you will meet lots of nice young men and fall in love with one of them.'

'Perhaps…' Julia looked wistful. 'Mama says that I should marry a man who can keep me in the manner I am accustomed to—and that I should look for a title if possible.'

'And what would you like?'

'I am not sure.' Julia frowned. 'I am looking

forward to my Season, Elizabeth, but…I think I should prefer to marry a man I can like and admire. I do not care for his fortune so much, but I do not think Mama would allow me to marry someone…' Her words trailed away unhappily.

'Someone like the Reverend Bell perhaps?'

'Oh…' Julia blushed. 'Have I been so obvious? I do like him very well, though I am not sure he approves of me. He thinks me frivolous and empty headed, and perhaps I am—but I hope my feelings have not been on view for all to see?'

'No, you have not been obvious at all,' Elizabeth assured her. 'I merely suspected that you liked him— but he is a pleasant young man. I dare say your parents believe you could do better, for he has little fortune.'

'I have some money of my own, left to me by Grandfather,' Julia confided. 'I think I could be quite happy to live quietly—but Mama thinks I shall catch at least an earl.'

'I see.' Elizabeth was thoughtful. Clearly Lady Giles was ambitious for her lovely daughter—and who was to say she was wrong? Julia was a pretty girl with a nice way about her. It was entirely possible that she would attract the attention of a rich and titled man—but would he make her happy? 'Well, no doubt in a week or two you will be wondering why you were anxious. I am sure you will have a wonderful time in town.'

'Yes, perhaps I shall,' Julia said, her spirits lifting again. 'I wish you were coming with us, Elizabeth. I should be sure of one friend then.'

'You will make lots of friends, believe me.'

There the conversation ended. They went in to have their lunch with Lady Isadora and Mr Elworthy, who had come down to join them and was feeling much better again. After the meal they repaired to the small sitting room and chose a play from the volume Elizabeth had used previously, but instead of her reading all the parts, they chose one each and passed the book from hand to hand. The play was called *Much Ado About Nothing,* and it was not long before they were all laughing so hard that the time passed very quickly.

After tea, Julia said she must leave. She had walked over because it was a fine morning, and Lady Isadora insisted on sending her home in the carriage.

'It will be late if you walk all that way,' she said. 'No, no, my dear, I do insist. Your parents may worry if you are late.'

'Yes, perhaps,' Julia said. 'Thank you for a lovely day, Lady Dora—and Elizabeth.' She smiled shyly at John Elworthy. 'You have all been so kind and I have enjoyed myself so much.'

'We have enjoyed having you,' Elizabeth said. 'Come, Julia, I shall see you to the carriage.'

The two girls walked outside together, kissing each other on the cheek. 'I am so glad that you have come to live here,' Julia told her. 'I hope we shall always be friends.'

'I am sure that we shall.' Elizabeth stood, waving her off, and then, as she felt a chill breeze in the air, shivered and went hurriedly inside.

'Well, that was most pleasant,' Lady Isadora said when Elizabeth rejoined her in the parlour 'I am glad she allowed me to send her in the carriage. I should have been anxious had she gone alone.'

Elizabeth smiled and agreed. Their young friend had walked the distance without harm that morning, but it would have made her late for dinner, and she would be safe enough in the carriage.

Chapter Six

'This is a particularly fine wine,' John Elworthy was saying as they finished their puddings a little later that evening. 'It goes so well with the cheese, Lady Isadora. Do you happen to know where Daniel found it?'

'I believe it was laid down by—' Lady Isadora was interrupted by the sound of voices in the hallway, and then Sir Henry Giles came into the dining parlour, looking flustered. 'Sir Henry—'

'Your pardon for intruding upon you at table, Lady Isadora,' he said. 'Lady Giles was worried when Julia did not come home in time for dinner. I thought her foolish, for it occurred to me that she might still be here, but your servants tell me that she left almost two hours ago.'

'Indeed she did,' Lady Isadora said, getting to her feet. 'She wanted to walk, but I told her I should not be happy unless she took my carriage since I did not wish her to be late home. Oh, dear—what do you think could have happened?'

'I was hoping to learn that from you, ma'am,' Sir Henry said. 'Will you please summon your coachman and have him explain what has happened to my daughter?'

'Yes, indeed, of course,' Lady Isadora said, preparing to leave the room. However, even as she reached the door, there was a commotion outside and a groom came bursting in, closely followed by an agitated footman still protesting that he was not allowed in the dining parlour. He was wearing a hastily improvised bandage about his head, which was stained with crimson. 'James! Goodness me! What has happened?'

'Forgive me for bursting in on you, ma'am. I know I should not, but it is important. There is something I must tell you! I came as soon as I was able, your ladyship,' the groom told her. 'Coachman was shot through the arm and they hit me over the head with a cudgel when I tried to stop them taking the young lady—'

'Taking Julia?' Lady Isadora turned pale and might have fallen had Elizabeth not been at her side to support her. 'Who took her? I do not understand…'

'There were three of them, my lady,' the unfortunate groom said. 'Dressed in black they was from head to toe and with mufflers over their faces, their hats pulled down hard. They was all armed to the teeth with pistols and they meant to kill Coachman, if you ask me. 'Twas a wonder the ball did not catch him in the chest. If I had not pushed him to one side, he would be dead.'

'The Lord have mercy,' Sir Henry said. 'My poor child! Who can have done this wicked thing?'

'She has been abducted,' Lady Isadora stated the obvious. The news had affected her badly and she was trembling. 'I must sit down, Elizabeth. I have never been so shocked in all my life. Such wicked goings-on! Who could it have been?'

'I do not know,' Elizabeth said. It had immediately crossed her mind that it might have been Mr Palmer, but she hesitated to point the finger of blame. Julia had told her that she was afraid of him, but that did not mean he was a part of this evil crime. 'It is a terrible thing to happen. Have you no idea who might have wanted to abduct her, Sir Henry?'

'Not for the life of me,' the anxious father said. 'There was someone who wished to press his suit with her—an acquaintance of mine—but I made it clear that he must wait until Julia had had her Season. I would not force her to take him or any man.'

'Julia said you would not,' Elizabeth spoke without consideration. 'I believe she did not quite like the gentleman, sir—his manner to her—but she was sure that you would not press her to marry him.'

'Indeed, I should not. There was a little matter of a debt…but it is paid and the thing ended.' He frowned. 'You do not think that he…?'

'Who was this gentleman?' Mr Elworthy inquired. 'Forgive me, sir. It is not my business, but I may know something of this…I too was shot and left for dead quite recently.'

'Palmer…Richard Palmer,' Sir Henry said distractedly. 'I met him through Sir Montague Forsythe. I was foolish enough to play cards with them a little too deeply for my pocket and had to sell a small part of the estate to pay the debt—but I have learned my lesson and shall not be so reckless again.'

'I see…' John Elworthy glanced at Elizabeth. 'Would you look after Lady Isadora, Miss Travers? I must speak privately with Sir Henry.'

'Yes, of course, sir.'

Lady Isadora had sat down at the table and was sipping her glass of wine. Her face was pale and she was clearly upset. Elizabeth guessed that she had taken in very little of Mr Elworthy's conversation with Sir Henry.

'Would you like to go up and rest, ma'am?'

'How could this happen?' Lady Isadora said, looking up at her in distress. 'That innocent child abducted—and after we had enjoyed such a lovely afternoon together. It is wicked and I am distraught. I feel it is my fault—I should have made certain she arrived safely at her home.'

'It was not your fault, ma'am,' Elizabeth assured her. 'You did all that you could—sending her home in your carriage….' She frowned as something occurred to her. 'That is rather odd, is it not? How would these rogues know that she was in your carriage? Have you sent Julia home in one before, ma'am?'

'No, for she has never stayed all day alone before,' Lady Isadora said. 'She has ridden over once or twice with a message from Lady Giles, and she has come to tea on many occasions, but with her mama.'

'Then…' Elizabeth began, then noticed Lady Isadora's expression. 'But let me take you upstairs, ma'am, for you look done up.'

'I do feel most upset,' Lady Isadora said. 'Please come with me, Elizabeth, and then go to Mr Elworthy and discover what this is all about if you can.'

'Yes, certainly,' Elizabeth said, for she wished to speak to him herself.

It took only ten minutes or so to settle her ladyship into the care of her attentive maid, and then Elizabeth came downstairs again. She discovered Mr Elworthy returning to the house, having seen Sir Henry on his way.

'Miss Travers,' he said. 'May I speak with you privately?'

'Of course, sir,' Elizabeth said. 'I was about to ask the same of you.'

He nodded and led the way into Lady Isadora's parlour, turning to look at her. 'I am not sure what you know of this sorry business, Miss Travers. I understand you spoke to Daniel about certain things?'

'Yes. He told me that he believes Sir Montague and his friends may be involved in some kind of a scandal concerning the abduction of young girls.'

'He did not tell you that Lady Elworthy's younger sister was almost abducted in a similar way to what happened near here this evening?'

'No, sir. He told me nothing of that…though he did say that there were things that he was not at liberty to divulge to me.'

John nodded his agreement. 'Yes, that is very like Daniel. Lady Elworthy's sister was a mere child and we have wished to keep it quiet—but there was also another young woman who disappeared and has not been found.'

'That is shocking,' Elizabeth said, her eyes wide with distress. 'How was the abduction of Lady Elworthy's sister prevented—if you do not mind my asking?'

'We happened to be riding that way quite by chance,' John said. 'The awful thing is that she was on my brother's own land and these villains were trying to drag her into a carriage. Maria fought them bravely and we were there before they could accomplish their villainy. Had she not acted with courage, they must have succeeded in their foul aim. Daniel fired over their heads and they broke and ran. We caught one of them, but he refused to talk. He is in prison now, but more afraid of his master than either imprisonment or us. Whether he will talk if they decide to hang him I do not know—but he hopes to be transported.'

'Yes, I see,' Elizabeth said. 'In the matter of Julia, I can tell you only that she was afraid of Mr Palmer—and since he turns out to be a friend to Sir Montague...'

'Yes, it appears to fit, does it not?' Mr Elworthy frowned as if trying to make sense of something. 'I could wish that Daniel was here. Sir Henry has taken some of Lady Isadora's servants and gone to the scene of the abduction, but I do not know if it will serve any purpose. They may be able to follow, but must be too far behind to catch up with the villains, and if they have gone to ground...' He shook his head—it was possible that Julia would never be found.

'There is one thing in all this that puzzles me,' Elizabeth said. 'How did they know that Julia would be in Lady Isadora's carriage?'

'That has also puzzled me,' John said. 'Unless they had a spy here, I do not see that they could have known.'

'Do you believe that any of Lord Cavendish's people would betray him?'

'I know he has taken on some new men,' John said and looked thoughtful. 'I dare say he trusts them—but I cannot see how else the rogues could have known.'

'Unless they did not know,' Elizabeth said. 'Might they have believed that one of us was in that carriage? It bears the Cavendish crest on the side panel, does it not?'

'My God!' John looked at her and she saw that he was struck by her words. 'I thought Palmer must be behind this when you mentioned his name, but perhaps he has nothing to do with this business…'

'If he wanted to marry Julia, is it not more likely that he would wait and try to persuade her before abducting her? I do not know the man and can have no idea of his mind—but if he loves her, what good will come of this? She will surely hate him for treating her so ill.'

'Yes. Unless he simply wishes…' John checked his speech, looking awkward. 'Forgive me. I did not think what I was saying.'

'I do not mind plain speech,' Elizabeth assured him. 'I know that her abductors may have something other than marriage in store for her, especially as her father refused to let Mr Palmer approach her. If Julia was the target, we must assume that we have a spy here— but if they were lying in wait for one of us…'

'I do not know what I ought to do,' John said. 'Daniel asked me to stay here to help protect you and his mama but I feel that he ought to know what has happened here.'

'Can you not send word to him?'

'Yes, I suppose that might serve us,' John agreed. 'But who to trust?'

'I believe you may trust the footman Forrest,' Elizabeth said. 'Unless you wish to go yourself?'

'I shall speak to Forrest,' John said. 'In the meantime, may I ask you to be careful not to leave the estate unaccompanied, Miss Travers?'

'I shall certainly take the greatest care when out walking,' Elizabeth said, 'though I believe Lord Cavendish has arranged for us to be well protected here—which was perhaps why the abduction took place beyond the village.'

'Yes, that is very true,' John said. 'I am glad that you are such a sensible young lady, Miss Travers. I think on reflection that perhaps the footman you spoke of would be of more use here. I shall go to London myself in the morning.'

'Then I must ask you to take one of the carriages and at least two grooms with you, sir. It is not long since you were the victim of a shooting that may have been intended to end your life.'

'Thank you for your concern. I shall certainly take

your advice, Miss Travers. I shall send word this evening for some of my own grooms to come here and take the place of Daniel's men until I return.'

'I shall hope to see you safely returned very soon,' Elizabeth said. 'And now I think I must go up and see Lady Isadora. She is very distressed by this unhappy business.'

'Yes, indeed, as are we all,' John said. 'At least this time we have some idea of where to start and I can only hope that we shall recover Miss Giles before...' He shook his head. 'It does not bear thinking of!'

Elizabeth could only agree. She was very anxious about the young girl she had befriended and could not bear to think of what might happen to her if she had indeed fallen into the wrong hands.

Daniel looked at the small pile of notes lying on the table before him, well aware that the man who had thrown them so carelessly into the pot could not afford to pay what he owed. He had known it before he sat down with Sir Fletcher Harding.

'So, you win again, sir,' the unlucky gambler said. 'It will take me a little time to raise the blunt, Cavendish.'

'More than a little, I dare say,' Daniel said pleasantly. 'What do you say to double or quits, Harding?'

His opponent looked at him in silence for a

moment, and then, 'You know I have no hope of paying such a sum, don't you?'

'Oh, I think there is a way that you can very easily pay me,' Daniel told him. 'There is certain information that I need.'

Sir Fletcher looked uneasily about the room—he knew what Daniel was after, and should never have put himself so deeply in his debt.

'And for that you will return my notes?'

'And some others that I have bought,' Daniel said, still with that pleasant easy smile on his lips. 'It is little enough, Harding—a few names, a few clues as to what went on…'

'The Hellfire Club was rumoured to be a Satanist association,' Sir Fletcher said. 'My father was a member and he introduced me when I was but sixteen. It was on its last legs by then and, though it went on for a while in some form or other after Sir Francis Dashwood died, it was never the same. From what I recall towards the end, it became merely an excuse for dressing up in weird costumes and drinking too much. And there were women called nuns, but I doubt that any of them truly were of that calling…nor yet the virgins demanded by the rituals.'

'Sir Montague Forsythe was also a member, was he not?'

'Towards the end of the time, when it had become a

pale imitation of the original,' Sir Fletcher said. 'He wasn't as old as I had been when someone brought him in, and I think he expected it to be more than it was. He and some others went off and formed their own club a few months later…' He glanced uneasily around him. 'I do not think they pretend to worship Satan— they are far worse, for they consider themselves lords of creation and believe that they are above the law.'

'Do you know what they call themselves?'

'No, and nor should you inquire too closely,' Sir Fletcher said. 'Most of the men who patronised the original Hellfire Club soon grew tired of it and ceased to attend the meetings, as I did myself—but Forsythe and his cronies have gone from foolish youths to…evil men. You should be careful, Cavendish. If they knew what we speak of this evening, they would think nothing of having us killed.'

'Would you stand up in court and condemn them?'

Sir Fletcher shook his head. 'I value my life too much. I would rather be ruined than in their hands…'

'Just why are you afraid of them?'

'I once saw something I should not have seen,' Sir Fletcher said. 'It was in the woods at Forsythe's place. I think that is where they hold their devilish rituals. I was returning home and my horse went lame. I thought to seek help at his house and took what I believed was a shortcut through the woods…' Sir

Fletcher shuddered. 'What I saw will haunt me for the rest of my life.' Daniel's brows rose, but he shook his head. 'It sickened me and I got out of there as fast as I could—but somehow he knew. He came to me at my house and told me that if I breathed a word of what I had seen I would die in agony. I do not have many years left to me, but I have kept out of his way rather than die in the way he described.'

'What you witnessed—did it involve a young woman?' Sir Fletcher nodded, but would not be drawn further. 'I see—well, I dare say I may imagine what took place. I have had my suspicions and you have confirmed them. For that I thank you and I shall return all your notes.'

Sir Fletcher reached for his wineglass, drinking deeply. 'I dare say you think me a coward? My conscience tells me that I should put a stop to their evil, but their influence is far reaching.'

'How long ago did you witness the scene that shocked you so?'

'About a year,' Sir Fletcher said and closed his eyes. When he opened them again, he saw that Daniel was watching him intently. 'I shall do one thing more for you, Cavendish. I have written a letter to be opened after my death, and I shall instruct that it be sent to you should I die unexpectedly.'

'Thank you. I do not wish for your death,' Daniel

told him with a grim smile, 'but that your courage may return and help you to take the step you know you ought.'

'It is not just for myself I fear,' Sir Fletcher said, forced to confession. 'I have a young granddaughter. She is just fifteen and very pretty…'

'Then I understand and shall not press you further,' Daniel said. 'What you have told me confirms my suspicions, and it gives me a clue to something I need to know. I shall do my best to unmask the members of this club and bring them to justice.'

'Call it a coven and you will be nearer the truth,' Sir Fletcher said. 'Sir Montague is their high priest, mayhap their god, for they worship evil and take pride in their wicked trade.'

'Thank you,' Daniel said. His expression was grim as he left the table and the club, unaware that he was being watched by a man he had never met nor yet would care to meet. Indeed, his thoughts were far away and he was wondering how much longer he must linger in town when he longed to be in the country.

'Good grief, John,' Daniel exclaimed as his friend walked into the library of his London home the following evening, where he was just drinking a glass of wine before going out. 'What are you doing here? You look like death, my friend!'

'In truth I feel it. I am done up by the journey, for I have not spared myself,' John Elworthy said, 'but Miss Travers agreed that you must be told what had happened immediately, and she said that Forrest must be taken into our confidence. He swore that he would defend her and Lady Isadora with his life, and I think he may be of more use to her than I at the moment.'

'What has brought you here in such haste?'

'I have grievous news,' John told him. 'It concerns a young woman and will distress you, I know…'

'Do not worry yourself about my feelings,' Daniel told him with a frown. It was clear that John had exhausted himself to bring the news, which meant that it must be something important. 'Drink this wine and rest a moment and then tell me the whole.'

Elizabeth was looking out of the upper-floor landing window that morning when a gentleman rode swiftly to the front of the house and dismounted from his horse. He was clearly in a state of high emotion and she ran down the stairs to meet him as he entered the hall.

'Sir Henry!' Elizabeth called as she saw him. 'Have you news, sir?'

'Miss Travers! I came to you in haste, for Julia begs that you will visit her,' the emotional father said, tears squeezing from the corner of his eyes to run down his face. 'She has been returned to us unharmed, thank God. One of my men found her at dusk last evening, wandering some distance from the house in a dazed state. We put her to bed and she slept for hours, for she was exhausted, but this morning she has woken and seems a little better. She is shaken and a little bruised, but otherwise untouched. It appears that she was taken somewhere, but then it was discovered that a mistake had been made and she was blindfolded, bundled back to the carriage, and driven to our estate where they put her out and left her.'

'Oh, that is wonderful news,' Elizabeth said, her voice catching as the relief swept over her. She had been restless since Julia's abduction, thinking of what her young friend might be suffering. 'But poor Julia, how terrifying it was for her to be put to such an ordeal. I can hardly believe that she was set free unharmed. Why was that, do you imagine?'

'That has puzzled me,' Sir Henry agreed and his voice shook with emotion. 'I feared that she had been taken for some evil purpose and that we should never see her again.'

'She must have had a guardian angel,' Elizabeth said, her throat tight. 'You must be so thankful, sir.'

'I shall never cease to thank God for it,' Sir Henry said. 'She is, of course, very distressed and says that she must talk to you—will you come?'

'Yes, sir, I shall,' Elizabeth said. 'I shall bring the governess's cart and three grooms to ride with us.'

'You are very wise to take such precautions,' Sir Henry said. 'I rode here without giving much thought to your return. I could not bear to look at her and think…' He shook his head, his voice harsh with emotion. 'But I have my pistols, Miss Travers, and I should not hesitate to use them in your defence.'

'I dare say they will not be needed, for the rogues that abducted Julia have lost the element of surprise and must know that we are on our guard,' Elizabeth said, 'but I shall ask the grooms to ride with us just in case.'

She asked that he would excuse her and ran upstairs to speak with Lady Isadora. That lady broke down in tears when the news of Julia's safe return was given her, and begged Elizabeth to go to her at once—and then in the same breath to take the greatest care.

'Yes, certainly, ma'am,' Elizabeth told her. 'I am to drive myself, but Sir Henry and three of Lord Cavendish's grooms go with me. I shall be well protected, I promise you.'

'I shall be uneasy until you return,' Lady Isadora told her. 'And yet you must comfort that poor child. That she should have been taken after visiting us…I cannot understand it.'

Elizabeth thought that perhaps she could, for it seemed to her unlikely that Julia would have been returned unharmed had she been their intended victim. It was more likely that they had hoped to capture either Lady Isadora or herself, because it would give them a hold over Lord Cavendish. However, she could not tell Lady Isadora of her suspicions and merely shook her head.

'We must be glad that Julia escaped as lightly as she did, ma'am.'

'Yes, certainly,' Lady Isadora said. 'Go, then, for she needs you or her father would not have come. I shall look for your safe return, my dear.'

'You need not fear. I am well protected, ma'am.'

After leaving Lady Isadora, Elizabeth went to her room to fetch her pelisse and the small pistol that her father had given her to protect herself.

'I do not think you will have cause to use it,' Sir Edwin had told her when he taught her to shoot straight as a young girl. 'But it is possible, Elizabeth. You like to walk alone and I would not have you afraid—but if you should be attacked, shoot the rogue and be damned to the consequences!'

Elizabeth had promised that she would, though she had seldom bothered to take it with her on her walks since she had believed herself safe on her father's land. However, the case was altered for there were dangerous men in the vicinity—men, it seemed, who

would stop at nothing to gain their ends. And yet—
why had they returned Julia to her home?

It was very odd—she might have heard or noticed
something that could lead to their exposure. Elizabeth
puzzled over it for some minutes, and could think of
only one explanation.

She arrived safely at Julia's home, and was taken up
to her rooms at once. Julia was sitting in a chair, her face
pale, some kind of restoring drink at her side and a book
on her lap that she was making no attempt to read.

'Oh, Elizabeth,' she said, the book sliding to the
floor as she jumped up. 'I asked for you, because I
must tell you—they thought it was you in the carriage,
not me. You must be careful never to go out alone.'

'Julia, my dear, how are you? We were all so
worried about you.'

'Did you hear what I said?' Julia asked, her voice
rising shrilly. It was obvious that her nerves were on
edge. 'They thought I was you—but then someone
told them they were wrong and they brought me back.'

'Where did they take you?'

'To a house; I do not know where. I was confined
upstairs in a horrid bedchamber. It was quite dark,
for they had not left me a candle. Then, when it was
morning, I heard shouting downstairs. It went on for
a while and then, after what seemed for ever, two

men came to take me away. I tried to struggle, but they were too strong. They blindfolded me and told me not to make a fuss because I was going home. At first I did not believe them, but they were grumbling amongst themselves about it being a natural mistake to make, and how were they to know it was the other one wanted…' Julia looked at her. 'They spoke of you, Elizabeth—for they said you were the companion…'

'Yes, I had wondered if it was a mistake,' Elizabeth said, looking thoughtful. 'For how could they know you were in Lady Isadora's carriage? They must have been watching for it…and it was more likely that either I or Lady Isadora would be inside.'

'But why should they want to abduct you or Lady Isadora?' Julia asked. Elizabeth's calmness was reassuring for, on her return, her mother had gone into a fit of hysterics, which had made Julia weep. 'I thought when they first grabbed me that it must be Mr Palmer abducting me, because Father refused his offer of marriage but…' She shook her head. 'It is stupid, I know, but I think I heard his voice…when they were arguing at that house. And later as we were leaving. He said that they were to do exactly as he had bid them or they would know the consequences.'

'That would not surprise me,' Elizabeth said for it accorded with her own thoughts on the matter. 'I believe Mr Palmer has a true regard for you, Julia— and that is why you are here now, unharmed. A mistake was made when you were snatched, but, having taken you, it was strange that they should let you go again. I believe that someone must have ordered them to do so.'

'Oh…' Julia's hand trembled as she put her fingers to her mouth. 'Who are those men, Elizabeth? I think they must be very wicked.'

'Yes, I believe they are,' Elizabeth said. 'I cannot tell you more, for it is not in my power—but you are very lucky to be here.'

'I do not think that I shall ever dare to walk out alone again,' Julia said and tears stood in her eyes. 'I have told Mama that I cannot go to London. I feel…' She shook her head. 'I cannot explain it, Elizabeth, but I think I was in great danger.'

'Yes, Julia, I am certain of it, but remember that it *was* a mistake. You were not the intended victim. You must not let this make you afraid to live your life as you always have.'

'I know that you are right,' Julia said, tears hovering on her lashes, 'but it was so horrible. I thought that I should die or be…' She gave a little sob. 'I cannot believe that they let me go.'

'You were very lucky,' Elizabeth agreed. 'I think you must not walk out alone for a time, but soon perhaps this unhappy business will be over and you will be safe again.'

'Why is this happening?' Julia asked, looking at her curiously. 'You know something of it, do you not?'

'Yes, a little, but I may not speak,' Elizabeth said. 'I can only apologise because you were caught up in something that did not truly concern you.'

'But if Mr Palmer was there, he saved me...' Julia looked thoughtful. 'Is that truly why I am here, Elizabeth? Had he some influence over the men who ordered it?'

'I do not know for sure,' Elizabeth said, 'but it is possible.'

Julia shuddered. 'I would rather die than marry such a man! He must be evil to know these rogues.'

'Perhaps...or a man caught up in something he does not like, but cannot break free of,' Elizabeth suggested. 'But you are safe now, Julia. Give yourself time to think about the future.'

'Yes, perhaps,' Julia said. 'I feel better now that I have seen you, Elizabeth. I was so afraid that something awful would happen to you. How did you come here?'

'I drove myself, but I have some of Lord Cavendish's grooms waiting for me.' In actual fact, the men waiting for her had the look of old soldiers and she suspected that they were some of the men Lord Cavendish had hired to protect his home and friends. She smiled as Julia looked doubtful and took a small pistol from the pocket of her skirt. 'And if someone should attempt to abduct me, I shall use this.'

'Oh!' Julia gasped at the sight of it. 'Would you dare to fire it?'

'Yes, indeed, if need be,' Elizabeth said. 'But I am well protected and I think it may be a while before those rogues try that trick again. They had the element of surprise when they took you, but it is lost now, and your father has informed the magistrates. There will be a watch kept at the tollgates.'

'Yes, I see,' Julia said and smiled oddly. 'I wish I was as brave as you, Elizabeth. I do not think I should dare to fire a pistol.'

'You might be able to do it if you were taught,' Elizabeth said gently. 'You might consider it, Julia, for it would afford you some protection if you wished to go out alone.'

'No! I could not…' She shuddered. 'Mama has said we shall go away for a while to my aunt in Bath. I think that perhaps I may feel able in a few days. Now I have spoken to you, I do feel a little calmer.'

'It was a frightening ordeal,' Elizabeth said with warm sympathy, 'but you are a brave girl, Julia, and I think you will conquer your natural fear. After all, why let these men win—and they do so if they succeed in making you afraid to live your life as you would wish.'

'Yes, I know you are right,' Julia said. 'Thank you for coming, Elizabeth. Perhaps you will visit me again another day?'

'Yes, of course,' Elizabeth said and smiled at her. 'I am determined that these men shall not intimidate me—and I think in time you will feel the same.'

They embraced and Elizabeth left her. She was thoughtful as she drove home, the three grooms riding protectively close to the governess's cart. Julia had been very lucky. It was, in her mind, clear that Mr Palmer had been Julia's saviour, which must mean he was neither as depraved nor as evil as his friends. She would speak to Lord Cavendish as soon as he returned—perhaps Mr Palmer might prove to be the weak link in the chain. If he could be prevailed upon to lay evidence against his friends, it might be the end of them.

Elizabeth was very much aware of being watched over wherever she walked in the gardens. It was good to know that she and Lady Isadora were being so well protected, though she doubted that it was truly necessary. Surely the rogues who had mistakenly taken Julia would not dare to try again?

The past few days had been peaceful enough for there had been no more intruders or abductions to worry them. She was steadily working her way through the estate journals and had now selected all the remaining volumes from the shelves, dusting them and arranging them in chronological order. She had listed them on a sheet of paper, and she had looked for any relevant letters or documents tucked inside the volumes, without success. There were letters and lists, but they were concerned only with estate matters. It seemed that either the fragment they had found was all that had been committed to paper or the intruder had been successful in taking what he needed.

Lord Cavendish had been gone six days, and Mr Elworthy four. Elizabeth had visited Julia twice at her home and she was planning to take flowers to the church the next day. For that purpose she had been discussing her needs with Mr Browning, and was on her way home with a single bloom from an exquisite orchid, which he had presented to her with a little flourish. As she drew near the house, she saw that a curricle had drawn up and for a moment her heart beat faster—she thought it must be Lord Cavendish. However, further inspection told her that she was wrong, and as she went into the house she heard a man's voice coming from the front parlour.

She hesitated outside, and then tapped the door before entering, still carrying her orchid.

'Elizabeth, my dear,' Lady Isadora said, and the tone of her voice was enough to warn her that all was not well. 'We have visitors. Lord Barton, who lives at Barton Hall, which is some twenty miles to the east of Cavendish, and his cousin...Sir Montague Forsythe.'

'Miss Travers, I believe?' Lord Barton looked at her, his eyes narrowed and cold. 'I was just asking Lady Isadora if we might impose on her hospitality for one night. We are on our way to London, you know, but I seem to have developed a chill...' He sneezed into his kerchief as if to illustrate the point. 'I have a weak chest and if I continue my journey immediately I may take harm.'

Elizabeth went gone cold all over and shivers ran down her spine. She could hardly believe that this was happening, and yet she knew that Lady Isadora was in an awkward position. How could she turn away a neighbour, a man she was obviously acquainted with, when he pleaded ill health?

'Indeed, I am sorry to hear it, sir,' Elizabeth said. Her expression was frozen and she could not bring herself to look at Sir Montague.

'I cannot do less than offer you a bed for the night,' Lady Isadora said, ringing for a maid. 'However, I would not wish to detain Sir Montague. I dare say he would prefer to continue his journey without delay?'

'Indeed, ma'am,' Sir Montague said, his eyes narrowed and hard as he looked at her and then Elizabeth. 'I have no need to presume on your hospitality. I shall continue on horseback for I may hire a horse at the local hostelry.'

'Oh, I am sure we can loan you a horse,' Lady Isadora said, her relief showing despite her efforts to hide it. 'May I offer you some refreshment before you leave, sir?'

'No, thank you. I came only to see my cousin safely lodged for the night. If he should take a turn for the worse, I would beg you to seek a physician for him.' Lord Barton sneezed three times in rapid succession.

Elizabeth had moved away to the window. She could hardly bear to be in the same room as Sir Montague. She suspected him of some evil intent in coming to Cavendish Hall, but she had no authority to send either him or his cousin packing.

'Miss Travers…' She stiffened as she heard his voice close to her shoulder, turning to glance at him. 'A moment, I beg you.'

'Sir?'

'I believe you have taken me in some dislike, Miss Travers? I am sorry for it, and I would wish you to know that I deeply regret your father's ill fortune.'

'Indeed?' Her eyes were bright with disbelief.

'I would not have had him die in such a way. Had he come to me, we might have found some way of resolving his difficulties.'

'I doubt that, sir.'

'Believe me, I have no quarrel with you, Miss Travers.' His eyes went to the orchid. 'You are fond of flowers?'

'Is not every woman?'

'My late wife enjoyed her gardens,' he said, an odd smile flickering on his lips. 'I shall be in London only a few days. It would please me to show both you and Lady Isadora the gardens at Forsythe Towers on my return.'

Elizabeth inclined her head, but did not give him a reply. He looked at her for a moment more, nodded briefly and strode from the room. Lord Barton was having another sneezing fit and, when the house-keeper arrived, she bore him off with her to one of the best guest chambers.

'Oh, my dear,' Lady Isadora said after they had gone. 'I am so sorry. I would have saved you the em-barrassment of having to meet them if I could—but it would be rude to refuse Lord Barton. I have been his house guest in the past and I could not show him the door when he so obviously has a chill.'

'No, of course not,' Elizabeth said. 'Besides, Sir Montague has gone and I have no dislike of Lord Barton.'

'He is well enough in his way,' Lady Isadora said. 'My husband and he were great friends when they were younger, you know.' She wrinkled her brow.

'They fell out over something—I know not what—and after that we did not visit. If Daniel had been here, I should have asked him to see them—he would have had no scruples in sending them away, but I do not have the stomach for it. And if Lord Barton remains in his room, we shall hardly know he is here.'

'No, that is true,' Elizabeth said. But would he? She made a mental resolution to keep both her window and her door shut tight that night. Lord Barton had not come here because he had taken a chill—so just what was his purpose in obliging Lady Isadora to offer him a bed for the night? 'We must hope that he is recovered enough to continue his journey on the morrow.'

She went away to put the orchid in water, thinking that she would speak to the young footman Forrest. It would be as well if he and some of Daniel's soldiers were to keep a vigil during the night.

Lord Barton kept to his room that evening. He seemed to be genuinely ill for the housekeeper was obliged to make him several tisanes and he declared himself too sick to come down for dinner, though he ate what was taken up to him on a tray.

Elizabeth was relieved that they were not forced to accept his company at table that evening. Believing his cousin to be guilty of several kinds of villainy, she could not acquit Lord Barton of having an ulterior motive in foisting himself upon them. Accordingly, she locked her door when she retired for the night, and it was arranged that one of the male servants would sit outside Lady Isadora's apartments all night. Elizabeth had no wish to alarm her, and so decided it was best to protect her without her knowledge.

Elizabeth read for a while, feeling too much on edge to sleep at once. She lay unconsciously waiting for a sound in the house—a door opening, creeping feet, a door handle being turned. Nothing of the kind occurred during the time she lay awake and in the end she fell asleep.

In the morning she was awake at half past six and downstairs by seven. She visited the library as was her usual habit, and immediately sensed that someone had been there not long before her.

A glance at the windows told her they were still firmly closed, so no one had come in from outside. She went immediately to the shelf containing the estate records and saw that three of them had been taken out and replaced hastily, breaking the order she had created. They covered the years following the journal that had been stolen, and she was certain that whoever had been here had been looking for the second part of the letter.

At least she was certain that they had not found what they sought for she had been before them. She looked for her own list of journals and discovered that it was missing. Why on earth should anyone want that list? It could surely be of no interest to anyone but Lord Cavendish. Elizabeth could not think for the life of her why her list had been taken.

She checked the journals thoroughly to be certain that none were missing. They were all in order as they had been, except that they had not been replaced quite as she had left them. Nothing more in the room had been touched.

Elizabeth turned to the shelf at the opposite end of the room. She had decided to clear it, placing the books on the drum table at that end of the long room. She wanted to store all the more serious works here—she believed that would enable Lord Cavendish to make his selection without searching the whole library.

She carried several piles of books to the table, noticing that there was everything under the sun from poetry to sermons, light fiction and histories. She laid them side by side on the table, looking at the titles. Should she arrange them in order of title or author? The books were all beautifully bound in leather, though some of the covers were red, others a dark green. They would look well if all the same colour were together, and she discovered that all the green bound books were works of William Shakespeare and other playwrights, whereas thc red were novels. None of them would be on this shelf eventually, she decided as she took down the last few books. And then, as she turned back to the bookcase, she saw something. A folded paper sealed with red wax and the Cavendish crest. She reached out to take it from the shelf and was looking at it when the door opened and Lord Barton walked in, wearing a very handsome dressing robe.

Elizabeth hid the letter behind her back instinctively. She was startled and it was a moment before she could find the right words.

'Are you unwell, sir?' she asked at last. 'May I request Mrs Bates to bring you something?'

'I am almost recovered, Miss Travers,' he said. 'I shall leave immediately after I have broken my fast. Your housekeeper's tisanes have done me much good and I shall beg the recipe from her...' He hesitated, then, 'It was to find her that I came down so early. I thought I should not disturb the household if a tray was brought up to me.'

'Ah,' Elizabeth said and smiled at him. 'I dare say you took a wrong turn while looking for the kitchens, sir. You must go out of this door and...but I am sure Mrs Bates would wait on you if you were to ring for her.'

'Yes, I dare say she might,' he said, barely able to conceal his annoyance at having been put in such an awkward position. 'I had not expected to see you down so early, Miss Travers.'

'No, sir, I do not suppose you did. However, I rise early, and, as you can see, I am cataloguing Lord Cavendish's library for him. There are some fine books here, but the order lacks conformity. I am trying to bring some harmony to these disordered shelves.'

'I wonder that you have the patience for it,' he said. 'I imagine the books were bought by the yard to fill the shelves, and that is why they are uniform in cover.'

'I dare say the works of Master Shakespeare may have been bought in that manner,' Elizabeth said, 'but do you not think that books should be easy to find either by title, category or author?'

'I had not thought of it,' he said and it was clear that he was put out about something. 'Excuse me, I shall return to my room and summon the housekeeper.'

Elizabeth frowned as the door closed behind him. She slipped the letter she had discovered into the pocket of her skirt and went back to her books, selecting the sermons from the piles she had laid upon the table and beginning to dust them.

She was almost certain that Lord Barton had visited the library twice that morning. His first search had revealed nothing—so why had he returned? He must have had further thoughts about where he might find the document he sought.

Lady Isadora had told Elizabeth that her husband had once been a firm friend of this man. It was therefore possible that he knew of the late earl's habit of tucking things inside books. Perhaps he had decided to look in some of the other volumes? He must be frustrated indeed to find Elizabeth at work.

Had he seen the letter she had hidden behind her back? Elizabeth had acted instinctively, but she could not be sure that he had not caught a glimpse of the folded paper she had tried to conceal. It was a pity that she had not put it away at once, for if he suspected her he might try to take it from her before he left. She considered hiding it in her room, but decided against it, for it was surely the first place someone would look if they knew it had been in her possession. And since Lord Barton had failed to find that which he sought, another attempt might be made to break into the house.

Elizabeth worked on for another two hours, beginning to arrange the serious works in order of their content—sermons, histories and political works—and then by author. She would make a list for Lord Cavendish, but this time she would find a blank journal and write it down properly rather than on a single sheet of paper.

When she had completed the task she had set for

herself that morning, Elizabeth went up to her room. She had left it unlocked for Amy to clean, and found the girl just finishing her work.

'Are you ready for your breakfast, miss?' she asked, smiling at Elizabeth.

'Yes, thank you, Amy,' Elizabeth said. 'But I have a small favour to ask of you—if I may?'

'Yes, of course, miss,' the girl said, looking curious.

'It is this letter,' Elizabeth said, taking it from her pocket. 'It belongs to his lordship and I want you to keep it safe for me.'

Amy looked surprised. 'Am I the proper person to have it, miss?'

'Yes, I believe so,' Elizabeth told her with a smile. 'I think it may be important, Amy. I have not read it and nor should you—but I think someone wishes to steal it and if I hide it here…'

'Yes, miss, now I understand,' Amy said. She took the sealed packet and slipped it into the bodice of her gown. 'No one would think of looking in my room. I'll take care of it for you.'

'It is only until his lordship returns,' Elizabeth told her. 'But we cannot be too careful in the meantime and you should tell no one that I gave it to you.'

'I wouldn't breathe a word,' Amy said. 'I'll fetch your tray up to you now, miss.'

'That is very kind of you.'

'It is no trouble, miss. You will tell me when you want the letter back?'

'Yes, thank you,' Elizabeth said. She was thoughtful as Amy went out, for there had been some intriguing developments of late. She went behind the screen to take off the plain gown she had worn earlier and to change into something a little smarter. It was a pleasant morning and she had decided that she would visit Julia for an hour or so.

Chapter Seven

Elizabeth drove herself to the estate of Sir Henry Giles after she had breakfasted. She felt that it was hardly necessary to take her gallant band of protectors, but, rather than risk something untoward happening, she allowed them to accompany her.

Julia was delighted to see her and thanked her warmly for coming. The past few days had brought them closer together, and Julia had benefited from the calm good sense of her friend, which was in stark contrast to the rather hysterical behaviour of her mother.

'Mama is in such a state over what happened,' Julia told her that morning. 'I have explained to her that I was taken by mistake and that is why they returned me to my home. She cannot believe it and is nervous of something similar happening again. Poor Papa is made to check the house at least twice every night lest someone should try to steal me from my bed.'

'I think that most unlikely,' Elizabeth said with a smile. 'But you seem more cheerful this morning, Julia. Are you feeling better?'

'Yes, I feel calmer,' Julia said. 'The Reverend Bell came to visit me yesterday afternoon, and he was so nice to me, Elizabeth. He condemned the wicked men who had abducted me and told me I have been in his prayers every night since then. We talked for quite a time, and when he left he said he would return soon to visit me. He told me I must be brave and trust in God, and we said a prayer together.'

'I am sure that helped you a great deal,' Elizabeth said for she could see that her friend was almost back to her old self. 'I am so glad, Julia. It was good of him to call on you.'

'Yes, it was,' Julia said. 'I told him that I was to go to Bath instead of London, and that I should be staying quietly with my aunt. He encouraged it and told me that I must try to enjoy myself and not worry about the ordeal I had endured.'

'That was kind of him,' Elizabeth said. 'I am sure there is nothing to stop you attending private affairs with your mama, and the Assembly Rooms are very respectable. I think you will be quite safe there, Julia.'

'I dare say I am safe enough here,' Julia said, for she had recovered her nerve. 'Had they meant me harm I should not have been returned to my home.'

'That is very true,' Elizabeth said. 'And besides, all this may be over when you return from Bath.'

'I hope that the culprits will be caught and punished,' Julia said, looking serious. Her ordeal had sobered her a little and she seemed to have grown up quickly. 'Because I fear it is you they mean to harm, Elizabeth. I do not understand why, but I believe you are in great danger.'

'Perhaps,' Elizabeth said. 'But I am well protected. I promise you that my guards go everywhere with me.'

A smile lurked in her eyes but Julia shook her head at her. 'It is not amusing, Elizabeth. These men are wicked creatures—if you fell into their hands they would not so easily let you go.'

'I know you are right,' Elizabeth said, 'but I do not think they will try to snatch me while I am so well protected.'

'You must take care,' Julia said. 'It would grieve me if harm were to come to you.'

'I thank you for your concern,' Elizabeth replied, feeling it time the conversation was turned. 'Now, tell me, Julia—have you had your new gowns made or shall you buy them in Bath?'

Elizabeth returned to the house after a happy morning spent discussing fashions and trinkets with her friend. She noticed something different as she walked into the house, and her heart jerked when she heard the sound of laughter coming from Lady Isadora's parlour. Approaching, she realised that they must have company for there was a buzz of voices and she walked in to find that the room seemed filled with gentlemen.

'Ah, there you are, dearest,' Lady Isadora greeted her. 'We were about to have nuncheon and wondered where you had got to, Elizabeth.'

'Forgive me if I have kept you waiting,' she said, her eyes moving round the room until she found the person she sought. Her breath caught as she saw the intense look in his eyes. He stared at her much as a thirsty man might look at an oasis in the desert. 'I have spent some time with Julia, longer than I intended—but she was feeling so much better and kept me talking.'

'Miss Giles is a fortunate young woman,' Daniel said, his expression giving little away. 'But I am remiss—may I introduce you to my friends, Miss Travers? Charles Hunter, Hilary Matthews and Robert Young, who is entitled to be called Lord Young, but does not care for it—gentlemen, Miss Elizabeth Travers.'

'Gentlemen…' Elizabeth dropped a curtsy, her eyes moving over them. All three looked to be attractive, obviously well bred, and wealthy by the way they dressed—but she thought that Charles Hunter looked haunted, his eyes dark shadowed, as if he had been ill or under some strain. 'I am glad to see any friends of Lord Cavendish.'

'Miss Travers,' Lord Young said, a gleam in his eyes. 'Cavendish has been keeping you a secret. I am dashed glad to meet you!'

'Miss Travers.' Hilary Matthews inclined his head, smiling slightly.

Charles Hunter merely looked at her before throwing himself into a chair by the window and staring moodily out at the park.

'Was Miss Giles much distressed?' John Elworthy asked. 'I was never so relieved in my life when I heard that she had been returned to her family unharmed.'

'She was shocked and tearful at first,' Elizabeth told him. She walked across to stand next to him in front of the fireplace. 'But I think she understands that she was taken by mistake and is recovering her natural confidence. The vicar visited her yesterday and that has cheered her a little, and I believe the cure will be completed when her parents take her to Bath next week.'

'Bath?' Daniel looked at her sharply. 'I thought she was to have gone to London?'

'She felt unable to face society on that scale, I believe. In Bath she may mix with her aunt's friends and perhaps attend the Assembly, but she will not be required to go out as much. In the circumstances it is probably for the best.'

'Yes, perhaps,' Daniel agreed. 'I must speak with you later, Miss Travers.'

'Certainly,' Elizabeth said and her pulses raced. 'Perhaps before dinner this evening. I have made certain developments that you may wish to approve in the library.'

'Yes, of course,' Daniel said, nodding. 'Before dinner then, Miss Travers.' Such a look had he given her that she swallowed hard, her mouth unaccountably dry.

They were called to the dining room then, and Elizabeth was content to listen to the gentlemen talking amongst themselves. It seemed that they planned to do a little shooting in the earl's woods that afternoon, and left soon after the meal was over. Mr Elworthy remained. He joined Lady Isadora and Elizabeth in the parlour.

'You will think your house turned upside down with so many gentlemen visiting,' he said to Lady Isadora. 'You must be wishing us to the devil, I expect.'

'Oh, no,' she said, 'though I thought Daniel might have invited a mixed party—but it seems that the gentlemen came down for a sporting week. I do not mind. It makes a pleasant change to have guests in the house—though we had one we did not wish for last night.'

'Indeed?' John looked at her. 'And who might that be? Not another intruder?' He realised his mistake almost at once. 'I meant who was the intruder, of course.'

'Lord Barton,' Lady Isadora said, frowning a little. 'And he brought Sir Montague Forsythe with him—though he did not stay, but merely borrowed a horse from the stables. Lord Barton had taken a chill and felt unable to continue his journey.'

'Indeed?' John looked startled, his eyes meeting Elizabeth's. 'Does Daniel know of this?'

'I did not think to mention it with all the company at once,' Lady Isadora said. 'But it was merely an inconvenience—he stayed in his room all the time and we hardly saw him.'

'I saw him the next morning before he left,' Elizabeth said. 'I believe he was feeling much recovered.'

'Oh, do let us forget the horrid man and his wretched cousin,' Lady Isadora cried, fanning herself as if the incident had made her overwarm. 'What shall you read to us this afternoon, Elizabeth?'

Elizabeth went down to the library as soon as she had changed for dinner. She had recovered the letter she had given Amy, and it was tucked into her pocket safely. She found the earl already waiting for her.

'You had visitors, I understand?' he said and looked grim. 'Have you anything to tell me concerning them?'

'I believe that Lord Barton visited the library during the early hours of the morning. I came down and started to remove some books from the shelf before seven and he entered the room. I think it was not his first visit, because a list I had made of your father's journals was missing.'

'Then why should he return?'

'I imagine he had not found what he sought.' Elizabeth withdrew the sealed letter from her pocket. 'I cannot say for sure, but I think he may have been searching for this...' She held it out to him. 'I discovered it seconds before he came in, behind the books at the end of the room near the drum table. He may have seen it in my hand, but made no attempt to take it from me.'

Daniel looked at the seal. 'You did not open it?'

'It was not mine,' Elizabeth replied. 'It is addressed to you, sir.'

'Yes, I see,' he nodded and turned it over in his hand. 'The ink is not faded and I would imagine it to have been written more recently than the fragment we found previously.'

'It may have no bearing on the matter you are investigating.'

'We may soon discover the truth,' Daniel said and broke the seal. He read through the rather spidery script and looked grim. 'It is not a continuation of that confession, Miss Travers—but it tells me things that I had suspected. My father had just broken off his friendship with Lord Barton when he penned this, and he warns me to have nothing to do with him. He had lost deeply at cards and believes that he was cheated of a great deal of money. He hints at the unsavoury character of Lord Barton's cousin and says that he should have made the break long ago. There are also other things that he wishes to tell me, but they do not concern this business.'

'Then it does not help you very much in your investigation, sir.'

'Not as such, but I now know that I was right to suspect Sir Montague and his friends of wickedness. It is no longer in question—though I still do not have the proof I need.'

'Sir Montague has gone up to London,' Elizabeth said. 'But he invited Lady Isadora and myself to visit him at his home when he returns.' She was thoughtful for a moment. 'Do you think that perhaps we should?'

'I think it is the last thing you should do!' Daniel was horrified. 'Surely you cannot wish to visit his home?'

'No, indeed, I do not wish it,' Elizabeth said, giving a little shudder of rejection. 'But it might be that I could find some clue that would help you.'

'If the clue is there, then it is up to me to find it,' Daniel said. 'And I may take advantage of his absence…'

'Would that not be very dangerous?'

'Less so for me than you, Elizabeth. You must know that I would never risk harm to you. I shall do what is needful myself—with perhaps a few friends to assist me.'

'Your old soldiers have been good bodyguards to me,' Elizabeth said with a smile. 'They follow me wherever I go and I am well protected.'

'I am glad of it,' Daniel said, and his smile nearly took her breath away. She could almost think that he cared for her—that his attentions were more than mere seduction. 'It would cause me much grief if harm should come to you through this business.'

'Oh…you must not…' she breathed a little faintly.

'What must I not, Elizabeth?' he asked and the note of tenderness in his voice made her turn her nails into the palms of her hands as she struggled against her feelings. 'Should I not admire you? You have such qualities that any man of sense would value them—and you.'

Elizabeth steadied her nerves. He was merely saying that he valued her as a person, not as someone for whom he had a *tendre*. She breathed deeply, smiling a little as she fought the odd mixture of emotions swirling inside her, one of which was most definitely disappointment.

'You are very good to say so, sir. I am really very ordinary.'

'Now that I shall not allow,' he said. 'You are far from ordinary…but I do not mean to distress you.

Thank you for finding this letter, which is of value to me in several ways. I shall not delay you further—our guests will be coming down shortly.'

'Has Mr Hunter been ill?' Elizabeth asked. 'He looks as if he is suffering under a great strain.'

'Indeed, he is,' Daniel said, 'but I am not at liberty to say more for the moment.'

'Yes, I see.' Elizabeth accepted it and kept her own thoughts. 'Excuse me, sir. I must go and see if Lady Isadora needs me.'

Daniel nodded, but said nothing. He looked thoughtful and, glancing back at him from the door, she saw that he was intent on his letter. She wondered if there was more than he had told her in the letter, but it was not truly her affair. She decided to put it from her mind, though she would of course pass on any further items of interest she might find amongst the books. Had she been privy to Daniel's conversation with certain of his friends a little later that evening, she might not have slept so soundly.

'If we are to do it, then tonight is as good as any other,' Daniel said, looking into the faces of his four closest friends. They had all served in the army together, watching each other's backs and on occasion saving each other's lives. They were bound together by bonds forged in the fires of battle, and he knew as he looked into their faces that they were with him to a man. And he wanted to have this thing finished, for only then would he be free to think of his own plans. 'Good, then it shall be tonight. He is believed to be in London, though we must not count on it—he may have lied when he called here.'

'They must have known that you were not here, Daniel,' John Elworthy said. 'And perhaps that I had left for London.'

'They took a great risk coming here,' Charles Hunter said. His eyes were like dark coals in his face, ringed with red, his thick hair longer than fashionable, as if he had no care for his appearance. It was many nights since he had slept for more than an hour or so. 'That makes me suspect that they grow desperate, Daniel.'

'I am certain that they have shameful secrets to hide, as I have told you,' Daniel replied. 'Are you prepared for the worst, Charles?'

'Yes, I am,' he said, his mouth a thin line of anger. 'If they have destroyed her, I would willingly give my life to see them on their way to Hell!'

'I do not doubt that they are destined for it,' Daniel said. 'But it would be better if they could be brought to justice, as a warning to other men who think as they do if nothing else.'

'You have more forbearance than I do,' Charles said.

'For myself a ball in the head is justice enough—and if nothing can be proved, I shall force a duel on Forsythe.'

'He is not the only one involved in this,' John said. 'What do you think of Mr Palmer, Daniel? Elizabeth seems to believe that it was because of his influence that Julia was set free and I tend to agree—having got her, why let her go? Someone must have prevailed upon them to do it.'

'Yes, you are right. I have been thinking how we may use him,' Daniel said. 'If he went against them for her sake, he cannot truly approve of what they do. Might he be willing to help us break them, do you think?'

'Elizabeth thinks it may be possible,' John said. 'She did not say as much, but I knew she thought it—she firmly believes that he was at the house to which they took Julia.'

'But does he have the courage to stand up against them?'

'If we had him in our custody, he would have to choose,' Charles Hunter said. 'Give me half an hour alone with him and I shall endeavour to persuade him for his own good.'

'Hush, man,' Robert Young said. 'You do yourself no good by this bitterness, Charles. We all care for your sister and we are sworn to avenge her. Whatever needs to be done shall be done.'

The four friends looked at each other, nodding their

heads in silent agreement. They were neither murderers nor yet violent men in their hearts, but they had faced war and survived it, and they had sworn to find Charles's sister and avenge her.

Elizabeth did not see or hear the small party of men ride out—she had gone to sleep soon after she blew out her candle, and though her dreams were muddled and a little disturbing at times, she had forgotten them by the time she woke. It was nearly half past seven when she went down to the library as was her habit, and she entered the room prepared to spend an hour or so at her work. She gasped as she walked in on a scene that shocked her. Three men were gathered round a fourth, and she saw almost at once that he was bleeding profusely from a wound to his leg.

'Forgive me,' she said, relief sweeping over her as the earl turned to face her. 'I did not know that you were here—but may I be of service to you?'

'Miss Travers, thank you,' Daniel said. 'As you see, Charles has been hurt badly; he lost a deal of blood as we brought him home despite our efforts to staunch the wound.'

'I shall fetch water and salves,' she said. 'Would you wish to tend him here or upstairs?'

'If we could bind him and stop the blood here,'

Daniel said, 'then we can carry him up. He has lost consciousness, as you see.'

Elizabeth went swiftly from the room. In the kitchen she found Amy and some of the other servants already at work. She beckoned to Amy, who understood her request and promised to bring the necessary items at once.

'I heard the gentlemen leave last night, miss,' she said. 'It was in my mind that there might be some trouble.'

Elizabeth returned to the library armed with her scissors. She went over to the injured man, noticing that his leg had been packed with cushions that were now soaked in his blood.

'We must cut his breeches away,' she told the assembled court. 'Amy is bringing bandages and water, also salves, but the sooner this is attended to the better. It is a more serious wound than yours was, I think, Mr Elworthy.'

'He was caught in the full blast of a shotgun,' John said. 'I believe they were expecting something…Forsythe knew that his visit here would draw us out, as it did.'

'Yes, I understand.' Elizabeth did not turn a hair as she worked, cutting the tight-fitting breeches from Charles Hunter's legs with such presence that the gentlemen looked at one another.

'May I help you?' Daniel asked.

'Oh, Cavendish,' Elizabeth said. 'Yes, please lift him now if you would. I must cut beneath him if I am to free him without causing more damage.'

'I'm here, miss.' Amy's voice from behind her made Elizabeth turn and smile. 'I've brought a towel to cover the gentleman's modesty…' She moved forward to lay it over Charles's lower regions as the breeches were stripped away.

'That was thoughtful of you,' Elizabeth said. 'Cavendish, lift him carefully if you will now…that is well done. Now, someone may cut away the rest of his breeches while Amy and I bathe his wound and bind him.'

A moan broke free from their patient as they cleansed the wound, which consisted of a wide area of buckshot wounds. The flesh had been badly mangled and looked raw, still bleeding profusely, but after examining it Elizabeth thought that he had after all been luckier than might have been the case.

'Bear up, old chap,' Lord Young said, bending over him. 'Miss Travers is seeing you right. I dare say you'll be better soon enough.'

For a moment Charles Hunter looked at him, and then, as the linen was wrapped tightly about his wound, fainted once more.

'There, I think the bleeding should stop soon,' Elizabeth said as she stood up. 'Amy and I have done what we could, gentlemen. If you could manage to get him upstairs between you, he will do better in his bed.' She looked at Daniel. 'Have you sent for the doctor, Cavendish?'

'Yes, Forrest went almost as soon as we returned, but if he should not be at home it may be some time before he arrives and Charles will be better for your interest. I was thinking of sending for you, but your excellent habit of rising early made it unnecessary. I am once more in your debt, Miss Travers.'

'I have done nothing that makes you obliged to me, sir,' Elizabeth said. 'And I shall ask only one question of you—did you succeed in what you attempted last night?'

'In part,' Daniel told her. 'Forsythe was not at home, but his bullyboys were—and it was probably a gamekeeper who shot at us as we left. However, the night was not unprofitable.'

Elizabeth nodded. 'Excuse me, I must go and tidy myself. I shall leave the rest to you.'

She left them to get their friend to bed and went upstairs to change out of her gown, which was spotted with blood. She heard a slight noise as she was washing her hands, and turned to discover that her visitor was Lord Cavendish and not Amy as she had expected.

'Sir?'

'You called me Cavendish earlier,' he said, a wry

smile on his lips as her eyes challenged him. 'Forgive me, I know that I should not be here—but I wished to speak to you in private.'

Elizabeth could not find it in her heart to be angry that he had invaded her room once more. Indeed, she had been thinking of him and it was somehow right that he should come to her. 'You are anxious about your friend, perhaps? I think the wound has bled too much, but it was not as deep as it might have been, you know.'

'I have been worried about Charles for months, and in some ways this wound may prove providential,' Daniel said, feeling the relief of being able to talk to her as he could not have to his mama or any other lady of his acquaintance. 'He has cause to hate Forsythe and his friends and he might have been reckless. His being confined to his bed may be beneficial—you see, he could otherwise do something rash.'

'I do not quite understand you, sir.'

'We entered Forsythe's house through a door carelessly left undone and found Mr Palmer drinking alone in Forsythe's library, and we took him prisoner. We have him now in one of the unused guest chambers.'

'Cavendish!' Elizabeth was shocked. 'You kidnapped Mr Palmer...that is a capital offence.'

'Indeed it is, and by telling you, I am making you an accessory to the fact,' Daniel told her. 'Though I should deny that you knew anything if it were to be discovered. But if we are to keep him here in secret, only a few can know the truth. I thought you might be trusted to keep us safe—Forrest and perhaps Amy, also—unless, of course, you forbid me to involve her in this business. Forrest is already involved and wishes to be of use to us. He is an intelligent young man and wasted as a footman. I think he could be of use to my agent and may rise to something of the sort—but that is for the future.'

'I think you have chosen wisely,' Elizabeth said. 'I shall speak to Amy, but she must protected if this should turn out badly.'

'Of course,' he said and smiled at her. 'I think I must thank Mama for her part in all this. What should we have done without you, Miss Travers?'

'You make too much of my part…' Elizabeth said, but then her breath caught as he moved towards her, looking down at her with such intent that she knew what he meant to do even before he reached out for her. 'Cavendish…'

His lips stopped her words. For a moment she stood stiffly within his arms, but then something opened up inside her and she melted into him, her warmth flooding through in the kiss she returned without restraint. In that moment, Elizabeth forgot prudence, forgot her mama's teachings and her notions of propriety. She would at that second have granted him anything he asked of her.

'Elizabeth…' Daniel smiled down at her. 'I should not have done that, you know—but I have been wanting to kiss you almost from the first time we met.'

'Sir…'

He placed a finger to her lips. 'It must be Cavendish now, you know. You cannot go back, my very dear Elizabeth. I know you now and I shall not let you pretend to a correctness you do not feel.'

'You are unkind, sir,' Elizabeth replied, but she was smiling.

'I dare say. I am many things, Elizabeth—but in this I shall have my way.'

'Very well, Cavendish.'

'Much better. One day it may be Daniel, but that is not yet. Many things may happen in the future, Elizabeth—but before I can attend my own wishes I have to settle this other business.' He laid a small package on her dressing table, smiling as he saw her look. 'A small token of gratitude for your help, Elizabeth. A flask of the perfume you like, I believe.'

'Thank you,' she said a little stiffly. 'It was thoughtful of you.'

'It is a mere trifle. Please accept it in the spirit it is offered. I make no demands, indeed I am already in your debt—please believe me.'

'Yes, I understand you,' Elizabeth said. He had spoken of his own wishes. She was not quite certain what they might be—was he thinking of offering her marriage or *carte blanche?* Surely it must be one or the other, for his look had been so particular when they exchanged glances in Lady Isadora's parlour. She felt a little shy all of a sudden—he might have taken her willingness to be kissed as an open invitation. Indeed, her behaviour had given him a perfect right. For a moment she had forgotten that she was merely his mother's companion.

'No, no, do not look like that,' he said, tipping her chin towards him with one finger. 'You know my feelings, Elizabeth. Keep faith. I swear I shall not hurt you.'

'Very well, Cavendish,' Elizabeth said, her practical side re-establishing itself. 'Pray tell me why you have brought Mr Palmer here as your prisoner.'

'To discover if he will tell us what he knows of Forsythe and his friends.'

'I believe it was his influence that set Julia free,' Elizabeth said, looking thoughtful. 'He may be their weakest link—but will he dare to tell you anything that may incriminate them in a court of law?'

'I have hopes that he may be inclined to share his burden,' Daniel said. 'He was drunk when we took him and he made no attempt to escape us. Why was that, do you imagine?'

'He may be uneasy in his mind. It might be that he is caught up in something from which he would like to escape, but either cannot or dare not…he may feel that he deserves some punishment.'

'Why are you so different from any other woman I have known?' Daniel asked her. 'Mama could not have followed my train of thought—nor yet any lady I have known intimately. I think that I have been sleeping, Elizabeth—but you have woken me to what life might yet be.' His smile set her stomach fluttering. 'If we could make him safe from them, he might trust us enough to tell us what we need to know.'

'But would he stand up in court? You need complete proof to convict men who have influence—men like Lord Barton and Forsythe can muster others to say that Palmer lies.'

'True enough,' Daniel said. 'But if the proof was plain enough to convince us four—then he might be tried before a natural court and brought to justice.'

Elizabeth looked into his eyes, a cold shiver running down her spine; she sensed that he could, if forced to it, be ruthless.

'But you will do all in your power to bring them to a court of law?'

'It is my intent and my wish,' Daniel said. 'But there are others who are not so nice in their intent.'

Elizabeth nodded. 'I believe I understand. And now, Cavendish, you should go before Amy comes—or I shall have no reputation left.'

He smiled at her, a challenge she could not quite read in his eyes, but he left her without another word. Elizabeth was thoughtful as she went downstairs to finish the work she had intended in the library that morning. Cavendish was caught up in a dangerous situation, and she did not doubt that what they had done would bring some form of retribution in its wake. They did not yet know the ending of this affair, and it would be sensible to take great care. Now that Cavendish had moved against Sir Montague, the battle was truly joined.

'Did I hear some commotion earlier?' Lady Isadora asked when Elizabeth went to her room later. 'I know we have gentlemen staying, but it was early even for them.'

'Oh, I think there was some kind of an accident,' Elizabeth told her, for she was mindful of Cavendish's strictures about keeping their adventures secret. 'I believe Mr Hunter had hurt himself and needed the doctor.'

Lady Isadora gave her a thoughtful look, but readily accepted her excuse. 'I have decided that we shall go visiting this afternoon,' she said. 'You have met some of my friends, but there are others I would wish you to meet, my dear.'

'That will be very pleasant,' Elizabeth said. 'It will be nice to go visiting again. Mama used to enjoy it of all things, but after Papa died she no longer cared for such things.'

Lady Isadora nodded. 'Are you feeling a little better in yourself, Elizabeth? You were suffering greatly when you came here, I think?'

Elizabeth realised that she had indeed been feeling better these past few days. 'I shall always be sad that Mama and Papa died in the way they did,' she said. 'And of course there are moments when I miss them terribly. But of late I have been too occupied in my thoughts to dwell on my grief.' In truth, she had been feeling very alone, but that feeling had passed.

'I am so glad,' her kind employer said with a smile. 'You have had much to grieve you, but you are young and the future may be brighter for you soon.'

'I am very satisfied as I am,' Elizabeth told her. 'It was so kind of you to ask me to come here. I am sure I should not have been as happy had I sought employment anywhere else.'

Lady Isadora was gratified by her answer and turned away to hide her smile. It looked as if things would work out much as she had hoped for her friend's daughter, though she was not sure that Daniel would oblige her by playing his part. With so many single gentlemen staying in the house, Elizabeth was able to choose the one she preferred—and she had noticed that at least two of Daniel's friends were paying attention to the girl. She was also fairly certain that something odd was going on in the house, and that Elizabeth was a party to it.

Daniel would try to keep it from her, for he did not like her to be anxious, but if anything out of the ordinary was happening the servants would soon be aware of it, and her maid would tell her.

Daniel watched his Mama's carriage leaving that afternoon. It would be followed at a discreet distance by the extra men he had detailed to accompany Lady Isadora and Elizabeth, so he had no fears for their safety and was pleased that they would be gone for a while. This was the opportunity he had been waiting for to question his prisoner.

He told his friends that they might be needed, warning them to come to him only if he sent Amy or Forrest to them, and went alone to the guest chamber where his unwilling guest waited to hear his fate.

'Good afternoon, Mr Palmer,' Daniel said, smiling pleasantly at the man, who looked up uneasily. 'I dare say you are wondering where you are—and perhaps why?'

'I know the answer to both questions now that you are come,' Palmer said. 'Forsythe is aware that you have been poking your nose into his affairs for a while. I dare say you have guessed that it was to have been either Lady Isadora or Miss Travers abducted when Miss Giles was mistakenly taken.'

'Ah, yes. I imagine it was you who had her returned to her home unharmed?' Only the slight flicker of a pulse at his temple showed that he was moved to anger by Palmer's words.

'Of course. I insisted on it. Had she been harmed I would have seen them hanged and be damned to the consequences. But neither Forsythe nor Barton was there and I had little trouble in making those rogues obey me.'

'You are very frank, sir.'

'It hardly matters what happens to me now,' Palmer said. 'The woman I care for would never look at me when she knows what I am—and if you do not kill me, Forsythe will.'

'Would you be willing to help me bring him to justice if I guaranteed your safety?'

'And how might that be achieved?' Palmer looked sceptical. 'Once Forsythe knows I've been with you, he will assume I have betrayed him and dispose of me.'

'He must needs find you first,' Daniel said. 'The world is a wide place and with money in your pocket you might go where you will.'

'Run away like a dog with my tail between my legs? I have thought of it many times since that night,' Palmer said gloomily. 'Forsythe has a hold over me, as you may imagine. I have a sister. She is married and old enough to be of no use to them in their rituals, but she has a daughter of ten years—and they would take her if I escaped.'

'They cannot touch her if they are behind prison bars or dead. And your sister's child can be protected.'

Palmer looked at him uncertainly. 'If they were dead, she would be safe. For myself I care little enough. That night haunts me and I have been close to ending it many times.'

'If you have real evidence it may be enough to hang them,' Daniel said grimly. 'I know that they are involved in some kind of pagan rituals and that they have mistreated girls of good family in the past—but I need evidence from a living witness about a more recent act.'

'You found it, then,' Palmer said, nodding. 'Forsythe knew that your father had something, for he threatened them with exposure. He said there was a letter that would shame and ruin them and, if anything violent happened to him, they would be unmasked. It kept him safe, for they believed he knew enough to finish them. After he died and nothing happened, they thought the danger over and began their evil work again…'

'I see…' Daniel frowned. 'Do you say that my father's influence kept them honest?'

'Oh, the rituals went on,' Palmer said, 'but the girls

were ignorant, silly things of no principle and agreed to take part for money. Most of them were frightened by Forsythe and disappeared into the brothels they had come from after he had done with them. However, after your father died, there was an innocent girl…' His face creased with an emotion that might have been grief or anguish and he paused for a moment, a shudder running through him. 'God forgive me! I played a part in it and I shall never ease my conscience of the evil done.'

'You do not seem to me of their ilk,' Daniel said enquiringly. 'How did you come to be involved with them?'

'It was soon after I first came upon the town with money to burn. Forsythe saw me for a flat and took most of what I had. He encouraged me to drink too much, and then told me that he could show me such delights…the kind of thing that men experience in their wildest dreams. He promised me that I should be a member of an exclusive group, and he tore up my notes, restoring my losses. Like a fool I jumped in with both feet.'

Daniel nodded, understanding how Forsythe had worked his evil spell, blinding the young man by a show of generosity and leading him into depravity.

'And what happened to give you a disgust of him and all that he stands for, sir?'

'He told me a little of their rituals. He spoke of potions that enhanced a man's strength to make him a very demi-god of love. I was a little drunk most of the time and it excited me. I admit it freely. He talked of virgin sacrifices and himself as the High Priest who would deliver this wonderful experience...' Palmer shuddered. 'That night he gave me a glass of wine to drink; it tasted a little bitter and I was told that mixed into it was an African root that would enable me to perform with the strength of a lion with its mate...'

'Go on,' Daniel said. 'I have heard of such things, but I think them dangerous.'

'I was out of my mind,' Palmer told him. 'Nothing seemed real. The images were sharper and yet everything I did was as if I were someone else, moving in a dream. We went to the woods where we disrobed. A young woman was lying on a bed of silken drapes. Her skin was pale and white in the moonlight. Forsythe began his rituals...' Palmer stopped, shaking his head as if the memory was almost too hard to bear. 'She had been given some kind of a drug, I imagine, but it was not strong enough for she came to her senses to find us capering about her in a grotesque dance and she started up screaming. She jumped to her feet and ran away and we chased after her.' He stopped abruptly, passing a hand over his eyes. 'God forgive me...'

'What happened next?' Daniel asked when he seemed unable to continue.

'I cannot be sure.' Palmer held up his hand as he saw the look of anger in Daniel's eyes. 'No, hear me out, I beg you.'

'Very well. I am prepared to listen, but if you lie it will not go well with you.'

'I remember that she screamed and we began to chase her, but…' He shook his head, passing a hand over his eyes. 'Everything became hazy in my mind after that and I believe I passed out. I remember waking in my bed the next day with a fearful head, but nothing more.'

'Did you ask Forsythe or Barton what happened?'

'Forsythe told me that she simply disappeared, but…' Palmer pressed a hand to his forehead. 'Barton told me later that a girl's body had been found in the lake weeks afterwards. Apparently, it lay too long in the water for an identification to be made and was buried as a suicide—name unknown.'

'You believe that it was the girl you were to have ravished in your foul ritual—and do you know the name of that girl?'

Palmer took a deep breath. 'That girl was Sarah Hunter—the sister of your friend Charles. But I cannot say for certain that she is the girl who lies in a suicide's grave.'

'My God!' For a moment Daniel felt such rage that he could see nothing but a red mist before his eyes. His hands tightened at his sides and it took all his strength of purpose not to spring at Palmer. In that instant, he could cheerfully have killed him, but as the mist cleared, he remembered his vow of safekeeping. He spoke in a strangled voice, holding his rage by a thread. 'I thank you for telling me. I have vowed to find Sarah, and at least now I know where she lies.'

'I would not blame you if you left me to Forsythe's mercy,' Palmer said and his face was creased with grief and self-hatred. 'I surely deserve it for the part I played that night—and my intention, for had she not woken I might have defiled her.'

'Was she untouched at this point? Forsythe or another of his cronies had not raped her?'

'Barton told me that she had not been harmed. It is part of the ritual that she remain a virgin until the sacrifice is made—and then, after the initiation, she would have been used by all of us. I know it is wicked beyond forgiveness and I have asked myself a thousand times what possessed me to join in such depravity.'

'You were an evil man's tool,' Daniel said. 'I have no doubt that he feeds on such as you. At least you have repented of your wickedness.'

'I swear it, Cavendish. I have been tortured by nightmares since that night, and I know that I am as guilty as they of her death. In justice I should stand my trial with them.'

'Yes, perhaps,' Daniel said. 'Yet I think that my friends might be inclined to show mercy. You have given us the proof and you were duped by that man, I dare say. I shall have pen and ink brought to you. You will write out all you have told me and sign it and we shall all witness it before you. I think such a statement ought to be enough to bring Forsythe and Barton to justice.' He frowned. 'Was it just the three of you that night?'

'I have tried to remember but it is not clear. There might have been one other…dressed in a long white robe. Yes, I think it was so, though I have no idea of his identity. I knew only Forsythe and Barton. Barton is a lecher—no maid in his house is safe from him— but Forsythe wants power more than gratification of the flesh. He is the core of the coven and without him it would die a natural death.'

'Yes, I have thought as much,' Daniel said. 'Are you prepared to give me a signed statement of all that you have told me?'

'And if I do?'

'You will be taken safely to the coast and seen on to a ship bound for the port of your choice.'

'Then you shall have it and welcome,' Palmer told him. 'I would be free of him and his madness, for madness it is—and if I find life or death overseas, at least it shall be of my own choosing.'

'Then pen, paper and ink shall be brought,' Daniel promised. 'Once it is done you may be on your way to safety. Until then, I must lock the door—for your safety and ours.'

Palmer laughed mockingly. 'Do you imagine that I am stupid enough to run away? If I do not have your promise of a safe passage, I am a dead man. Forsythe kept me on his string, a puppet for his amusement, but I have known that my time was short. I know too much. He would sacrifice anyone to keep his own neck safe.'

'But still I shall lock the door, until that paper is safely in my hands.'

'You shall have it,' Palmer said. 'You have my word on it.'

'I shall return when you are ready.'

Daniel left him to return to his friends, locking the door and pocketing the key. Forrest had the match to it and no other—despite his promise, he did not trust Palmer not to try and escape.

'Well, that was very pleasant, was it not?' Lady Isadora said to Elizabeth as they returned from their jaunt that afternoon. 'Did you enjoy visiting Lady Roxborough, my dear? I know her reputation is somewhat murky—her husband was a terrible rogue and much of his misdoing has rubbed off on her, I dare say. Personally, I like her—she has a sense of humour. We do not live in each other's pockets, but visit now and then.'

'She is always very friendly,' Elizabeth said, for the woman had a bright, cheerful manner and had been particularly warm towards her, talking to her of a shared love of poetry and reading for most of the visit. 'She has a distinctive voice, does she not? Deep and husky with a hint of humour. I remarked it particularly when she dined with us. And when she read that poem to us it took on true meaning.'

'Yes, indeed. Now you mention it, her voice is distinctive—a little masculine, perhaps?'

'Yes, but attractive.'

Lady Isadora nodded. 'Well, she is but one of our neighbours, after all—and we shall go away to the sea soon,' Lady Isadora told her. 'I wonder if poor Julia and her parents have left for Bath yet.'

'I believe they go tomorrow,' Elizabeth said. 'Julia is looking forward to it. I think she has recovered from her distress quite well, and much of the credit for that must be due to Mr Bell's kindness to her.'

'Ah, yes,' Lady Isadora agreed. 'I believe Julia likes him, but her parents would not be happy with such a match.'

'No, I suppose not,' Elizabeth said. 'It is a pity that he has no fortune. In most other ways I believe he would be a kind husband for her.'

'You have no thoughts in his direction yourself?'

'Me?' Elizabeth was surprised. 'No, ma'am. I like him very well, but I would not wish to marry him. Besides, I believe that beneath his censure of her silly ways, he likes Julia more than he may have realised.'

'You may be right,' Lady Isadora said, mentally striking the reverend from her list of suitors for Elizabeth. 'Well, I believe I shall go up and rest for a while, my dear. What will you do?'

'I think I shall go down to the library for an hour before I change for dinner.'

'Do not tire yourself over those books,' Lady Isadora said. 'Cavendish might employ a librarian if he wished them to be catalogued.'

'But I enjoy the task, ma'am.'

'Very well, Elizabeth.' Lady Isadora left her in the hallway and proceeded up to the landing, where her maid was waiting for her with some news. 'What is it, Phipps? What have you to tell me?'

'It is a little odd, your ladyship, just as you thought. Perhaps we should go into your apartments?'

'Yes,' Lady Isadora said, struck by her maid's look of self-importance. 'Perhaps we should…'

* * *

Elizabeth was about to leave the library, having finished listing the books she had cleaned and arranged in order earlier that morning. The door opened abruptly, startling her as the earl walked in. She knew at once from the look on his face that something was wrong.

'What has happened?'

'Did you tell my mother that we were holding Palmer prisoner?'

'No, of course not,' Elizabeth said, feeling shocked that he should ask her in such an abrupt way, almost as though he were accusing her. 'You should know that I would not. I was most careful not to say anything that might arouse suspicion.'

'Then it must have been that maid!'

'Amy? I am sure she would not. Why are you so angry?'

'Because Mama was told and she demanded the key from Forrest. He had no choice but to give it to her, though he came at once to find me. Unfortunately I was at the stables and by the time I returned to the house it was too late.'

'Too late?'

'Mama had told Palmer that he was free to leave. I had got his promise to sign a written confession and now he has fled and there is nothing to show for it.'

'And you are the worse off because he will take great care not to be caught again.'

'He was a fool to leave. I cannot understand why he fled when he knows what lies in store for him.'

'What does he know?' Elizabeth frowned. 'I suppose Sir Montague Forsythe may suspect him of betraying him and—' Her eyes widened, for his expression betrayed it all. 'He may be killed?'

'He will certainly be disposed of,' Daniel said and looked grim. 'He has signed his own death warrant and he knows it. I cannot understand why he should go when I had pledged to help him escape Forsythe.'

'Perhaps he thought you had changed your mind and abandoned him to his fate when Lady Isadora told him to leave?'

'Yes, it is possible.'

'It was unfortunate that she set him free. It might perhaps have been better had you told her what was going on at the start. I think she would not have interfered had she known what was at stake.'

Daniel looked rueful. 'Indeed, you are right. She was angry with me for not telling her and for abducting him in the first place.'

'Have you explained why you were holding him?'

'No. I was too annoyed that he had gone and his confession with him.'

'It is a setback for you. Perhaps your one chance of proving Sir Montague's guilt in court…'

'I doubt it will come again.' Daniel frowned. 'But we know the truth now and shall act upon it…'

'You will take the law into your own hands?' Elizabeth was shocked. 'But…you cannot!'

'We shall do what must be done.'

'No,' Elizabeth said. 'No matter what Sir Montague and his friends have done, no matter how wicked they are—they must be brought to trial in the proper way.'

'You know that there is little chance of that now. Would you have me let them go free?'

'I do not know,' Elizabeth said. 'Could you not expose them in a way that leads to their social ruin? I am sure it may be done…'

'And is that enough for the abduction of a beloved sister? Sarah Hunter was taken from near her home and subjected to… Suffice it that she has suffered things that no young girl should! She may be dead even now. Consider, is mere social ruin payment for that or your father's ruin? And his murder—for it was murder, Elizabeth. I have no doubt of it.'

She raised her head, gazing into his eyes, shock and grief mingling. 'No, it cannot be enough,' she said and her voice was raw with emotion. 'I would rejoice in Forsythe's punishment if it be administered by the law—but if you are his murderer, then you are no better than he…'

'If that is what you believe then there is no more to be said.'

The sizzle of his anger crackled between them for a moment. Elizabeth watched as he turned and left the room abruptly. A part of her wanted to run after him and beg his pardon, but something held her back. She loved him. She knew in her heart that she would always love him, but she could not accept what he meant to do…

Chapter Eight

'Well, I think it was very rude of Cavendish to go off like that and desert us all,' Lady Isadora announced at dinner that evening. 'I am sure I do not know what has got into him these days. Abducting a gentlemen and holding him prisoner—and then to ride off without a word to anyone!'

'No, no, ma'am, you misjudge him,' John Elworthy said in awkward defence of his friend. 'You do not perfectly understand Daniel's purpose in bringing Palmer here. I do assure you that he had excellent motives.'

'Indeed?' Lady Isadora was plainly upset with her son. 'Perhaps you can explain them to me—and why Mr Hunter is lying upstairs with a terrible wound to his thigh?'

'I shall be pleased to tell you all you wish to know, ma'am,' Elizabeth told her. 'Unless you would wish to do so, Mr Elworthy?'

'No, no, Miss Travers,' John said hastily. 'I am sure you would handle the business much better than I could.'

'Shall we leave the gentlemen to their port?' Elizabeth asked, concealing her own fears and regrets as best she could. 'I am very willing to explain, ma'am, for it would have been much better had Lord Cavendish taken you into his confidence at the start…'

Lady Isadora got to her feet and led the way into the drawing room. She sat down in her accustomed chair and looked at Elizabeth.

'Perhaps you can explain what is going on, Elizabeth? I suspected you of knowing what was taking place and it seems that I was right.'

'Please do not be cross, ma'am. I was sworn to keep Lord Cavendish's secret, but I think it right that you should know the whole. It concerns Sir Montague and certain friends of his—and it is a harsh tale that I am sure will shock you.'

Elizabeth did not spare her. She told of the partial letter they had found, written by her late husband, and of Daniel's suspicions. She explained that the men who had stolen Julia had meant to take either her or Lady Isadora herself to gain a hold on Daniel and force him to give up his investigation.

'It was Mr Palmer who persuaded them to return

Julia,' Elizabeth said. 'Had it not been for him, she might have disappeared without a trace.'

'But why did he make them release her?'

'Because he cares for her—and because of that he is the weak link in the chain. He had some important evidence about their activities and was about to sign a confession, which, if placed before the right people, would have brought Sir Montague and his evil friends to justice. Now that may not happen—and Lord Cavendish is angry.'

'And that is my fault,' Lady Isadora said, looking bewildered and upset. 'But how could I know? I thought it was some shocking jest…the kind of thing that men in their cups get up to now and then. Naturally I went at once to release him.'

'Yes, of course. It was the proper thing to do for you could not know why he had been brought here under duress.'

'I should not have interfered if Cavendish had explained,' Lady Isadora said crossly. 'I exonerate you for you had a right to know the truth—this concerns your father and you helped bind the wounds of both Mr Elworthy and Charles Hunter.' The annoyance vanished as she suddenly saw how very serious the situation was now. 'What will happen to Mr Palmer? If he was willing to betray his friends to help Daniel, will that not place him in danger?'

'Daniel had promised him safety—perhaps in another country. I believe he fears that they will kill him rather than let him live to betray them again.'

'No!' Lady Isadora looked stricken. 'It will be my fault if the poor man is murdered.' Her hand crept to her throat. 'I had no idea…this is terrible.'

'Lord Cavendish ought to have told you at least a part of it,' Elizabeth said. 'You are not to blame, ma'am.'

'I may not have known what I did by releasing Mr Palmer, but I am certainly to blame,' Lady Isadora said. 'I only wish that Daniel had explained, but, of course, I know why he did not. He believes me a weak creature and thinks to protect me.'

'Then he must learn to know you,' Elizabeth told her, a sparkle in her eye.

'Unfortunately, it is too late for this affair.'

'All may not be lost. I imagine that Cavendish has gone to look for him, perhaps to bring him back.'

'Oh, I see,' Lady Isadora said, somewhat relieved. 'I shall apologise to him for the action I took—but he must learn not to keep me always in ignorance.'

'I imagine he may have learned his lesson, ma'am.'

'Let us hope it may be so,' Lady Isadora said. She glanced towards the door. 'Do you think the gentlemen will join us this evening—or have they other plans?'

Even as she spoke, the door opened and John

Elworthy walked in. He smiled a little awkwardly at them.

'Forgive me if I intrude?'

'Of course you do not,' Lady Isadora said. 'We are glad to have your company. Are the other gentlemen to join us?'

'I believe they may have gone to the billiard room—or perhaps to see Charles.'

'No, Mr Elworthy,' Elizabeth said. 'That will not do. I know that you mean to spare us, but we shall have the truth if you please.'

'Well, they have gone after Daniel,' he said. 'Robert is afraid that he may be in some danger. He went off in such a temper!'

Lady Isadora gave a little cry and fanned herself, clearly distressed. 'If anything happens to him, it will be my fault!'

'Do not worry,' Elizabeth said. 'I believe Lord Cavendish to be capable of taking care of himself—and he was, I think, more angry with me than you, for we had quarrelled.'

'You had quarrelled?' Lady Isadora looked startled. 'Oh, my dear. I had not realised.'

'It was a matter of disagreement rather,' Elizabeth said. 'I dare say it is forgotten by now.'

'I would have gone with them,' John said. 'But it was thought best that I should stay here just in case.

Forsythe may try some kind of reprisal after what happened—though he may be still in town. It is certain that he will come down as soon as he knows of it.'

'I am glad you are here,' Lady Isadora said. 'I am glad to know what is going on, but it is very worrying.' She smiled wryly. 'Yes, I know that you would have spared me had I let you—but then I should have been imagining all kinds of things.'

'Shall we play individual whist?' John suggested. 'Since there are only the three of us…'

'An excellent idea,' Lady Isadora said, seizing on the idea. She glanced towards the window. 'It will help to pass the time—and it is no use my going to bed early, for I shall not sleep a wink.'

Lady Isadora was finally persuaded to go up at a little after midnight. Elizabeth would have followed her, but John detained her, waiting until they were alone to speak.

'Daniel planned to go to Barton's place,' he said. 'He thinks that Palmer will go there to ask for help. Barton is a fool and a lecher by all accounts, but I believe it is Forsythe who should be most feared.'

'I am sure you are right,' Elizabeth said. 'But do you think that Mr Palmer will dare to show himself there—or anywhere that he is known?'

'I cannot be certain, but he will not go near For-sythe's estate. That much we may be sure of.'

Elizabeth nodded her agreement. They parted and she went upstairs to her bedchamber, but after un-dressing, she sat by the window looking out, her mind in turmoil. However, it was not more than ten minutes later that she saw something that drew her attention in the garden. At first it was indistinct, a mere shadow amongst the shrubbery, but then a cloud passed away from the moon and she knew that what she had seen was a man creeping towards the house. From his manner, he was furtive and very much afraid. She hesitated for a moment and then went downstairs. She found Forrest sitting in the porter's chair in the hall. He had his eyes shut, but as she approached he opened them.

'Miss Travers—is something amiss?'

'I think we are about to have a visitor, Forrest.'

'Right, miss. I'm ready for him…' They both heard the tinkle of broken glass and looked at each other. 'The library… You wait here, miss. I'll deal with him.' He took out the pistol Daniel had given him, a determined gleam in his eyes. However, as they started towards the library, a man came from it.

'Stay where you are! I'll shoot if you do not obey,' Forrest commanded and the intruder raised his hands at once.

'Don't shoot! It is me,' a voice cried. 'I left the house when Lady Isadora bid me, for I did not know what else to do, but I have been waiting for the chance to return…'

'Mr Palmer?' Elizabeth was incredulous, but it could be no one else. Forrest had been shielding her with his body, but she stepped out from behind him. 'You have returned to give yourself up?'

'Cavendish promised me a passage to safety,' Palmer said. 'I ran when I had the chance, but then I realised I had been a fool and returned to beg for his charity. In truth, I have nowhere else to go. I thought of applying to Lord Barton—he is not as much a monster as Forsythe—but then I knew it would be useless and I came back.'

'How sensible,' Elizabeth said and smiled at him in approval. 'We are very glad to see you alive, sir—but I am afraid you must allow Forrest to lock you up once more. It is not that we think you would try to escape again, but for your own safety.'

'Anything,' he said and looked at her oddly, hesitated, then, 'If you are Miss Travers, and I believe you must be, I should like to apologise for what happened to your father.'

'You were there?'

Palmer nodded. 'Sir Edwin was given wine that contained a drug and he knew not what he did, Miss

Travers. The wager was suggested to him and he agreed without understanding what he said—and then, when he sobered up and said that he had been cheated, Forsythe put the pistol to his head and killed him. I was not there at that moment, but I heard him boast of it later that same day to Lord Barton.'

Elizabeth felt the sting of tears as she fought to control her grief. 'Would you add that to your confession, sir? It cannot help my father, but may bring justice for my brother.'

'Willingly,' Palmer said. 'It was none of my doing—though I am guilty of other crimes.'

'Perhaps not of your own free will?'

'You are generous, Miss Travers.' A look of shame and regret entered his eyes, as if he wished that he had not put himself beyond the bounds of decency and was free to live as a gentleman again.

'Let me take him up, miss,' Forrest said. 'And then I'll come down and mend that window again. I thought someone was supposed to be watching out for intruders.'

'I suspect that Lord Cavendish may have given them other duties this evening,' she replied. 'But I shall wait for you in the library. Give me your pistol, Forrest. I shall use it if anyone else tries to take advantage of our vulnerability.'

'Are you sure, miss?'

'I assure you that I know how to use it.'

Forrest handed over the pistol and Elizabeth proceeded to the library to look at the broken window. She thought that perhaps another bolt ought to be fitted; as it was, it made them vulnerable to any intruder. She lit three candles and was about to light others when she heard a sound behind her and turned to see the door slowly opening. Lifting her arm, she levelled the pistol at the door and waited until the man came in.

'Elizabeth! Damn it,' Daniel exclaimed as he saw the pistol pointed in his direction. 'Please put that down if you will. I did not know you were here. I was following someone and I thought he came in here.'

'If you mean Mr Palmer, he did,' Elizabeth said, lowering her arm with relief. 'Forgive me. I thought for a moment that we had another intruder. Forrest is locking Mr Palmer into his bedchamber for his own safety and I promised to guard the library until he could fix the window.'

'I believe you would have shot me,' Daniel said, a wry smile on his mouth—she looked perfectly calm and capable of doing whatever was needed. Was it her composure that made her such a delight to him, the sweetness of her smile—or that wicked tongue of hers? 'So Palmer realised that he was safer here, did he?'

'Yes, of course,' Elizabeth replied. 'I am afraid you have had a wild goose chase, sir.'

'Not quite. I have discovered something significant…Lord Barton is dead. I went there because I
thought Palmer might have gone to him in desperation. I think he was not as evil as his cousin, but lived
in fear of Forsythe. When I got there the house was
in uproar. Barton had put a gun to his head. It appears
that it was arranged to seem a suicide, but I think we
both know who was responsible, for even if he took
his own life it must have been out of fear. He must
have believed that Palmer would confess and that he
was at the very least ruined and might end at the
hangman's noose.'

'You mean Sir Montague Forsythe,' Elizabeth said.
'It would not the first time he has killed that way. My
father was his victim.'

'Palmer told you that?' Daniel's brows rose.

'Yes. Forsythe boasted of it later that day. Mr
Palmer has promised to add it to his confession.'

'That is excellent news. We have him now, Elizabeth.'

'Yes, sir. I believe we have.'

'Not Cavendish?'

'I was not sure…' She stopped as he came towards
her. 'Cavendish?'

'Surely you know how I feel about you?'

'You were angry earlier.' She raised her clear eyes
to meet his. 'I believe I offended you.'

'I did not like the picture you painted for me,'

Daniel said honestly. 'But you were right, of course. Forsythe shall be brought to justice in the right way.'

'I am glad,' Elizabeth said and smiled at him 'It is as well that Mr Palmer decided to return.'

'Yes, indeed, for his own sake as much as ours,' Daniel said. 'With his confession Forsythe is done for. As soon as I have it safely in my possession, I shall have him arrested. But first I must see Palmer safely on his way. I have promised him money and a safe conduct to a ship. He may go where he pleases and good luck to him. I bear him no ill will—even though he is not free of guilt.'

'I think he is not the only one to have been corrupted by Sir Montague Forsythe,' Elizabeth said. 'What will you do now?'

'Hilary and Robert will take Palmer to safety,' Daniel said. 'Once he is on board a ship of his choosing, they will join me in London. We shall all put our names to the document as witnesses that it was a free confession...' He smiled as Elizabeth questioned with her eyes. 'No force was used—save that needed to bring him here the first time. He unburdened himself freely, and has returned of his own accord.'

'Yes, that is true,' she agreed. 'It must be enough to have Forsythe arrested and sent to trial, I believe. Though I dare say he has influential friends who may help him?'

'He may have a hold over some of his acquaintance and so we must expect that they will try to have him freed, but I think others will be secretly glad to see him locked away.'

'They will welcome the end of his power over them,' Elizabeth said and nodded. 'I wish you success with your quest, Cavendish. We shall all be the safer when that man is locked behind bars. When do you leave?'

'In the morning. Elizabeth…' he said as she turned to leave. 'Will you not stay a while longer?'

'Lady Isadora does not know of your safe return,' she said, hesitating uncertainly; the look in his eyes had made her heart race and she knew that if he took her in his arms she could not resist him. 'I shall go to her and—' She broke off as the door opened and Forrest came in, closely followed by Lord Young. 'You will have things to do. I must leave you now, sir. Goodnight.'

'Goodnight, Elizabeth,' he said, frowning a little as she went out.

Elizabeth was thoughtful as she walked upstairs. Now that this business with Sir Montague was drawing to its close, she ought to give some thought to the future.

Elizabeth rose a little later than usual the next morning. She had spent half an hour talking with Lady Isadora before returning to her bed, and even then she had not been able to sleep. She had been conscious of footsteps in the house, doors opening and closing, and then the sound of horses' hooves—at least three or four horses, she guessed. Mr Palmer must be on his way to the coast with an escort to keep him safe.

When she met Amy coming from the breakfast room, she asked her if the gentlemen had left, and was told that only Mr Elworthy remained.

'And Mr Hunter, miss,' Amy said. 'The doctor said yesterday that he was to stay in bed for another week, though it goes against the grain with him. He was trying to get out of bed when Forrest went into him this morning, but was persuaded to stay where he was after a visit from Lord Cavendish.'

'Has his lordship left yet?'

'He went only a few minutes ago. He asked for you, miss, but I told him you were not down and he said that I was not to disturb you.'

'Thank you, Amy. I believe this awkward business is over now, and we may be ourselves again.'

'Yes, miss,' Amy said and smiled. The earl had given her twenty guineas for her part in the affair, which was little enough for she had done no more than carry a tray upstairs a few times. It would be added to the little store of money she was saving against the day she married and was almost as much as she might have earned in a year.

* * *

Elizabeth spent the day quietly. Lady Isadora seemed to be lethargic and dozed on her sofa throughout the afternoon while Elizabeth worked on the altar cloth they were making. John Elworthy looked in on them for a moment and left again when he saw that Lady Isadora was sleeping.

When Elizabeth saw him at tea he told her that he had spent most of the day with Charles Hunter, who was feeling restless and wished to be up and about again.

'He sent you his thanks for tending his wound and hopes to thank you in person in the morning, Miss Travers.'

'I did very little, sir. The doctor did all that was necessary, I believe, when he arrived. I am pleased to have helped and that Mr Hunter is feeling a little better.'

'He wishes to be up and about again.' John looked at her uncertainly. 'I think that you may not know the worst of this affair, Miss Travers—and I may not tell you, for it is not my secret. It concerns Charles and his sister.'

'Say no more,' Elizabeth told him. 'I have been told a little and, as you say, it is not for us to discuss—but Mr Hunter has my sympathy. I understand something of what he is feeling in this terrible business.'

'Yes, of course. Your father.' John looked grim. 'Had

I guessed what was happening that day, I might have done something to help him.'

'It was not your fault, sir. I am simply glad that Sir Montague will now receive the punishment he deserves.'

'Yes, indeed. We may all rest the easier for it,' John said. 'I for one shall be glad to hear that Forsythe has been arrested.'

'Yes, indeed. We are in agreement on that, sir.'

'I think perhaps we should agree on most things,' John said a little diffidently. 'I have seldom met with a lady I find so agreeable.'

Elizabeth felt her cheeks begin to burn, but at that moment a visitor was announced, which saved her blushes. The Reverend Mr Bell walked in, looking a little flustered.

'Please excuse this interruption, Miss Travers,' he said. 'Lady Isadora—Mr Elworthy…I bring such news. Lord Barton is dead—murdered, they say, by Mr Palmer, who is an acquaintance of Sir Henry. They are saying it was he who tried to have Miss Giles abducted and he has now fled the country.'

'Indeed?' Elizabeth said, looking at Mr Elworthy in alarm. How could such a lying tale have got about? 'Where did you hear such a tale, sir?'

'Oh, it is common gossip in the village,' the Reverend said. 'I was much shocked, I can tell you, and relieved that poor Julia had gone to stay with her aunt and was not forced to hear all the speculation. Sir Henry will be very distressed when I write to him of the matter.'

'Yes, I dare say he might,' Elizabeth said. 'But can you be sure that the tale is true, sir? Might it not just be gossip and speculation?'

Mr Bell looked struck by her question. 'Well, it was spoken of as fact, but it might be best to exercise a little caution. Yes, perhaps it might be as well to wait for a while until we are certain what has happened. I am very glad that I came here, Miss Travers. They were saying that Sir Montague Forsythe had set the Runners upon Mr Palmer for the murder, but that may be just another tale.'

'I think you should wait before you pass on gossip, sir,' Lady Isadora said, seeming to wake up for the first time that afternoon. 'Besides, if you wait a few days, you may go to Bath and take a message from me to Lady Giles. I have decided to take a house in Brighton for the summer and I should be glad of their company when they tire of Bath.'

'That would be a much better idea,' Mr Bell agreed. 'I must leave you now, for I have another call to make this afternoon. I shall hope to see you all at church on Sunday.'

'Will you not stay for tea?' Lady Isadora asked. 'I can ring for more water.'

'You arc vcry kind, ma'am,' Mr Bell said. 'But I have a sick parishioner and my duty is to him.'

'Then we shall not delay you,' Lady Isadora said.

'I shall see you to the door, sir,' Elizabeth said, for there was more she wished to ask him. 'We should not keep you if you are needed elsewhere.'

She waited as one of the footmen handed Mr Bell his hat and gloves, and then went outside with him. He stood for a moment, hat in hand.

'Do you know if Sir Montague has been seen in the vicinity recently, sir?'

'I have not heard.' Mr Bell looked at her and frowned. 'Such odd goings on. I declare I do not understand it. All this upset of late has been so very disturbing, Miss Travers. I had meant to call on you before, but...' He paused, drew a deep breath and went on in haste, looking conscious and slightly awkward. 'You must know that I have formed a great regard for you...' He faltered as she began to speak.

'How kind of you to say so, sir. I believe we are friends and I hope that we always shall be.' Elizabeth gave him a direct look. He opened his mouth as if he would press his claims, then shut it again as she went on, 'Please give my love to Julia when you see her again. You must know that I am truly fond of her and I hope to see her happy one day—and, indeed, I know she was helped by your kindness to her in her misfortune, Mr Bell. In all honesty, I think you were the saving of her. She is fortunate to have your regard. Excuse me now. I think I must return to Lady Isadora.'

'Oh…very well,' he said, putting on his hat rather crossly. 'I suppose I understand you, Miss Travers.' He tipped his head to her, turned and walked away quite fast.

Elizabeth looked after him, a smile on her lips. She was certain that he had been on the verge of proposing to her and was pleased to have averted it. Returning to the parlour, she heard Lady Isadora's voice raised as if in distress.

'I thought this business was settled?'

'Indeed, it will be once Daniel has laid his evidence,' John said as Elizabeth entered. 'But it is just the kind of clever, wicked thing that Forsythe would do—if he could lay the blame for both Barton's murder and Miss Giles's abduction at Palmer's door, he might hope to avoid prosecution.'

'It must have been he that set the rumours going, mustn't it? I asked Mr Bell if he had been seen in the district, but he did not know. But you have the evidence against Forsythe…' Elizabeth frowned as she considered the matter. 'It is, of course, only one man's word against another's.'

'Yes, unfortunately,' John agreed. 'We believed we had all the proof we needed with Palmer's signed testimony, but Forsythe is very clever…devious. It would be too bad if he were to wriggle out of this with his lies.'

'Indeed it would,' Lady Isadora grumbled. 'I do not wish to be embroiled in this kind of affair. I doubt that my nerves can stand it. I shall be glad to leave for Brighton at the end of this month. It will do us all a world of good to benefit from some sea air.'

Elizabeth guessed that Lady Isadora's irritation came from anxiety. Sir Montague Forsythe was a dangerous enemy, and had killed more than once. If he escaped detention by placing the blame on Mr Palmer—what was to stop him plotting against Lord Cavendish and his family?

'I think we must put our faith in Lord Cavendish,' Elizabeth said, refusing to waste time in idle speculation. 'He knew that Forsythe had friends and he may be prepared for some such eventuality. I believe we may be worrying for nothing.'

'You are such a comfort to me,' Lady Isadora said with a sigh. 'When you came here, you know, I had it in my mind that I should be glad to arrange a marriage for you—but now I am not sure that I could be persuaded to part with you. I do not know what I should do without you, Elizabeth.'

'Well, you need not think of that just yet, ma'am,'

Elizabeth said, a smile on her face. 'No one has asked me and I do not think it likely…' She caught John looking at her oddly and looked away quickly. 'I have another two weeks of strict mourning for my mother, you know—and I would not even consider any kind of attachment until that is over.'

'That is very proper,' Lady Isadora said approvingly. 'But that will be over when we go to Brighton, you know. I think we shall both need some new clothes, my dear. Tomorrow, I shall call for the carriage early and we shall go into York. We may stay at the inn overnight and the next day visit a seamstress I patronise from time to time. She will come to us for the final fittings, but she has a large stock of silks and we shall see more if we visit her. Besides, I have not been to York for an age and I have a fancy for it.'

'That will be pleasant,' Elizabeth said, 'especially if the day be fine.' She looked at John. 'Would you care to accompany us, sir?'

'Yes, indeed I should,' he said. 'I must think of returning to my home soon, Miss Travers. Lady Isadora, I have been a guest here for some days when it was my intention only to dine here. I ought to go home and attend to my affairs—but they may wait until after tomorrow.'

'Then it is arranged,' Lady Isadora said, looking pleased. 'I must go up and change now, Elizabeth.

Perhaps you would play for us after dinner this evening?'

'Of course. I shall be very glad to do so.' She made to follow Lady Isadora from the room, but was detained by John's hand upon her arm. 'Sir...you wished to tell me something?'

'This is a worrying business.'

'You mean the tale that Sir Montague has set running?' Elizabeth frowned. 'Yes, indeed. If he should escape justice, he will be a dangerous enemy.'

'But if he has set the tale running does it not mean that he must be in the vicinity? I do not think he could have gone to London when he told you.'

'Yes, I think it must have been a lie, perhaps to hide his true intentions,' Elizabeth said. 'It is as well that Daniel left his men to guard us. I think we must all continue to be very careful...'

A sense of slight unease hung over the company that evening. The brooding atmosphere was perhaps the more so because Charles Hunter had dragged himself from his bed to join them. His darkly handsome face was set in lines of grief and pain, and they could only guess at what torments he suffered. He hardly spoke during dinner, but afterwards came up to Elizabeth, sitting by her on the small sofa.

'I have much to thank you for, Miss Travers. I think

I may have been brusque, even rude when I first came here—but I had much on my mind.'

Elizabeth gave him a look of sympathy. 'I understand that you have had sadness to bear, sir. I have not been told all, but I believe you are grieving for the loss of a loved one.'

'My sister Sarah. That devil Forsythe and his friends abducted her—and God alone knows what else they did to her. I shall not distress you by telling you the shocking details. I believe she may be lying in a suicide's grave, driven there by those wicked men—' He broke off with a choke of misery. 'I shall not rest until she is at peace, at home with us where she belongs.'

'I am so sorry,' Elizabeth said. She had not known the whole of it until now, though she had guessed that Daniel believed Sarah dead. 'I wish that I could say something that would ease your pain, Mr Hunter, but there is no answer in such a case.'

'Only time may heal,' he told her. 'That and justice. If I can see Forsythe hang for his crimes, I shall feel I have answered Sarah's pleas for justice.'

'It must be the hope of us all,' Elizabeth told him. She silently prayed that Forsythe and his evil friends would be prevented from causing such grief to others. She had remonstrated with Daniel when he spoke of natural justice, but, seeing Charles's suffering, she was filled with rage. The man who had brought him to this must be punished! 'I wish that I might help you to find justice, sir, but I fear there is little I can do...'

'Daniel persuaded me that it was right to bring him and his friends to judgement under the law,' Charles said and a hard look came into his eyes. 'But if he is not made to pay for what he has done I shall kill him. I do not care what happens to me—but he shall not be allowed to live. I swear it on my sweet sister's memory.' Charles looked desperate. 'She was such a sweet, loving child—' He broke off. 'I loved her so and she did not know it.'

'I am sure she did, sir. She must have known. I am certain you were a kind brother.'

'Perhaps. Thank you.'

Elizabeth looked at him, warm sympathy in her eyes. She had denied Daniel in his righteous anger, but she could not deny Charles Hunter. Sir Montague deserved to lose his own life at the hangman's noose.

'I am certain of it, sir. Whatever happened, your love will have sustained her.'

'You are as good as you are lovely,' Charles said. 'Had I met you before this business...but you see before you the shell of a man. I have no love or gentleness in me, Miss Travers. There is only hatred.' He gave her a wry smile. 'Besides, Daniel was there before me and I could not hope to win you from him.'

Elizabeth shook her head, a faint blush in her cheeks. Had she been an open book to all of them? 'Sir, you should not…'

'If he has not spoken, he will,' Charles said. 'And now I must beg you to forgive me. It has cost me much to come down this evening, but if I lie too long abed I shall lose my strength—and I must bring Sarah home.'

'I'm sure that Lord Cavendish will do all he can to help you, sir.'

'Yes, you are correct. He has done everything anyone could do. Daniel has been a good friend to me in this, Miss Travers. He deserves you.' He stood up and bowed towards Lady Isadora and John, who were talking. 'Forgive me, I am tired. I must wish you good night.'

'That poor man,' Lady Isadora said as the door closed behind him. 'To bear such a burden of grief— and to have been wounded like that! I dare say he may have a limp for the remainder of his days.' She sighed and looked at John. 'And you, Mr Elworthy—does your shoulder pain you now?'

'Hardly at all, ma'am. I was fortunate to have it attended by the best of nurses. If I had continued to lose blood at such a rate, I might still be lying on my bed instead of on my way to recovery.'

'Elizabeth is very good at these things,' Lady Isadora agreed. 'But then, she does everything well. Will you play for us now, dearest?'

'Yes, of course,' Elizabeth said and got up. She sat down by the piano and opened the sheet music, flexing her fingers. Even as she did so they heard a loud noise in the garden, which could only have been a shot. She looked round, startled, and saw that there were men everywhere in the garden, some carrying flaring torches. 'Oh, I think something must have happened…'

'Come away from the window,' Lady Isadora begged her as John got to his feet. 'If you mean to discover what is happening, I beg you will take care, sir.'

'You have no need to be anxious for me, ma'am,' John said. 'Excuse me, I shall see what is going on. Please stay here and away from the windows until I return.'

'Oh, dear,' Lady Isadora cried as he left. 'Will this sorry business never end? Daniel told me faithfully that it was over.'

'He is doing his best to bring it to an end,' Elizabeth told her. 'Please do not be too anxious, ma'am. It may be nothing at all.'

'How can it be nothing? Lady Isadora asked plaintively. 'We all heard the shot.'

However, when John returned a few minutes later, he told them that a shot had been fired in error. 'One of the men thought he saw someone approach the house and fired a warning shot, but now he believes he was mistaken and it was merely one of the dogs moving in the shrubbery.'

'Well, please tell him to be more careful,' Lady Isadora said a little crossly. 'My nerves are already ragged and I dare say I shall not sleep a wink all night.'

'I think we may all sleep the sounder to know that we are so well protected,' Elizabeth said. 'For myself I shall not let this small incident disturb me. And now I shall play for you.'

She walked back to the pianoforte, her manner calm, almost regal as she sat down at the instrument and began to play an elegant piece with soft, sure strokes. She had known from the moment Mr Bell told them of the tale set about that Sir Montague would not let things rest. He would seek some way of avoiding capture—and to punish Lord Cavendish, he would strike at those dearest to his heart.

They must all be on their guard, but it would be foolish to give way to nerves—that would be to let their enemy win. She refused to let them make her afraid. She would put her trust in Daniel—she was sure that he would do all that was necessary to keep them safe.

It was very pleasant to visit the bustling city. York had come to prominence through its flourishing wool trade and there were many elegant houses to hold testimony to the wealth of merchants, both past and present. Elizabeth looked about her as the carriage drew up before a prestigious inn that fronted the busy square. It was a fine-looking building and the grooms sprang to attention as their carriage swept under the arch and into the yard.

One young lad swept a path before the ladies as they walked towards the entrance, making sure that there was nothing to soil the hem of their gowns. Mr Elworthy tossed him a coin, and Elizabeth thanked him with a grateful smile. Inside the inn, the host came hurrying to greet them.

'Lady Isadora. It is a pleasure to welcome you here again.'

'Did my man inform you of our needs?' she asked. 'I hope you have kept the three best rooms for us— and a private parlour so that we may dine alone?'

'Yes, of course, your ladyship. An important gentleman was here last night, but he moved out this morning and the best chamber is free, also my second-best bedchamber and one that will suit the gentleman. You shall have the parlour to yourselves for the duration of your stay, ma'am.'

'Thank you, Mr Hanlon,' Lady Isadora said. 'If your wife will show us to our chambers, we shall tidy ourselves and partake of dinner when we come down. We shall stay for one night, and leave you after nuncheon tomorrow if all goes well. We are here to see our dressmaker.'

'I shall send a message to Mistress Barber and tell her you will visit her in the morning,' the innkeeper said. 'If your ladyship should wish it?'

'Yes, that will do very well,' Lady Isadora nodded. 'She may wait on us here this evening if she wishes and we shall arrange a time convenient to all in the morning.'

The innkeeper's wife came bustling through then to take them upstairs. She obviously knew Lady Isadora from past visits and talked naturally, repeating much of the gossip of the town and telling them of riots that had taken place in the surrounding district some days earlier.

'It is all some nonsense that folk have taken into their heads over a fire at a local mill,' she told them. 'The workers have complained of conditions there for some time and they are blaming the manager, though in common truth he does only what the owner tells him.'

'Was anyone hurt?' Elizabeth asked. 'In the fire?'

'Yes, there were several workers burned and three died,' Mrs Hanlon told her. 'The workers decided enough was enough and started a protest, and that set a few others off in their turn. It was quite nasty for a few days and the magistrate ordered the militia out—but it seems to be over now, miss.'

'And who is the owner of the mill?' Elizabeth inquired. 'Will he make some compensation for the workers' injuries?'

'That is unlikely, miss. Sir Montague Forsythe is not known for his generosity in these parts. I should say he was the most hated employer of any I know…and there are some hard men in this part of Yorkshire.'

'Yes, I see,' Elizabeth nodded. 'That is certainly unfortunate.'

She was thoughtful as she followed the woman upstairs. It seemed that Sir Montague was not only a murderer and a cheat, but the worst of employers. Surely he could not remain above the law forever?

They dined pleasantly in the inn, and then Mr Elworthy suggested a little stroll so that Elizabeth might enjoy the fine evening by gazing into the windows of some of the most fashionable shops. She readily agreed, though Lady Isadora cried off, saying that she would prefer to sit comfortably in the inn-keeper's private parlour.

'I shall speak to Mistress Barber when she comes. It will be as well if she knows what we are expecting from her before we visit her establishment, Elizabeth.'

'Would you rather I stayed with you, ma'am?'

'Not at all, my dear. Enjoy your stroll with Mr Elworthy. I shall be quite comfortable here.'

Elizabeth rose from her chair, pulling her pelisse about her as they stepped out of the parlour and into the street. It was not as crowded in the town as it had been when they arrived, but several people were strolling about the streets in which the best shops were situated.

'This is very pleasant,' John said. 'I believe this is your first visit to York, Miss Travers?'

'Yes, indeed. I passed through it on my way to Cavendish Hall, of course, but I did not have a chance to look at the shops.'

'I think some of them are the equal of London's best,' John said as they paused to look at a display of silverware in the window of an exclusive emporium. 'Living in this part of the country is not to be despised, though of course my mother always spent several weeks of the Season in London.'

'Indeed? I dare say she enjoyed meeting her friends there?'

'Yes, very much so—though we have some good neighbours living about us at Elworthy. I have perhaps neglected them a little, for I was busy when I first returned from the army, but when I marry I shall put all to rights.'

'I am sure that you will,' Elizabeth said. They had reached the end of the street and she could see a fine park beyond. 'I have visited London but once, sir. For myself I like the country well enough, though the Season has its merits, I believe.'

'Yes, I am sure that it does,' Mr Elworthy said. 'I like to spend some weeks there myself. I understand that Lady Isadora means to visit Brighton at the end of the month. I do not particularly care for it myself, but I may visit for a short time—' He broke off as she laid a hand upon his arm. 'Something disturbs you?'

'I thought I saw… Is that not Lord Cavendish? Do you see him at the entrance to the park? He is driving his curricle and…there is a lady with him.'

'Ah, yes, I believe you are right, Miss Travers. Would you wish to speak with him?'

'No, I do not believe so,' Elizabeth said and frowned. 'I thought that he had gone to London.'

'Did you? I am not perfectly sure,' John said. 'He has friends in York, you know—one of them an influential magistrate. He might have decided to lay his information before Lord Sawston.'

'Yes, perhaps,' Elizabeth said. 'Perhaps I mistook his meaning for we spoke of many things. I think we should return to the inn now.'

It had surprised her to see Lord Cavendish in York—and with a rather beautiful woman. The woman had been smiling at him with the intimacy of long acquaintance and Elizabeth could not hide it from herself that she had felt a pang of jealousy. So wrapped up in her thoughts was she that, when they passed the windows of a coffee house where gentlemen were sitting in full view of passers-by, she failed to notice Sir Montague Forsythe. She turned to smile at her companion, quite unaware that the gentleman left the coffee house soon after she had passed, following at a discreet distance until they entered the inn at which they were staying.

Chapter Nine

'Ah, there you are, my love,' Lady Isadora said when Elizabeth joined her in the parlour a little later. 'Did you enjoy your stroll?'

'Yes, very much,' Elizabeth replied. She considered telling Lady Isadora that she had caught a glimpse of Lord Cavendish, but decided against it. It really was none of her affair whether he chose to lay his evidence against Sir Montague in York or London—and as for his driving with a beautiful woman…well, that did not concern her either, despite his hints that he found Elizabeth attractive.

Yet had he said as much? She could not recall. He had commended her on her coolness in an awkward situation, but he had not truly spoken to her as a man might to the woman he loved. No, of course he did not care for her in that way. If she had begun to think it—to hope for it—she was blinding herself to the truth. She felt a swift, overwhelming surge of pain about her heart, but apart from a small flicker of her eyelashes there was nothing to show outwardly that she has suffering the pangs of unrequited love.

'Mistress Barber called while you were out,' Lady Isadora told her, looking pleased with herself. 'I have explained that we need at least two new gowns each for daywear and two for the evenings. That will be sufficient for the time being, I think. We can purchase more in Brighton, when we see what is being worn presently. I have remarked no great change in fashions here in York, but it may be different elsewhere. I was not sure what were your favourite colours, Elizabeth—but I thought possibly greens and blues might suit?'

'They are two of my favourites,' Elizabeth said, 'though the yellow silk you purchased for me has been tempting me these past weeks. I may not wear it yet, but I shall certainly do so when we are in Brighton—if you think it suitable for a companion?'

'You are as dear to me as my own daughter,' Lady Isadora told her with a look of affection. 'I offered you the post of companion for your pride's sake, Elizabeth—but you have become my friend and much more than a companion. I would wish to keep you with me always, my dear.'

'You have been so kind,' Elizabeth said. 'And I have

been happy in your home. I should be sad to leave it…'
She held back a sigh, for she was not sure what the
future might bring. It might be that she would find it
impossible to stay with Lady Isadora, though she
would be loath to leave her. And yet how could she stay
if Lord Cavendish brought home a beautiful bride?

They dined without Mr Elworthy that evening for he
had begged to be excused on business, and then spent
the evening talking in a companionable way, mostly of
the happy times that Lady Isadora had spent with Elizabeth's mother when they were girls. It was clear that
they had been great friends, and Elizabeth felt that she
had learned things about her mother that she had never
known. At nine o'clock Lady Isadora declared herself
ready for bed and they went upstairs together.

Elizabeth was not yet tired and sat on a little box
seat near the window, looking out. Her thoughts were
with Lord Cavendish and she was not aware that in
the shadows someone watched her window.

'Damn it, John!' Daniel said, frowning. 'Could you
not have persuaded them to put off their visit for a few
days—at least until this business was finished?'

'Lady Isadora was upset over the whole sorry business,' John said, looking rueful. 'I do not think she
would have listened to me had I tried to persuade her.
The best I could do was to accompany them.'

'Well, it is not your fault. I dare say Mama would not have listened had you tried to put her off. I hope you brought some of our men with you?'

'I told them to follow at a discreet distance,' John said. 'But I had hoped the danger might be over by now.'

'I laid the matter before Sawston, but Forsythe had been before me—not to Sawston, but to another magistrate. He has laid the blame for Barton's murder at Palmer's door—and that means it is a matter of one man's word against another. Sawston believes me completely, of course, but he says his hands are tied. Even if he had Forsythe arrested, it might be only a matter of time before he managed to bribe someone to release him.'

'Then what are we to do?'

'Forsythe is in York. He frequents a gaming club here. I shall try to meet him this evening, and I shall challenge him to a duel. If he accepts...then the problem is solved either way.'

'You mean that one of you will be dead,' John said a grim expression on his face. 'It is the honourable way, I grant you, Daniel—but does he deserve it? There are men who would slit his throat for a handful of guineas. Surely that is good enough for such a man?'

'I have been tempted,' Daniel admitted, a rueful look in his eyes as he recalled Elizabeth's scorn as she told him what she thought of such a plan. 'I doubt that many would shed tears for him—but it would be murder and I should be little better than he for ordering it.'

'A just killing,' John argued. 'He has been found guilty of several crimes, for we have tried him in his absence. I believe that Palmer spoke the truth concerning Sarah Hunter's abduction and their plans to use her in their wicked rituals. We cannot know for certain if she lies in that suicide's grave, but it seems likely. We know that he was responsible for the murder of Miss Travers's father and therefore deserves his punishment. If there were no other way, I would take the guilt of Forsythe's execution upon myself. Let me do the business.'

'Let me try whether he will meet me first,' Daniel said. 'If I cannot force him to a duel, then it seems that we shall have no option but to order his execution.'

'Very well,' John agreed. 'But you will have to kill him. It will not be enough to wound him and consider honour served.'

'Yes, I know,' Daniel said. 'It may be that I shall be obliged to leave the country for a while—just until the scandal blows over—but I consider it a price worth paying.'

'If you do not kill him, Charles will,' John said. 'He forced himself from his sickbed to dine with us the night before we left Cavendish—he is in haste to have Sarah's body taken home. Once that is done, he will come looking for Forsythe.'

'I believe Sir Montague's days are numbered one way or another,' Daniel said. 'But how did you know I was in York?'

'Miss Travers saw you driving from the direction of the park this afternoon. I knew it was your habit to stay here and so I came in search of you.'

'Then she also saw Lucinda Sawston,' Daniel said frowning.

'She was surprised to see you—she believed you had gone to London.'

'It was in my mind at one time,' Daniel said, 'but I felt it better to speak to Sawston. He has a good legal mind and I wondered if Palmer's statement would be enough.' He cursed inwardly, for it must have looked odd to Elizabeth. She could not know that Lucinda Sawston was his friend's sister and already engaged to be married. 'How long does my mother intend to stay in York?'

'A visit to the dressmaker in the morning, I understand, and then I believe she intends to return home.'

'I shall call on Mama tomorrow at mid-day if all goes well.'

'You will allow me to be your second in this duel?'

'Yes, of course, if you wish it.'

'I shall stand with you in this until the end,' John said. 'I may wish that you would take another course, but I shall abide by your decision.'

'In that case we shall dine together before visiting the gaming club.'

Elizabeth slept reasonably well, for the beds were comfortable and properly aired. However, she was up by seven o'clock and went downstairs to the parlour, where she was greeted with a look of surprise from the landlady.

'I wasn't expecting you down just yet, miss,' the woman said. 'If you should care for it, your breakfast may be brought up to you in twenty minutes or so.'

'Thank you,' Elizabeth said. 'I thought I would go out for a short stroll. If it will not be too much trouble, I shall breakfast in the parlour in about an hour.'

'That will suit me very well,' the landlady said, thinking what a pleasant-mannered young lady she was. 'There won't be many about yet, miss. You'll have the streets to yourself—apart from the milk-maids and early birds.'

'It will give me an appetite,' Elizabeth told her. 'I saw a pretty bonnet last evening in the window of a milliner's shop and I thought I should like to look at it again, for I might buy it.'

'That's right, miss,' the landlady said. 'You can

look at it properly on your own. Gentlemen don't understand these things.'

Elizabeth smiled at her and went out. She had a few guineas in her purse, which hung from her wrist, and she thought that the blue velvet bonnet might bridge the gap between her blacks and the colours she would start to wear when they went down to Brighton. It was kind of Lady Isadora to buy her some new gowns, but she would like to keep a little of her independence.

A dray wagon rattled by as she walked away from the inn. The milliner's shop was on the other side of the Market Square, and she had no qualms about walking that short distance alone, for she must be safe enough here in the middle of the town. There were only a few costers going about their business. A milkmaid carried a yoke on her shoulders, balancing her pails at either end as she cried her wares, and a woman had come out into the square to shovel the droppings left by a passing horse into her bucket. Two children were playing with a wooden hoop, and a market trader was beginning to set out his wares.

Elizabeth walked as far as the shop, gazing into the window for some minutes as she tried to decide whether or not she ought to buy the bonnet, which was certainly very attractive and would suit her colouring. She was turning away as a small boy came running up to her, begging for a penny for some bread. She hesitated and then opened her purse. The urchin snatched it from her and set off down the street. Elizabeth went after him as he turned into a side alley.

As she did so, a well-dressed man stepped out and grabbed the boy. He boxed his ears and took the purse from him. The urchin wriggled free and went running off at speed, and the man turned to Elizabeth, smiling at her as she came up to him.

'Thank you,' she said, a little out of breath; she had run fast to keep up with the boy. 'There is not much money in it, but I did not want to lose the purse.'

'Then I am glad to have been of service to you, miss.' He held the purse out towards her, a smile on his face.

Elizabeth took two steps towards him, reaching out for the purse, but just at the last moment she hesitated, feeling that something was wrong. It had all happened too easily and she was suddenly wary as she saw the gleam in the stranger's eyes. She paused, thinking what best to do, for she was certain it was a trap, but even as she tried to turn, an arm went round her from behind and she felt herself clasped in a firm hold.

'Keep still and you won't be harmed,' a voice grunted in her ear. 'He wants you alive…'

Elizabeth opened her mouth to scream, but the man's hand closed over her face and he was holding a pad soaked in some foul-smelling liquid, which made her swoon into his arms. She was still conscious when the carriage drew up beside them, but overcome by the fumes that were claiming her senses…

'He knows that you are searching for him,' John said to Daniel that morning when they breakfasted together at the inn where both had spent the night. They had passed the previous evening visiting the various gaming clubs to look for Sir Montague without success. 'He has gone to ground because he knows that you will not let this matter rest.'

'Perhaps…' Daniel looked thoughtful. 'He was here the night before last—he was seen at the club. I thought he meant to brazen it out, call my bluff as it were—but I feel that something has changed…'

'He has cut and run,' John said. 'Perhaps he is more afraid of your evidence than you thought.'

'I wish I thought it might be that,' Daniel said. 'But I am uneasy, John. I think I shall visit Mama as soon as we have breakfasted.' He did not know why, but he was conscious of a pit of fear at the base of his stomach—fear that Sir Montague had once again outwitted him.

'You do not think that Lady Isadora or Miss Travers may be in danger?'

'I think it possible,' Daniel said. 'If Forsythe has discovered that they are in York, it may be that he believes it is his opportunity to strike against me.'

'Then let us go immediately,' John said, becoming agitated. 'I have no appetite—I shall not rest until I know that they are safe.'

'Yes, you are right,' Daniel said. 'We shall go at once.'

It was about the time that they were leaving the inn, where they had spent the night, that Lady Isadora came downstairs to the parlour for the first time that morning. She met the landlady leaving the parlour with a tray, and inquired whether she would find Elizabeth within.

'No, indeed, she is not, ma'am,' the landlady said. 'She went out for a walk much earlier, my lady, and ordered her breakfast for an hour later—but she has not been back. I was removing the tray because the chocolate has gone cold.'

'That is very odd,' Lady Isadora said with a little frown. 'Did she go alone?'

'Why, yes, ma'am. The gentleman did not come in last night—his bed was untouched when my girl went in to tidy the room this morning.'

'Now that is most singular.' Lady Isadora was beginning to feel anxious. 'Did Miss Travers say where she was going?'

'I believe it was her intention to look at something she saw last night in the milliner's shop across the square. She said that she would not be long.'

'I shall wait in the parlour for her,' Lady Isadora

said. 'Would you send her to me, please, when she comes in? And if Mr Elworthy should return...'

'Yes, of course, ma'am,' the landlady said. 'As soon as I see him.'

Lady Isadora went into the parlour. She stood at the window, looking out for some minutes, undecided whether she ought to go out into the town and look for Elizabeth herself. The girl did not know York at all, and it was possible that she had taken a wrong turning in one of the streets. She was about to send for her maid to go in search of her young friend when the door opened behind her. Whirling round, she saw first Mr Elworthy and then her son, and gave an exclamation of relief.

'Thank God you are come! Elizabeth is missing...' she cried. 'She went out early this morning for a walk and did not return in an hour for her breakfast as she promised.'

'Good grief!' John looked at Daniel in dismay. 'Do you think he has taken her?'

'What do you mean?' Lady Isadora cried, frightened by their grim looks. 'Who has taken her? Not that dreadful man? I had imagined that was all over, Daniel. Why has he not been arrested?'

'It seems that Palmer's confession was not enough,' Daniel said. 'I believed it must be acceptable in court, but Sawston says we need more. In truth, Forsythe has been too clever for us, Mama. He laid evidence against Palmer before I could lay mine and that means Palmer's evidence is only one man's word against another's.'

'Then what are we to do?' Lady Isadora was most upset. 'Why did you get embroiled in this mess in the first place, Cavendish? If anything happens to Elizabeth, I shall hold you responsible.'

'No more than I,' Daniel said, an oddly bleak look in his eyes. The sting of regret, of remorse that he had failed to keep her safe, the aching longing to have her with him was so strong that he could hardly bear to speak. 'Has anyone started a search for her?'

'No—for I have not long learned of it and I was not perfectly sure what to do.'

'Then, if you will excuse me, Mama, I shall arrange that it begins at once.' He looked at his friend, the agony he could not quite quell in his eyes. 'John, we have work to do.'

'But what shall I do?' Lady Isadora asked as her son turned away.

'Stay here for the moment,' Daniel said. 'Ask your dressmaker to call or go to her, but I cannot protect you if you go home. I need all the men I have here to search for Elizabeth.'

'Daniel…' Lady Isadora cried a trifle plaintively. Her son had never spoken to her so sharply before and it upset her, especially when she needed comforting.

'Please excuse us,' John said, seeing her distress. 'This is serious, for if we do not find her...' He left the rest unsaid and hurried after Daniel.

Lady Isadora stared at the parlour door for some minutes after it had closed. She felt like weeping, but that would do no one any good. Nor was there any use in sitting here and worrying. She would visit the dressmaker after all and order some silks for their new gowns, and then when Elizabeth was back with them they could be made up into the gowns she needed.

She would not allow herself to think of a future that did not contain Elizabeth, because she was so very fond of her—and so was Daniel. It suddenly struck Lady Isadora that her son's brusque manner must mean that he cared for the girl more than she had guessed.

'Please do not let anything happen to her.' Lady Isadora's prayer was fervent. 'Please let Elizabeth come back to us safely.'

What could have happened to her? How could she have disappeared from the streets of a busy town without someone seeing her abduction? Surely they must have done so?

As Lady Isadora summoned her maid to accompany her to the dressmaker, she little guessed that her thoughts echoed what Daniel was even now saying to his men. She could not even begin to understand the thoughts that pricked and tortured him as he thought of Elizabeth at the mercy of evil men.

Elizabeth was aware of a headache. She had never quite lost consciousness—in the struggle to capture her, the cloth had not covered her nose and she had inhaled only a small amount of the foul substance that had overcome her. She had been lying on the seat of the carriage for a while now, her eyes closed as she fought against the faintness and the sickness in her stomach, fully conscious of the fact that she had been abducted.

As time went on and she began to feel a little better, she understood what must have happened. Sir Montague must be in York. He had seen and recognised her, and, because he knew that evidence was being laid against him, he had decided to kidnap her in the hope of blackmailing Daniel. Or was she simply to be used as revenge?

For a moment the fear that this thought aroused was so strong that she could not think clearly, but Elizabeth had never been one to give into her fears and she told herself not to be foolish, but to look at her situation logically. Had Sir Montague merely wished for revenge, he could have had her killed instantly. Therefore, it was more likely that he was afraid for his own neck and would try to strike a bargain with Daniel for her safe return.

Now that she was able to think calmly, Elizabeth wondered what she might do to avoid letting Sir Montague win and escape his just punishment. Should she try to escape? If she pretended to be still under the influence of the drug they had given her when they came to take her into…where would they take her? Presumably to a house, she imagined. Either a property owned by Sir Montague or…a house of ill repute where she would be strictly watched.

So perhaps she should try to escape before that by throwing herself from the carriage when the chance came her way. It might slow down at a turnpike or the driver might want to stop for some reason and she could perhaps take them by surprise.

If she did that, nothing would have been gained from this, Elizabeth realised. Even if she managed to escape, she had no proof that Sir Montague Forsythe had ordered her abduction. He would be free to continue his evil work. If, on the other hand, she allowed them to think her cowed by her situation, she might discover the proof Daniel so sorely needed to bring his enemy to justice. She might in the end be the means of saving his life by helping to destroy his enemy.

Had she the courage to play this through to the end? Elizabeth thought about it and wished that she had her father's pistol with her, but that had been left behind at Cavendish. She had nothing but her wits to help her.

She might end by wishing that she had taken her chance to escape as soon as she was able, but she was not easily cowed and there was a certain satisfaction in the thought that she might play a part in an evil man's downfall.

The thought that the tables might yet be turned on him lifted her spirits. She would not try to escape, nor would she give way to missish fears. Now was her chance to do something to thwart the man who had so callously destroyed her family. Somehow she would endure whatever happened to her until Daniel came. And he would come. She felt the sting of tears in her eyes as she thought of him. Perhaps she had been wrong to think that he cared for her, but he respected her as a person and he would not simply abandon her.

'She cannot simply have disappeared into thin air,' Daniel said. 'Forsythe must have had her abducted.'

'I am sure that you are right,' John said. They had spent the best part of the morning riding about the town searching for Elizabeth and were now on their way to report to Lady Isadora. 'If she had simply been lost, we should have found her by now. Where do you think they will have taken her—and what is his next move?'

'If I knew that, I should not have wasted the day in

a futile search,' Daniel said. His nerves were on edge—he was aware that every hour lost brought Elizabeth closer to danger. 'She may have been taken to his home or…' he shuddered. 'God forbid that she should be imprisoned in a whorehouse!'

They dismounted in the inn yard and went inside, asking for Lady Isadora, who was, they were told, in the private parlour. She had been sitting staring into space, but started up eagerly as they entered.

'Has she been found?'

'No, Mama,' Daniel said grimly. 'We have found no sign of her.'

'She must have been abducted like poor Julia,' Lady Isadora said. 'Do you think they will let her go?'

'I cannot—' Daniel was interrupted by the landlady, who came in carrying something in her hand. 'Yes, what is it, madam?'

'Begging your pardon, sir. But this letter just came for her ladyship.'

'A letter? Give it to me!' Daniel took it and broke the seal, which was merely a blob of wax with no impression or crest. He read the brief lines and frowned. 'Is this Elizabeth's hand, Mama?'

Lady Isadora took it from him and read the few lines quickly. She frowned over them. 'It is something like, but I am not sure… but Elizabeth would not write this, Daniel.'

'What does it say?' John asked.

'That she has had to go home unexpectedly,' Daniel said. 'No, John, I agree with Mama. Elizabeth would not go so abruptly or send such a letter. She would have told Mama if she had bad news—besides, she has no home of her own. Depend upon it, this letter is to buy Forsythe time.'

'But why?' Lady Isadora asked. 'I do not understand, Daniel. If he wants to ransom her, why not say so at once?'

'Perhaps it is part of the torture he wishes to inflict,' he said, looking grim. 'We are meant to discover the grief of being unsure what has happened to her and to feel the pain of her loss.'

'So that we are willing to pay any price when a chance is offered to recover her,' John said. 'The man is fiendishly clever, Daniel. How are we to get the better of him?'

'You must do something!' Lady Isadora cried. 'I cannot bear to think of Elizabeth being mistreated. She must be so frightened.'

'Do you think so?' Daniel looked thoughtful. 'Elizabeth is not usually at a loss in a crisis. It might be that this will be his undoing.' He had clung to his belief in Elizabeth's courage, her calm fortitude in the face of a crisis, and by that means retained his own sanity.

'What can you mean?' Lady Isadora was too distressed to be placated. 'She is in terrible danger.'

'Yes, that cannot be denied,' Daniel said, 'for we cannot be certain of his purpose in taking her—but she knows what has happened and I have great faith in her resourcefulness.'

'I don't know how you can be so calm! Do you not care for her at all?' Lady Isadora accused.

'No, no, ma'am, you misjudge him,' John said. 'Daniel is as concerned as you or I.'

'Perhaps more so than you can imagine,' Daniel said, his lips white with tension. 'But this letter has reassured me on one thing. He does not mean to make her disappear into a whorehouse.'

'You think that he will take her somewhere close to him?'

'This is to put me off the scent,' Daniel said. 'I think he acted on impulse and needs time to think his plan through. I am sure that he has taken her to his estate. And that is where I shall go to look for her.'

'What would you have me do?' John asked.

'I should be grateful if you would escort Mama home,' Daniel said. 'I have two men I need to accompany me, but the others may go with you. I beg you will remain at Cavendish until you hear from me. And should Hilary or Robert return, please tell them that they may be needed.'

Daniel turned and strode from the room. He did not turn his head even though he heard his mother's little cry of distress. Too much time had been wasted already, and despite the words that were meant to deceive his mother, he could not be certain what Forsythe had in mind for Elizabeth.

What had possessed her to go walking alone? Yet how could she have guessed that Forsythe was in York? She was not to blame in any of this. Daniel placed the blame squarely where it belonged. He had begun this investigation from a desire to help recover Charles Hunter's sister, and in a spirit of adventure. Bored with the delights of society, he had missed his army days and believed that a little risk was well worth the taking. He had never dreamed that he might lose something so very precious.

And he had never told her!

Elizabeth sensed that the carriage was slowing. Her nails turned into her palms as she tensed, knowing that she had a part to play. She must not let these men suspect that she had long ago recovered her senses. She lay quietly as the carriage pulled to a halt, hearing the rattle of gravel beneath the wheels, forcing herself to lie still. It was growing dusk, so she knew that they had travelled some distance—but in what direction?

She could hear voices and then the carriage door

was pulled open and she was aware that someone was staring at her. The silence unnerved her and she gave a little moan for effect, fluttering her lashes, but not opening her eyes.

'Has she slept all this time?' a voice asked and she knew it at once. Sir Montague Forsythe! 'I hope you have not overdone it, Syrius. I want her alive and in good shape when he comes looking for her.'

Elizabeth's heart raced. Clearly Sir Montague had a plan in mind to bring Daniel after her—but why? Did he want to make a bargain with him for her life? Or was there a more sinister reason? Was he intending to kill his enemy? Was she the bait that would bring Daniel into a trap?

She almost wished that she had somehow managed to escape on the journey and yet she knew that Daniel and his friends would never be safe, nor would they rest until Sir Montague was brought to justice. He had somehow managed to turn the tables on them, and might do so again unless... Somehow she must deceive her captors until she could find some way to warm Daniel or to escape, for Sir Montague was guilty of having her abducted and that was enough to hang him.

If Daniel were to bring the law here and she was found on the premises, he would have all the proof he needed. She must put all thoughts of escaping from her head and trust in Daniel to rescue her.

'Well, get her out then, man,' she heard the note of irritation in Sir Montague's voice. 'Take her upstairs and lock her in. Roxie will take care of her when she wakes.'

'I am not sure that she will care to be embroiled in this affair, Forsythe.'

'She has enjoyed the benefits of our arrangement,' Forsythe growled. 'She will do as I tell her or face the consequences. If I hang, so will the rest of you.'

'Damn it, Forsythe! You know I shan't split on you the way Palmer did.'

'He was always a fool. I should have silenced him after that girl drowned. I kept him close for he might have inherited a fortune had his uncle died—but I knew that he had a conscience over that night.'

The man called Syrius had climbed into the carriage and was bending over Elizabeth. She could smell a heavy cologne on his clothes and guessed he was the man who had arranged the incident with her purse. She was aware of him bending over her and it took all her courage to remain still with her eyes closed as he pulled her into a sitting position and lifted her, calling to another man to help him get her out of the carriage.

They made heavy weather of it, for Elizabeth had deliberately let her body go limp and her arm banged against the side of the carriage as she was hauled out and finally hoisted over someone's shoulder. It was a most undignified way to be carried, and all her instincts cried out against the treatment she was being given, but somchow she managed to avoid opening her eyes or crying out as she was carried into a house and up some stairs. She heard the sound of a door being opened, and then she was dropped on to a bed, which was thankfully soft.

'Is she ill?' a woman's voice asked. 'You should not have brought her here. I want nothing to do with this…'

'I'm doing what he told me,' a man's voice grunted. Not the one called Syrius, Elizabeth judged, so perhaps the one who had tried to drug her. 'Tell him you won't have her here.'

'Oh, get out of here,' the woman snapped. 'Since Forsythe has seen fit to involve me I must accept it— but if he thinks I shall hang for him he is mistaken.'

Elizabeth heard a door shut with a snap and knew that only the woman remained. She felt the touch of a soft hand on her forehead and her heart raced. How much longer could she keep up this pretence?

'You have no need to pretend with me,' the deep, husky voice said. 'You are not dealing with those fools now. Open your eyes and look at me. We have something to discuss if either of us is to survive this mess.'

Elizabeth sighed and opened her eyes, easing herself up against the pillows. 'Lady Roxborough,' she said, for she had recognised the distinctive voice immediately, even though she had met its owner but twice.

'Where am I? I thought I was being taken to Sir Montague's house—or perhaps a house of ill repute.'

Lady Roxborough gave a harsh laugh. 'Some might say that my house is exactly that, my dear. My husband had tastes that many would disapprove, but I did not. I knew when I married him that he was a rogue. However, he left me a fortune when he died and I do not regret that I indulged him. Forsythe imagines that he still has a hold over me because of Roxborough's past sins. He brought you here because he believes he can intimidate me as he has others, and no doubt Lord Cavendish will go straight to Forsythe's own estate. Forsythe is clever and cunning, that is why he has succeeded in evading discovery for so long—but I do not fear him. For my husband's sake I endured his presence in our house and kept his secrets—but I shall not stand by now. I believe we may come to an agreement, Miss Travers.'

'I am very glad of that, ma'am,' Elizabeth said, sounding much calmer than she felt inside. 'What exactly are you offering me?'

'I shall keep his dogs at bay,' Lady Roxborough said. 'You will not be harmed while you are under my roof and I shall think of some way to help you when the time comes.'

'You mean when Lord Cavendish has been successfully lured here, of course. Tell me, what does Sir Montague propose to do with him—and me?'

'I imagine he plans to kill you both eventually,' Lady Roxborough said. 'Once Cavendish receives the ransom note the fat will be in the fire. If Forsythe imagines he can make a bargain, he is more of a fool than I take him for, Miss Travers. Cavendish is not easily overcome. And if he were dead... Naturally, you could not be left alive to testify—unless I help you.'

'But you know that I would not keep quiet, do you not? Therefore your price is my silence on the part you played in this, am I correct?'

'That and perhaps a little more—should I be able to prevent either of you being killed.'

'I have no money,' Elizabeth replied. 'I cannot speak for his lordship, but I would keep your secret, Lady Roxborough.'

'Call me Roxie, my dear. I liked you when we first met, and when Lady Isadora brought you to visit I realised that you were the girl I should have liked my daughter to be had life been kinder to me. Forsythe had spoken of you as being too proud, but it amused me that you had managed to probe beneath his skin. Very few people can do that, though in my youth I had him at my feet. He is completely depraved, but I knew how to make him beg for my favours. Unfortunately, I can no longer please his jaded palate, but I still have some influence with him. Do we have an agreement?'

'I have told you that I will keep your secret.'

'And the rest?'

'I make no promises for Lord Cavendish.'

'Then nor shall I,' Roxie said, her eyes glittering. 'We shall see what happens. I believe you would do best not to try and deceive Forsythe when he decides to visit you. Be proud and remote, it will impress him more than weakness.'

'I thank you for your advice, Lady Roxie.'

'I shall have food and wine sent up to you. You may eat and drink freely. I give you my word that it will not be drugged or poisoned.'

'Thank you,' Elizabeth said. 'I believe I could eat something since I missed my breakfast.'

'You are very cool headed,' Roxie said and smiled oddly. 'Had we met under other circumstances, I think we should have been friends, Elizabeth.'

Elizabeth did not answer. She merely inclined her head as Roxie went out, locking the door behind her. As soon as she was alone, Elizabeth put her feet to the floor. One small candle had been left for her, which was sufficient to show her that she was in a bedchamber that must be one of those reserved for less important guests. It was adequately furnished, though not provided with all the things that made life more comfortable. However, there was a dressing mirror, brushes and combs, and in the corner of the room a screen behind which she discovered the items she needed to relieve her physical discomfort.

She had made herself comfortable and was sitting on the edge of the bed when she heard a key in the lock, and then a man came in, carrying a tray with some food and a glass of wine. He looked at her, but did not speak as he set the tray down and then went out again, locking the door after him.

They were taking great care that she should not escape, Elizabeth reflected, but she was not yet ready to do so. She had Lady Roxborough's word for it that Sir Montague Forsythe was at the back of her abduction, and she had heard his voice when she lay in the carriage, but she wanted to meet him face to face. She had no particular concern for her own safety. She was certain that she was the bait to lure Daniel into Sir Montague's trap. Somehow she must work out how she could warn him that he was in danger. He would come for her; she had no doubt of it—and she must be ready.

The house was in darkness when Daniel arrived. He stood outside watching for a few minutes before making his way to the back of the building. They had found a door unlocked the night they discovered Palmer drinking alone in the library, but it took only a few seconds for Daniel to discover that this weakness had been rectified. He was just debating which window it would be easier to break open when a man came round the corner. Daniel stepped back out of sight. From his appearance, Daniel judged the newcomer to be one of the footmen, perhaps returning from his night off…which he appeared to have spent at the local inn.

He was whistling, a little unsteady on his feet as he tapped at the door, clearly expecting to be let in. Daniel covered the ground between them swiftly, grabbing him from behind just as the door opened and a young girl appeared carrying her candle.

'Don't scream,' Daniel warned her as he bundled his hapless victim inside. 'I mean you no harm. Answer my questions truthfully and you shall have a gold sovereign for your trouble.'

He had let go of his victim, who fell senseless to the floor, clearly overcome not so much by Daniel's attack as the ale he had taken that night.

'A sovereign?' the girl asked, impressed, for it was more than she earned in a month. 'What did you want to know, sir?'

'Has you master had visitors today? Has a young lady been brought here?'

'No, sir. I have been on duty all day, sir. Mrs Raunds—she's the housekeeper—she told me that he would be away for a few days.'

'That is the truth?'

'Yes, sir.'

'Do you know where he went? He was in York a day or so ago—have you any idea of where he might have gone?'

'No, sir.'

'Roxie doxie…' a thick voice said and Daniel looked down at the man he had grabbed so unceremoniously. 'They took her to Roxie's house…one of them…'

Daniel looked down at him. 'Who is Roxie? Where does she live?' For answer he received no more than a gentle snore. Clearly his victim was now dead to the world.

'I think that might be Lady Roxborough,' the girl ventured a little uncertainly. 'I do not know who you are, sir, and I may lose my place for it—but some bad things have happened around here and I have thought of leaving. But I know that Lady Roxborough was present at those ceremonies in the woods sometimes…'

Daniel put his hand in his pocket and pulled out five gold sovereigns. 'Here, share this with your friend,' he said. 'And if you are in need of a place, go to Cavendish Hall. You will be found work there if you choose.'

'Thank you, sir,' the girl said and slipped the coins into the pocket of her gown. 'I hope you find the young lady you are looking for—we don't want more trouble like what happened in the woods before, do we?'

'Do you know anything of that?' His eyes

narrowed, intent on her face. 'You know what happened to that girl?'

'He does,' she said, looking at the man snoring at her feet. 'Fred knows what happened. They made him do things he didn't like—and he would testify if you paid him, sir. We're planning to wed once we can find enough money for a small tavern of our own.'

'Bring him with you when you leave here, and if he is willing to testify in front of a magistrate, you shall have your tavern,' Daniel said. 'Pray tell me your name, girl.'

'Mary Meadows, sir,' she said and smiled at him. 'You'll have what you need in a day or so. Fred will need a little persuasion, but I'll bring him round.'

'If you can do it, you will not be sorry,' Daniel told her. 'I thank you for your help, Mary.'

'You were one of the gentlemen what took Mr Palmer,' she said. 'He wasn't like the others, sir. I should be glad to know what happened to him.'

'He has gone abroad for his health,' Daniel said, 'and now I had best leave before we wake the house and cause trouble for you and Fred.'

'Oh, there aren't many house servants now,' Mary told him. 'Most of them upped and went after Mr Palmer disappeared. Sir Montague were in a tearing rage when he found out what had happened, and he had one of the lads whipped. After that, there were only a handful of us stayed on. And Mrs Raunds is to go at the end of the month.'

Daniel nodded, his mouth set in a grim line. Apparently, Forsythe's people were deserting him—like rats leaving a sinking ship. It seemed that his world was crumbling round him and there might be more than one way of bringing him to his just deserts—but first there was the matter of Elizabeth.

Somehow he was not surprised to discover that Lady Roxborough was involved in this unsavoury business. Her husband had been known for his depravity, and was probably one of the first to join Forsythe's group. He had died of his excesses at the age of forty, leaving a fortune to his wife. It was whispered that Roxie had had affairs with various grooms and footmen, and it was possible that she had taken part in the pagan ceremonies held in Forsythe's woods.

It was plain to him why Forsythe had taken Elizabeth there. If only a handful of loyal servants remained to him, he could not have been sure of keeping her presence in the house a secret, or of holding her securely, but, in Daniel's opinion, he had made a mistake. Lady Roxborough was not a fool. She was unlikely to become involved in something that might lead to a hanging, which meant that Elizabeth was safe enough for the moment.

Chapter Ten

'Thank goodness we are home,' Lady Isadora said, sinking down into a chair in her parlour. 'I do not think I have ever endured such a journey. I was on edge the whole time and I feel as if I want to weep. Where is dear Elizabeth? And what is happening to her? I really do not think I can bear the agony of not knowing for much longer.'

'You must try not to worry,' John reassured her. He too felt that he would never wish to endure such a journey again, but for rather different reasons. John was the most patient of men, but Lady Isadora's anxiety had made her petulant and fretful. 'You will be able to rest now, dear lady—and, if you will excuse me, I shall go up to see how Charles is feeling this evening.'

'Yes, yes, do what you think best,' Lady Isadora said. 'I dare say I have been a trial to you, sir—but I do care so very much for her.'

'Of course. We all do,' John said and left the parlour a little abruptly. He had been patient with her during the journey, but in truth was as concerned as anyone about Elizabeth's whereabouts. It was as he was about to go upstairs in search of Charles that his friend came out of the library. He hailed him, relieved to see that, apart from a heavy limp, Charles seemed to be mending well. 'I was just about to seek you out.'

'I am glad you are back,' Charles said. 'I am going to set things in motion for Sarah's homecoming, John. I shall be glad if you will accompany me to the churchyard at Little Marsh Meadows tomorrow…' He broke off as he saw John's face. 'What is it? Something has happened!'

'Miss Travers has been kidnapped.'

'Forsythe, no doubt,' Charles said, his eyes glittering with anger. 'I had hoped he would be in prison where he belongs by now.'

'Unfortunately, he was too clever for us,' John said. 'Daniel has gone after her. He thinks Forsythe may have taken her to his estate.'

'Unlikely,' Charles said, looking grim. 'He knows that we are aware of his actions and he will seek a hiding place somewhere that we should not dream of looking…'

Hearing the sound of knocking at the front door, the two men looked at each other, for it was late for callers. Forrest, standing at his usual position in the hall, looked at them, raising his brows as if to question whether to open the door.

'Yes, answer it,' John said, and drew a pistol from the pocket of his coat. 'I am prepared for any eventuality.'

However, he was not prepared for what happened next. Forrest opened the door to a servant dressed in a sober brown coat. He handed a sealed packet to Lady Isadora's footman, tipped his hat and left smartly.

'What is it, Forrest?'

'It's a letter—or I should say a packet for Lord Cavendish, sir.'

'A packet?' John was curious. 'Let me see…' He took it, feeling it and finding it soft to the touch. 'It is rather strange to be delivering a packet at this hour, do you not think?'

'Open it,' Charles said. 'In the circumstances I think Daniel will understand.'

'Yes…' John tore away the wrappings to discover a lace kerchief with a light but distinctive perfume clinging to the fragile material. 'This is Elizabeth's…' He looked through the package, but there was no accompanying message. 'What does this mean?'

'Forsythe is telling you he has her,' Charles said. 'Damn him! If only we knew where she was being held.'

'Perhaps I might help, sir,' Forrest said. 'The

fellow who brought it—I know him. We have wrestled together at the fairs. He works for Lady Roxborough—or Lady Roxie, as he calls her. He brags that he has been her lover, sir, though I do not know if he lies.'

'You are sure?' Charles asked and his eyes gleamed with excitement as Forrest confirmed it. 'Then Forsythe has made his first mistake. We know where Elizabeth is. This was meant to puzzle and frighten us, but now we have the advantage.'

'If only Daniel were here…'

'It would be easier if there were three of us,' Charles agreed, 'but we have the element of surprise, and I dare say we could find one or two of Daniel's men who would come with us…'

'You can count me in,' Forrest said. 'I agree that we should act swiftly, sir. I have a pistol Lord Cavendish gave me—and there are two others I know of who would risk themselves for his lordship and Miss Travers. With your permission I'll tell them to prepare enough horses for us and be ready to leave in twenty minutes.'

'Well, I suppose…' John looked at their eager faces uncertainly. It seemed a little risky to go off without a plan to rescue Elizabeth, and yet he could not deny that they did have the element of surprise on their side. 'We might be fortunate enough to take them off guard…'

* * *

Elizabeth sat staring out of the window. She had eaten a little of the food that had been brought for her, but left the wine untouched, drinking a few sips of the water left in a jug for her personal use. Lady Roxborough had promised her that her wine would not be drugged, but she was not sure that she completely trusted her. She had blown out her candle earlier— she wished to save what little there was and she preferred to sit in the darkness staring out.

Time passed slowly. Clouds shadowed the moon, and sometimes she could see clear across the lawn to the shrubbery, but at other times it was quite dark. Now at last the moon had almost disappeared. It must be nearly morning and she would be able to see the view from her window more clearly. She had already discovered that she was being held two floors up from the ground and that there was nothing to help her climb down to safety, had she wished to escape that way.

Suddenly she stiffened. Something was moving in the direction of the shrubbery. Elizabeth strained to see, but a cloud passed across the moon and it was lost. She could not be sure that she had seen anything and yet she was almost certain that she had seen something.

Supposing it was Daniel? How could he have discovered her whereabouts so soon? It was hardly possible and yet her senses told her that he was near.

She had almost decided to light her candle and signal to him when she heard the sound of a key in the lock and moved away from the window, sitting on the edge of the bed as the door opened and a man came in, carrying a branch of candles.

'Ah, so you are awake,' Sir Montague said as she stood up, her hands clasped behind her back. His voice was slightly slurred and she guessed that he had spent the night drinking. 'Roxie told me she thought you had recovered from your faint. I do apologise for that, Miss Travers. I should have much preferred you to come of your own accord.'

'I do not imagine that you truly expected it, sir. Hence the subterfuge you used to trick me.'

'Rather clever of me, was it not?' he said, looking pleased with himself. 'Once you were out of sight of the inn, I knew I had you.'

'And now that you have me, I demand that you set me free immediately,' Elizabeth said, her head held high. 'I do not see how you can hope to gain anything from this foolish action, sir.'

'Do you not, Miss Travers—or may I call you Elizabeth? I think we could be friends, my dear.' His thick lips curved in a sneer. 'I believe I could teach you to welcome me in time. I have tamed wilder wenches than you, Elizabeth.'

'Indeed,' Elizabeth said, lifting her head proudly.

'But then, you have had great experience, haven't you? Miss Hunter was not the only young lady you have abducted, was she? I dare say there have been far more than anyone knows.'

'I see that you appreciate me, Elizabeth. Sarah Hunter was a fool. It was a pity that she awoke too soon. I could have got good money for her from some friends of mine after she had served her purpose.' He looked angry. 'The stupid girl ran from us—if she drowned that night it was her own doing.'

'If she drowned?' Elizabeth looked at him intently. 'Then you do not know for certain?'

'She disappeared into the night.' Forsythe scowled. 'Had I found her that night she would have learned her lessons well…'

'In one of the whorehouses you frequent,' Elizabeth accused. 'But perhaps they are your own? I do not think that you would care for the regular entertainment they offer, sir. It would need something a little darker to interest you, would it not?'

'What a proud beauty you are,' Sir Montague said. 'I knew you had spirit when we first met—but I had not realised how intelligent you are, Elizabeth. I have never cared for dull-witted females, you see— that is why lowborn whores have no interest for me. I like a woman with character.' He looked at her speculatively. 'I had thought it would be best to dispose of you once you have fulfilled your purpose, which is to bring Cavendish to the rescue. After he has had time to dwell on what is happening to you, of course. He chose to meddle in my affairs and now he must pay.'

'You mean to kill him?'

'Yes, certainly. That is the reason you are here, Elizabeth. I expect Sir Galahad to come charging to the rescue…when he discovers where you are, of course.' He smiled unpleasantly. 'But that will not be until I choose…a few days. Enough time for me to enjoy your undoubted charms, Elizabeth. And who knows, if you please me, I may keep you for a while before I let you join your sisters in the whorehouse.'

'Do you imagine that your insults will bring me to tears, sir?' Elizabeth asked. 'I care not what you think of me nor what you say.'

'But you will learn to care,' Forsythe promised her. 'Did you know that there are whips that can inflict terrible pain and yet leave a woman's skin unmarked? I know how to use them and other things…drugs that will destroy that fine mind of yours.'

'And then I should be like the dull-witted whores you despise,' Elizabeth told him scornfully. 'Where is the point in that, sir? Perhaps the whips might bring me to my knees. I should hate you, but I dare say you have never known a woman's love. Is that why you hate them so? Or perhaps it was your mother who turned you sour? Did she neglect you in your cradle?'

Forsythe lifted his hand, striking her across the cheek. 'Witch! You will pay for your defiance. Yes, the whips will bring you to your knees. You will crawl to me for favours, beg me to take you.'

'Leave her alone, Forsythe,' Roxie spoke from behind him. 'I told you I wouldn't have her harmed. If you meant to break her, you should have taken her to one of your houses. Did you imagine that I would stand aside while you amused yourself? I fear you were sadly mistaken, sir. I may have played your game while it pleased me, but no longer. If you lay another finger on her, I shall kill you.'

Forsythe had whirled around to face her as she spoke, and now Elizabeth could see that the older woman was carrying a small pistol and it was directed straight at his chest.

'Damn you, Roxie! I could ruin you as easily as I would swat a fly,' he raged. 'This is none of your affair. Leave me to my business and I'll leave you to your pretty boys.'

'You made it my business by bringing her here. A foolish mistake on your part,' Lady Roxborough said, her eyes glittering. 'I have hated you for years and now you have given me my chance to be revenged upon you. Leave her alone—and give the key of this door to me. You are not going to ruin her as you have so many others, Forsythe. Roxborough was depraved—but you were his mentor. Had it not been for you, I might have saved him from himself.'

'You cannot blame me for that drunken sot,' Forsythe said. 'Damn you! You shall pay for this…' Suddenly he lunged at her and they struggled for the pistol.

Elizabeth watched with a strange kind of fascination. She would have made her escape, but they were between her and the door and she could not move for fear of what might happen. And then the pistol went off, making an ear-splitting noise, and she heard Lady Roxborough scream. A moment later she had slipped to the ground, where she jerked for a few moments and then lay still.

Elizabeth could not take her eyes from the blood trickling from the wound in Lady Roxborough's stomach. She shivered, because she knew that the brave woman was dead. No one could suffer such an injury and live.

'You have killed her,' Elizabeth said. Her stomach was churning and she felt sick, but she knew that she must not give into her feelings. If she showed herself to be vulnerable, she would be lost. 'You murdered her. I saw you…'

'The woman was crazed,' he said, his face white. For a moment his eyes had the look of a maddened wolf as fear and savagery mingled. 'You saw that she threatened to kill me…'

'But you killed her,' Elizabeth said. She held back her desire to scream or weep, knowing that she must hold her advantage for as long as she could. And then she glanced beyond his shoulder and saw what she had been hoping to see for the past several minutes. Her rescuers had arrived. 'You cannot let me live now, sir, for I can hang you. And I shall. You may do what you please to me, but I shall—'

'Damn you!' Sir Montague cried. He lifted his arm to aim the pistol at her, but even as he did so, a man hurled himself at his back, knocking him to the floor. The tiny pistol went sliding across the floor to end at Elizabeth's feet. She bent down swiftly to pick it up, her eyes hardly leaving the desperate struggle before her. She would know what to do should the wrong man gain the upper hand, though she had no fear that he would.

'We have all the evidence we need against him,' she cried as the struggle went on. Daniel had his man on the ground now, sitting astride him, his hands about his throat. Forsythe was gasping for breath as the iron grip tightened, cutting off his breath. 'I believe he has no other weapon, Daniel. Take him alive…he deserves to hang!'

The fight lasted for a few moments longer, but then

Forsythe put out his hands in a gesture of surrender. Daniel let go of his throat, getting to his feet to stand over his beaten opponent. Elizabeth breathed a sigh of relief, though she had hardly doubted who must win. Daniel was younger and stronger, and he was fighting for her and justice. Sir Montague had fought like a cornered dog, growling, biting and punching as he hit out against his attacker, but he was no longer young and the end had always been inevitable. He lay winded on the ground, holding his bruised throat as he struggled to recover his breath.

'You're finished, Forsythe,' Daniel said as he got to his feet and stood looking down at him. 'I have several witnesses to take the stand against you. You won't get away with murder this time. Elizabeth saw you murder Lady Roxborough and I heard you—and there are others to testify that you drove Sarah Hunter to her death.'

'Damn you,' Forsythe snarled, voice hoarse from the bruises on his throat. He wiped the blood from his mouth, glaring up at Daniel. 'You think yourself so clever, but I'm not finished yet.' He hauled himself to his feet and stumbled towards the door, leaning against it as he called out, 'Help me! Syrius! Redfern! Get up here and bring your pistols.'

Daniel ignored him as he went to Elizabeth. His eyes moved over her anxiously, making her heart leap as she saw the tenderness there. 'Has he harmed you? Are you all right, dearest?'

'I am not harmed,' she told him with a smile that hid her inner weakness. 'You came just in time, Cavendish. Another hour or so and…' She could not hold back a little shudder. 'But we shall not think of that… Poor Lady Roxborough. She did her best to defend me, Cavendish. We must be grateful to her—did she tell you I was here?'

'No, I discovered it for myself…' He turned his head as Forsythe stumbled out of the door and they heard the sound of his feet clattering down the stairs. 'Do not concern yourself. I have men waiting downstairs. He will not escape.'

'I did not think it,' Elizabeth said. 'I am sure you have planned it all. I thought I saw someone in the shrubbery just before he came into my room. I was about to light the candle and signal my whereabouts.'

'Yes, that would be just like you,' Daniel said, a little smile on his lips. 'I dare say you hardly needed my help at all, my sweet general in petticoats.'

'Well, I think I might have escaped before we got here,' Elizabeth said, a sparkle in her eyes for she was recovering now, her calm no longer entirely assumed. 'You see, they thought I was drugged, but they made careless work of it. However, had I done so we should have been no better off than before. Now we have all the evidence we need to hang him. I saw him kill Lady Roxie.'

'Yes, indeed we do, Elizabeth.' Daniel grinned at her, hugely enjoying her tale. Her calm acceptance of what had happened, her practical thoughts were exactly what he had hoped. Inwardly, he was singing hymns of praise, but he held back the words he longed to say, held back the raging desire to hold her close. It was not the time to press his claims. 'You are a constant delight to me, dearest Elizabeth, for you have upheld my faith in your ability to cope with all eventualities. However, I believe this is finally over and you may—' He broke off as they both heard the shot from downstairs. 'Damn it! Now what has happened? I gave orders…Forsythe was to be restrained, but there was to be no shooting unless absolutely necessary.'

He started from the room, but even as he did so John came charging up the stairs. 'Are we too late?' he asked breathlessly. 'We heard the shot as we arrived…' He looked past Daniel and saw Elizabeth, relief lighting up his face. 'Miss Travers—thank God!' His gaze fell on Lady Roxborough lying in her own blood and a shudder went through him. 'Forsythe's work, I make no doubt. The man deserved his fate!'

'What was that shot?' Daniel asked, frowning. 'Forsythe is done for. We have all the evidence we need…'

'We shall still need it,' John said, 'though not to hang him. When he saw us he grabbed a pistol that was lying on the table, where one of his men had left it when they ran off. He realised that he was cornered and started waving the gun about—and then Charles went for him. They wrestled for a moment and Forsythe's pistol went off, killing him. It was an accident. If Charles had not stopped him, he would have killed one of us.'

'Damn it!' Daniel said for this was just what he had hoped to avoid. 'I wanted him taken alive for there is much we still need to learn of this affair.'

'What do you mean? 'John looked puzzled. 'Surely it is ended now? We know that Sarah lies in a suicide's grave…'

'We cannot know for sure. It may not be her, John.'

'No, for Forsythe said that she escaped him that night,' Elizabeth said, remembering. 'He may have lied—but it could be that some other girl was drowned in the lake.'

'Then where is Sarah?' John frowned. 'If Charles knew that there was some doubt…'

'He must not know yet,' Daniel said. 'I shall make further inquiries. For the moment he is coming to terms with her death. I would not give him false hope.'

'Charles has suffered enough,' Elizabeth said. 'We should not let him go on hoping for something that may never come about. It may be Sarah in that grave. It would be cruel to let Charles believe she is still alive until there is some proof.'

'Leave this with me for the time being. Forsythe may have hidden her away in one of his whorehouses. And there will be other girls who have been imprisoned in such circumstances. Now that he is dead it must be investigated.' He looked grim. 'We can do nothing more here tonight. Shall we go home? We could all do with our breakfast.'

'An excellent idea,' Elizabeth said, 'for I believe I am hungry.'

She smiled at him—she would not spoil his belief that she was able to take all this in her stride. It was only by keeping the appearance of calm that she managed to stop herself falling against his shoulder to weep. Not for Sir Montague, who deserved his fate, or for Lady Roxie who had repented of her own sins and done her best to save Elizabeth, but with the sheer exhaustion that was beginning to creep over her.

'Oh, Elizabeth, my love! You are safe. I have been having nightmares all day. Truly, I did not know how to bear it. I swear I shall never bear to be parted from you again.' She fell on Elizabeth, weeping as she held her close. 'I thought that you would die and I should never see you again.'

'I am sorry that you were so worried,' Elizabeth said. She had had time to recover her own composure in the carriage that brought her home and was able to comfort her friend. 'Now, do not weep, dearest Isadora. I assure you that it was much worse for you than for me. I do not believe I was ever in real danger, you know. It was Cavendish that Sir Montague meant to kill…and it is all over now.'

'Truly over?' Lady Isadora drew back and looked at her anxiously. 'Daniel told me it was over before we went to York and then you were stolen from me.'

'Sir Montague killed Lady Roxborough,' Daniel said. 'He ran off when I arrived and Charles shot him as he tried to escape…in self-defence.' It was the story they had all agreed on and he offered it without a flicker of remorse.

'Oh, thank goodness that wicked man is dead,' Lady Isadora said. 'How did Lady Roxborough come to be involved?' she asked and then shook her head. 'No, no, do not tell me. It is enough that Sir Montague Forsythe is dead and Elizabeth is safe. Now we may all be comfortable again.'

'Yes,' Daniel said and directed an odd look at Elizabeth over his mother's head. 'I shall leave you together, Mama. There are a few details that need to be tidied up—which means that I shall have to go to York first thing in the morning.'

'You are not going away again!' Lady Isadora was outraged at his words. 'How can you think of leaving us at such a time?'

'We are quite safe now,' Elizabeth said. 'We shall be perfectly content here together, ma'am. Lord Cavendish has a great deal to do, you know. There are a lot of loose ends to be sewn up. Lady Roxborough told me that Sir Montague had several houses of ill repute…and there will be girls there that need help.'

'Oh, the poor things,' Lady Isadora said. 'Go then, Daniel. We do not need you after all. Elizabeth and I have each other.'

'Yes, Mama. I am sure you will be comfortable with Elizabeth to care for you,' he said and looked at Elizabeth. 'I shall return as soon as I am able.'

'We shall be pleased to see you, sir.'

'Elizabeth…' He threw her a darkling glance. 'I shall have something to say to you when I return. And my name is Cavendish.'

Lady Isadora looked at her as he left the room. 'Are you really unharmed, Elizabeth?'

'Yes, quite unharmed,' Elizabeth promised her. 'But do you know, ma'am, I am very hungry.'

'Then you shall have a tray in your room,' Lady Isadora said. 'Ring for someone now—and please do not go back to calling me ma'am. We are friends, and I would have you call me Dora as my closest friends do.'

'Very well,' Elizabeth said and smiled. 'You know, Dora, I was very sorry not to have seen your dress-maker.' Her change of subject was well met, for Lady Isadora immediately brightened.

'Well, she is coming here to wait on us next week—and I have chosen several rolls of silk that you may like, though she may bring others with her.' She smiled a little mistily. 'You see, I could not bear to think that you might not come back and so I behaved exactly as if you had simply gone visiting.'

'And that is all it was, Dora,' Elizabeth said, resolutely shutting out the picture of Lady Roxborough bleeding on the floor in front of her from a fatal wound. 'It was merely a visit to an acquaintance and I am back now.'

Alone in her room, Elizabeth stared out of the window. It was afternoon now. The clouds had rolled away from the sky at last and it was a beautiful day. She had rested on her bed for a while, but been unable to sleep for her mind was too busy. It was a relief to know that the danger that had hung over them was gone, but now she must begin to think about the future.

She recalled Daniel using an endearment when he found her, but he had been under some strain and she must not take too much from that—or the look in his eyes when he had told her that he would have something to say to her when he returned.

Did he care for her, really care for her? She could not be certain of it—and if he did, what were his intentions? He had not scrupled to come to her room—to kiss her in a manner that had brought her close to swooning with pleasure—but was that the behaviour of a man who thought of marriage? She rather thought it more the reckless action of a man who sought a mistress. Was it in Daniel's mind to offer her *carte blanche?*

She supposed that after what had happened to her she could hardly expect more. She was penniless— there was no guarantee that the portion her father had set aside for her could be recovered. And her reputation must at least be tarnished by her abduction. Nothing had happened to her, but there was bound to be speculation and gossip once it all came out.

It might be that she could expect nothing better than an offer to be Lord Cavendish's mistress…but did she want that? Elizabeth looked into her heart, shaking her head when she realised that the question she ought to be asking herself was actually whether or not she had the strength to refuse.

Sighing, Elizabeth tidied her hair and her gown. It was time for tea and she had wasted too much time in daydreaming already.

Elizabeth did not rise as early as was her habit the next morning. She had slept very little and she was feeling subdued, a little tired, which, as Lady Isadora said, was only to be expected given the ordeal she had endured. Elizabeth was suffering from delayed shock had she but known it, for she could not quite put the sight of Lady Roxborough lying dead on the floor from her mind. After she had eaten breakfast, she sat late at the parlour table, wondering what she ought to do with herself. She did not have the energy to begin work in the library, and was feeling decidedly vaporous, which was not at all like her usual self.

'Miss Travers…'

Elizabeth turned as she heard the maid's voice behind her. 'Yes, what is it, Amy?'

'Mr Browning is here and asks if you will see him.'

'Yes, of course,' Elizabeth said taking a firm hold on herself. Sitting moping would not solve anything. 'Please ask him to come in, Amy.'

She stood up as he entered carrying the most beautiful bouquet of flowers she had ever seen in her life. It consisted of lilies, orchids, irises and other delicate flowers and ferns and was so huge that it almost hid the man who carried it.

'Oh…' Ridiculously, Elizabeth felt tears spring to her eyes. 'Are they for us, Mr Browning? How beautiful they are. You are spoiling us.'

'They are for you, miss,' the gardener said in voice that Elizabeth suspected was choked with emotion. 'It is a tribute from all of us who work here—to welcome you back. We was all very worried about you, miss.'

'For me...' Elizabeth could hardly speak for a moment, but then, all at once, she was smiling as her silly mood was swept away. 'Thank you so very much, Mr Browning. I love them—and I do appreciate the honour you pay me by giving me such precious things.'

''Tis nothing, miss,' he said, a bright red flush in his cheeks. 'But we all wanted you to know we was glad you was back.'

'You are very kind—all of you.' Elizabeth was not fooled—she knew that no one else would have dared to suggest picking so many prize blooms. 'Amy, come and help me because we must put all these wonderful flowers in water straight away.'

'Yes, miss, they are lovely, aren't they?' She grinned as the head gardener disappeared the way he had come. 'I reckon as you can add Mr Browning to your list of admirers, miss.'

'I haven't got any admirers, Amy.' Or none that she cared for. Surely if Daniel loved her he would have spoken before this?

'Is that so, miss? Well, I must have got it wrong then,' Amy said, but she was still smiling as she helped to carry the flowers to the small room kept for the purpose of arranging them.

Elizabeth was back to her normal calm self by the time that she had filled six vases with flowers, which Amy carried into the main parlours, taking one upstairs for Lady Isadora's boudoir and another for Elizabeth's room.

Lady Isadora came down for nuncheon, but she too was a little lethargic, and they spent the afternoon quietly, Elizabeth reading aloud for a while. After tea, Lady Isadora went up to rest and Elizabeth took a stroll in the gardens for it was a warm afternoon. It was just as she was about to go in that she saw Mr Elworthy coming towards her.

'How are you feeling?' he asked solicitously. 'I have been most anxious for you, Miss Travers. You must have been so distressed by all that happened to you.'

'It was indeed very distressing that poor Lady Roxborough died trying to help me,' Elizabeth said, 'and I still felt a little tired this morning, but I am much better now.'

'I am glad to hear it,' he said. 'You look very well. Indeed, you look lovely, as always.'

'You are very kind, sir. Pray tell me—do you know what is happening? Will Mr Hunter be charged with his death or is the story of the accident believed?'

'I believe all is satisfactorily concluded,' he said. 'The evidence against Forsythe was so overwhelming that there can be no doubt of his guilt. Therefore no inquiry will be made into his death. He resisted just arrest and there is an end to it.'

'Oh, I am so glad!' Elizabeth said. 'Mr Hunter has suffered enough.'

'Yes, that cannot be denied,' John said looking grave. 'I have just come from a ceremony he arranged. He is planning to have Sarah's body taken back to her home, where she will be buried in the family vault. They will hold a remembrance service for her in his local church. She was refused the rights she ought to have had when she was first buried, but now she will be at peace—and I think perhaps Charles will find peace too.' He frowned and shook his head. 'I worry what he will do if Daniel tells him that it may not be Sarah they have buried…'

'We can only wait and pray,' Elizabeth said. 'Lord Cavendish will do what is right. But tell me, do you come alone, sir—or is Cavendish with you?'

'He had some business that delayed him for a day or so longer, I believe,' John said. 'I have come only to take my farewell of you, for I must return home now. There are things that require my attention.'

'Yes, of course. You have been away longer than you would wish.'

'If ever you should need a friend you may call on me,' John assured her.

'Yes, I know, thank you,' Elizabeth said. 'And

thank you for coming to my rescue as you did—you and Mr Hunter.'

'We were hardly necessary—Daniel had done it all,' John said a little ruefully. 'But the intent was there and we are both glad that you were not harmed.'

'Thank you,' Elizabeth said. 'I think I must go and change for dinner. Shall you stay, sir?'

'I thank you, no. I merely came to say goodbye. I dare say we shall meet in Brighton in a few weeks.'

'Yes, certainly. I shall look forward to it,' Elizabeth said and turned towards the house. She would miss John's calm good sense.

Elizabeth looked for Cavendish to return for the following three days, but he did not come. However, the dressmaker arrived on time and took Elizabeth's measurements. Several happy hours were spent discussing the length of a sleeve or how the neckline should drape, and at the end of the day everyone was pleased with the outcome: Lady Isadora because she had persuaded Elizabeth to let her order six new gowns for her as well as a charming pelisse; Elizabeth because she had prevented her kind friend from ordering twice as many; and Mistress Barber because she had received a large order from Lady Isadora on top of what she was to make for Miss Travers.

She was to stay that night at Cavendish and return to York the next morning. She had promised faithfully that all the gowns would be delivered within one week because she would put all her girls to work on their order.

'You should have had the straw satin as well as the white evening gown,' Lady Isadora told Elizabeth the next morning. 'But it does not matter—we may order more gowns in Brighton.'

'I am sure I shall not need more,' Elizabeth said. 'I have not yet begun to wear those you had already bought for me.'

'I wish that you would,' Lady Isadora said. 'You always look elegant, Elizabeth, but I long to see you in colours rather than grey.'

'Very well,' Elizabeth said. 'My mourning is finished tomorrow, so I shall wear the yellow gown tomorrow evening—and the green afternoon gown, perhaps.'

'Ah, yes,' Lady Isadora said, looking pleased. 'We shall go visiting in the afternoon, for I like to see my friends…' She sighed. 'I shall miss Lady Roxborough, no matter what she did, for she was a witty and generous woman—and at the end she did try to help you, Elizabeth.'

'Had she not acted so bravely…' Elizabeth gave a little shudder. 'Well, we shall never know and there is no point in speculating.' She held back her own sigh. 'You have heard nothing from Lord Cavendish, I suppose?'

'I despair of him,' his mother said and scowled. 'He has never been one for writing letters, but I am sure he need not be away all this time.'

'He must have some reason for doing so,' Elizabeth said. She glanced round as one of the maids came into the room carrying a silver salver, which she offered to Lady Isadora. 'Is it a letter?'

'Yes, but not from Daniel.' Lady Isadora broke the seal and began to read. She gave a little cry of surprise. 'This is from Sir Henry Giles,' she said. 'You will never guess what has happened…'

'Is it something pleasant?' Elizabeth asked, for Lady Isadora was looking pleased rather than distressed.

'Well, yes, I believe it may be,' she said. 'It seems that Julia is to be engaged to the Reverend Bell…'

'I think that is wonderful,' Elizabeth said, 'for I know it was Julia's wish to be his wife and I suspected that he liked her more than he understood until she was abducted.'

'I am glad that I sent him down to Bath now,' Lady Isadora said. 'Her parents must have felt it the best thing for her in the circumstances. How nice it will be to have Julia settled in the vicarage. We shall be able to visit her more often, and she us.'

'Yes, that must be pleasing,' Elizabeth said, though

she could not help wondering about her own future. If Lord Cavendish should ask her to be his mistress, it might mean that she must find herself another position. Or accept his offer, which would mean that she would lose Lady Isadora's friendship for she could not be expected to receive her son's mistress. Oh, what a coil it all was!

'Is something troubling you?' Lady Isadora looked at her in concern. 'You seem a little down, Elizabeth—and that is not like you.'

'Oh, no, I am not troubled by anything,' Elizabeth said untruthfully. 'I was just thinking that I have neglected the earl's library of late. I must spend an hour or so there in the morning.'

'He does not deserve that you should,' Lady Isadora said, feeling cross, for she suspected the reason for Elizabeth's mood. 'Daniel can be very thoughtless at times. He really can!'

Elizabeth smiled and shook her head. In truth, Daniel had done nothing to arouse false hopes. Perhaps he had flirted with her a little, but men often did so. If she was suffering from low spirits, it was entirely her own fault.

Chapter Eleven

'Daniel is returning today,' Lady Isadora said when Elizabeth responded to an invitation to visit her in her bedchamber the next morning. 'I have had a brief note from him.' She waved it at her. 'He gives no news of anything—now is that not just like him? He must know that we are dying for news.'

'It would be good to hear how things go on,' Elizabeth agreed, trying to conceal her restlessness. 'Does he say what time we should expect him?'

'No, merely that he hopes to be here before dinner.'

'I see…' Elizabeth smiled. 'If you do not mind, Dora, I think I shall go for a walk. I shall see you at nuncheon.'

'No, of course I do not mind.' Lady Isadora shook her head. 'That son of mine is always so provoking!'

'Oh, no, it is just a little headache,' Elizabeth said. 'I shall see you later, dearest.'

Elizabeth walked as far as the village. Despite the

warmth of the sun there was a pleasant breeze and she enjoyed the exercise. Her heart was beating quite fast as she approached the house. Would Daniel be there?

He was not and she found it difficult to swallow her disappointment as she went up to change. Oh, why would he not come? How much longer must she wait in this uncertainty?

'Well met, Elizabeth,' Daniel said as she came downstairs that evening. 'I was hoping that we might have a moment to ourselves.'

'And I,' Elizabeth said. Her heart had started to thump wildly at the sight of him. She had not realised that he was back, but she managed to appear calm despite it. 'I wanted to ask you if there was any news about Sarah?'

'Let us go into the garden. I do not wish to be overheard.'

'Your mama knows nothing of your doubts,' Elizabeth said. 'I thought it best to keep it to myself until you have something more to go on.'

'We have discovered three houses of ill repute that were directly owned by Forsythe,' Daniel told her. 'All have been closed and the girls given their freedom—though most of them will go straight to another establishment of the same nature.'

'I suppose they have little choice,' Elizabeth said. 'Was there no sign of Sarah?'

'None at all,' he said and frowned. 'I suppose we must accept that she lies in that grave…'

'And yet you are still doubtful—why?'

'I should not be,' he said. 'But something nags at me…'

'You will not abandon the search entirely?'

'My agents will continue for a while,' he said. 'Though in truth I have little hope after all this time. Tell me, Elizabeth—' He broke off as someone came across the lawn to join them. It was the Reverend Bell, newly returned from Bath. 'Yes, sir? How may I help you?' Daniel frowned—he had hoped to have longer alone with Elizabeth.'

'It is an awkward matter…' Mr Bell looked at Elizabeth.

'I shall leave you together,' she said. 'I shall see you at dinner, Cavendish.'

'Yes, of course…' Daniel glanced after her as she walked away and then looked at the vicar. 'Now, sir—what is the problem?'

Elizabeth spent another restless night. Cavendish had ridden off with Mr Bell on an urgent parish matter and she had not seen him before she retired. She dressed early and went downstairs to the library where she spent two hours taking books down and dusting them. Some of them had not been touched in years and she was covered in a fine dust when she left the library and went up to her room. She had taken off her gown behind the screen and was wondering whether she had enough water to wash her long hair, which was now loose about her face and shoulders, when she heard the door open.

'Is that you, Amy? I need to wash my hair because those books were so dusty. I should really like a bath, but I do not wish to be a nuisance. If I could have a can of hot water…'

She came out from behind the screen wearing only a linen shift, which clearly revealed the contours of her slim figure, stopping in dismay as she saw that her visitor was not Amy. Reaching for a dressing gown that lay over a stool nearby, she held it to her, trying to cover herself as best she could. She was trembling inside, but hoped that she had not given herself away.

'You should not be here, Cavendish.' Her eyes met his with a swift challenge.

'I could not resist it,' he said, his eyes intent on her face. 'At least here I can be sure of being alone with you! I have thought of you so often, Elizabeth, and the days have been long. Besides, what does it matter that I am here? Convention means nothing to us. You know that I care for you…want you to be mine. Modesty is wasted, my darling, for we belong together. You know it as I do…' He moved towards her, taking hold of the dressing robe and wresting it from her grasp. He reached out to touch the slender arch of her white throat. 'So beautiful. I have dreamed of touching you like this…of having you in my arms, my bed.' He pulled her close, holding her pressed against him so that she could feel the throbbing heat of him through her shift. 'Have you any idea of the agony it caused me when I knew that devil had you in his power? The despair I felt because I had not protected you as I ought?'

'How should I? You have not told me.'

'Perhaps not in so many words, but you knew it—please tell me you knew it, Elizabeth.' He looked at her with such intensity that she felt her stomach clench with something that could only be desire.

'I have felt an attraction between us,' she admitted, her cheeks pink. 'I cannot say that I had any insight into your feelings.'

'You must have known that I have wanted you from the first?' He looked incredulous. 'Elizabeth, do not be missish. Not you! This is not like you, my darling.'

'I have sensed that there is a physical attraction on your side…'

'Not yours?' He frowned at her.

'Yes, I feel…perhaps I feel more than mere physical attraction,' Elizabeth said, for only plain speaking would help her now. 'I do not wish to be merely your mistress, Cavendish. I have considered it, but—'

He broke away from her, turning his back to her for a moment. 'Is it marriage or nothing with you then?' he asked, keeping his back towards her. 'Is that your ultimatum?'

'No, I make no demands,' Elizabeth said. 'But your mother loves me, Daniel, and if I came to you as your mistress I could never see her again.'

He turned towards her, a gleam of wickedness in his eyes. 'And is that your only quibble, my sweet idiot love?'

'Daniel?' Elizabeth stared at him as she saw the mockery in his face. 'I pray you, do not tease me.'

'Why should I not when you say such stuff to me?' he demanded, a martial light in his eyes. 'Tell me, Elizabeth, where did you get the notion that I wished to make you my mistress and not my wife? Did you think me a fool that I should not recognise true quality when I saw it?'

'Oh, but…I do not think you a fool by any means.'

'Then I must think you one in this instance,' he said. 'Why would I wish to mistreat the woman I adore? Why should I make you my mistress and see you only occasionally when I can wake each morning to find you in my bed, Elizabeth? When I can spend all my days with you, share my life with the only woman I have ever truly loved and admired? I should be a fool indeed to settle for less.'

'Oh…' She felt her throat catch with tears. 'But you could do so much better. I have no fortune and my reputation must be tarnished by what happened.'

'Why should anyone but those we trust know of it?' he asked, his eyes narrowing. 'As for your fortune, I do not know what may be rescued from the estate after Forsythe has done his worst—but it is your brother's, as in truth it always was, and your portion is for him to provide if he can.'

'How did you manage that?'

'It took some legal wrangling,' Daniel told her—it was the reason he had delayed his return some days. 'But it was done. I have written to your brother and invited him to stay with us in Brighton—and then we shall see what may be done to help him restore his estate.'

'You are too good,' Elizabeth said, overcome by what he had done. 'I do not know how I shall ever thank you…'

'I want no gratitude,' Daniel said, his eyes intent on her face. 'Just a simple answer, my dearest. Do you love me enough to take pleasure in becoming my wife?'

'Oh, Daniel,' Elizabeth cried, her eyes shining, though whether from tears or happiness it would be difficult to say. 'You know I do…'

She went into his arms as he kissed her, melting into

his body, her love flowing to him as she responded eagerly. In that moment she was lost to all but the pleasure of being close to him. He looked down at her, smiling as she reached up to touch his face, tracing his mouth with her fingertips.

'I never believed that such happiness could be mine,' she said. 'I do love you so very much, Daniel. I think I have almost from the first.'

'I was sure that you felt as I did,' he said, 'for we were always so much in accord—my little general in petticoats.' His eyes teased her, making her blush as she remembered that she was wearing nothing but her petticoat.

'What would your mama say if she knew you were here like this with me?'

'She would say it was time that I did what she has been telling me for as long as I can remember—and that is to find myself a wife I can love and she can enjoy as a friend. I believe she can have no complaints for surely you must wed me now, if only for your reputation.'

'You are a shocking tease, sir!'

'I dare say you are right, but you would not distress Mama by telling her that I have just proposed and you refused—even if you are in your petticoats.'

'No, for she is as fond of me as I am of her,' Elizabeth said. 'But I think she would be a little shocked if she knew you were here all the same—and you must go, for I need Amy to help me wash my hair if she is not too busy.'

'If you want to bathe you shall bathe,' Daniel said. 'The water shall be carried up immediately—and if Amy is too busy to wash your hair, I shall be your attendant.'

'Daniel, behave yourself, my love,' Elizabeth said. She could see the wicked gleam in his eyes and knew that he meant his threat. 'You must go now—I shall have no reputation left if Amy finds you here.'

'I dare say Amy knows that I am here,' he said grinning triumphantly. 'I do not think that my intentions will come as a surprise to your maid, my love—even if they did to you. Besides, she would never betray a word to harm you, she is too loyal.'

'Yes, that is true. Leave me, then, and tell Dora that we are to marry,' Elizabeth said, 'and I shall come down when I have made myself decent.'

'I think perhaps I prefer you indecent,' Daniel said and planted a kiss on the end of her nose. 'But I shall not tease you any more, Elizabeth. Instead I shall go and tease Mama…'

'Daniel can be so provoking,' Lady Isadora complained when Elizabeth came downstairs later that morning. She was wearing a green silk gown that fitted into her slender waist, the sleeves finishing at the elbows with a froth of exquisite lace dyed to match her gown. Her hair had been freshly washed and arranged in soft waves about her face in a new style that became her well. 'You look so beautiful, my dear—and where is he? He should be here to see you come out of your mourning. What must he do but ride out to visit one of his tenants! Truly, I have no patience with him.'

'You must forgive him,' Elizabeth said, a happy smile on her face. She knew herself loved and nothing could dim the light that shone from her like a beacon. 'I'm sure it was important or he would not have gone.'

'But you look so fresh and lovely,' Lady Isadora wailed. 'And he tells me you are to marry and I shall have to part with you.'

'But we shall meet often,' Elizabeth said. 'You know that I love you as dearly as my own mother, Dora. I would never desert you. We shall spend many happy times together through the years.'

'Oh, well, as long as you are happy,' Lady Isadora said and sighed. 'I suppose I must manage with Miss Ridley. I have today had a letter from her asking if she may return to her duties, and I could not have refused her. Not that I should have parted with you, my dear! I suppose it will work out very well, for you are exactly the wife I should want for Daniel—even though he is so very provoking.'

'I have always been provoking, Mama,' Daniel said, striding in at that moment. He looked every inch the wealthy landowner he was, dressed in pale breeches and a coat that fitted his broad shoulders almost as a second skin, his boots polished to a high gloss. 'Elizabeth you look more beautiful than ever. Is that a new gown? You should wear more green. I like it on you.' He smiled at her. 'But in truth I hardly notice your clothes, for you are always lovely—is she not, Mama?'

'Yes, indeed she is,' Lady Isadora said, looking at him with approval. His compliment was everything even she could desire. 'I am glad that you are back. We are going visiting this afternoon and you may accompany us—unless you have more pressing business?' She threw him a look that dared him to plead another appointment.

'No, I have nothing more important to do,' he said. 'Except to give this to Elizabeth.' He took a velvet box from his pocket and offered it to her. 'I believe it will fit…'

Elizabeth took the box and opened it to reveal a beautiful diamond ring in the shape of a daisy. 'Oh, Daniel, this is lovely,' she said. 'You could not have chosen better.'

'A beautiful flower for a beautiful lady,' he said,

taking the ring from its box. 'Give me your left hand please.' She held out her hand and he slid the ring on to her finger, looking pleased because it fitted so well. 'Ah, I thought it would fit, my love. There, Mama, are you not pleased? She cannot change her mind now, can she? She must marry me or appear a heartless jilt.'

'Do not be so ridiculous,' his mama replied crossly. 'Why should Elizabeth run away? It is entirely suitable—and now I really must insist that we have nuncheon.'

'Yes, Mama, of course,' Daniel said, and his eyes sparked with laughter as he looked at Elizabeth. 'We are entirely at your disposal for the remainder of the day.'

'Thank you, Daniel,' his mother said. 'I am well aware that you find me amusing, but I shall forgive you. At least I know that my dearest Elizabeth will be cared for and loved as she ought to be.'

'Then you think me worthy of her?' Daniel cocked an eyebrow at her, his face the picture of innocence.

'Daniel, you are incorrigible,' Elizabeth said, reproving him with a stern look. 'Pray stop teasing your mama and let us go in before the chef throws a tantrum and leaves…'

It was a warm evening and pleasant, and the rosebuds were just beginning to open, bringing perfume and colour to the borders as they walked together before dinner.

'It is good to have you to myself for a while,' Daniel said, taking her hand in his. 'I thought that Mama would never tire of talking to Lady Brackly. I am sure she is determined that the news of our engagement shall spread far and wide.'

'She is very happy with the arrangement,' Elizabeth said. 'Miss Ridley is to join us at Brighton, you know. I am glad of that—I should not have felt happy leaving Dora alone when we take our wedding trip. She was very lonely before I arrived, Daniel.'

'Well, she may stay with us whenever she chooses,' he said. 'I do not know at which of my country houses you would wish to reside—though of course we shall go up to town for some months of the year.'

'I like it here very well,' Elizabeth said, 'but naturally I am happy to be wherever you feel most comfortable, Daniel.'

'You are very obliging, Elizabeth,' he said. 'I am putting some changes in place at my home in Hampshire, and we shall visit when we return from our wedding trip. If you like Hallowsdene, we may live there—or here. Or perhaps we shall move from house to house…'

'When we are married…' She stopped and looked up at him, her eyes bright. 'How good that sounds,

Daniel. I had given up hope of ever finding someone I could happily spend my life with, until I met you and then I thought you might break my heart.'

'Did you think me so careless and cruel?' His wicked blue eyes were suddenly dark with inner tension.

'No, how could I? But I could not think why you should be interested in me when there are so many lovely women you could choose…' She remembered seeing him with one very beautiful lady in York. 'And then I saw you with someone, a very pretty lady, and I was sure that she must mean something to you—you were laughing at what she was saying…'

'In York, you mean?' He raised his brows. 'Were you jealous of Lucinda, Elizabeth?'

'Yes, a little,' she admitted and he laughed in delight. 'No, it is not amusing, Daniel. She was very beautiful.'

'Oh, indeed she is,' Daniel said. 'Also very spoiled and very much in love with her fiancé. I do value Lucinda Sawston. She is the sister of one of my best friends—but she would never have done for me or I for her.'

'Oh…' Elizabeth felt the warm glow of satisfaction as she took his arm and they began to walk once more. 'Look at that gorgeous rose, Daniel. Such a delicate colour.'

'Shall I pick it for you?'

'From Mr Browning's show beds?' Elizabeth was horrified. 'No, of course not. He would be terribly upset.'

'But they are your roses,' Daniel said. 'As my wife you must do exactly as you please, Elizabeth. All I have is for you to order as you will.'

'But it is so much more satisfying to be given flowers as a tribute,' Elizabeth said. 'After you had gone away to settle things this last time I had a fit of the megrims, and then Mr Browning brought me the most wonderful bouquet from his glasshouses. It made me feel so much better because he loves those flowers as if they were his children. Had I picked them for myself, they would not have been half as valuable.'

Daniel laughed. 'How wise and lovely you are, Elizabeth. I believe I shall spend my whole life thanking my good fortune in finding you—though in truth it is all due to Mama. I have sometimes thought her a little inclined to melancholy, which I believed mere foolishness, but I must do so no more—for if she had not brought you here we might not have met…'

Elizabeth shook her head at him. He reached out, drawing her close, gazing down into her eyes for a moment as he prepared to kiss her.

'Oh, I say, Beth,' a voice hailed them from behind

and they turned to look as a young man came striding towards them. 'Lady Isadora's maid told me you were in the gardens and I came at once to find you.' He looked at Daniel. 'You must be Cavendish. I got your letter, sir, and came at once to thank you for all you have done for me—and Beth, of course. If it is true that you are going to marry her?'

'Yes, it is true,' Daniel said, giving a sigh of resignation. 'I believed we should meet in Brighton, Travers?'

'Well, yes, but I was a little impatient to see you, sir—and Beth, of course. I thought if I came here before you left…well, I am anxious to go home and see what damage that rogue has done.'

'Yes, of course, though I believe you will discover everything is in hand. However, now that you are here we must talk, but it must wait until after dinner,' Daniel said. 'You must understand that we are ruled at Cavendish by Mama's chef. She suffered too long with a bad cook and will do nothing to dis-oblige him.'

'By Jove, yes,' Simon agreed at once. 'We all know how awful that can be. Should I go up and change, do you think—or would Lady Isadora prefer me at table as I am?'

'As you are,' Daniel said, a wicked light in his eyes. 'For otherwise we shall commit the unforgivable sin of being late…'

* * *

After dinner, the earl disappeared into his library with Elizabeth's brother. They were gone for no more than half an hour, but whatever was said must have pleased them both, for they appeared in high good humour.

It had been decided that Simon would depart for his own estate in the morning. He would remain there and join them at Cavendish in three weeks, when they would have returned from Brighton.

'I shall bring the Wentworths with me,' he told his sister when they met again after his private meeting with his future brother-in-law. 'Cavendish is persuaded you will want them here for the wedding, and since it is to take place two days after your return from Brighton...'

'Yes, please do so. Lady Wentworth was very kind to me—and to you, Simon. I should like them to be here for the wedding.' She smiled at him. 'At least you may leave Oxford now and know that you have your own home to go to, dearest.'

'Yes, thanks to Cavendish,' he said. 'I have much to thank him for, Beth—and I am glad that you are to marry him. He is as decent a fellow as you could find.'

'Yes, I believe him to be everything a gentleman ought to be,' she said, though when Daniel looked at her she gave him a challenging look. It was news to her that the wedding was to be but two days after their return from Brighton.

'Pray tell me what I have done to deserve such a look?' Daniel asked when he came to her a little later.

'I have been given to understand that our marriage is already arranged...'

'Ah...' His eyes gleamed with mockery. 'I see that you are impatient to be wed, my love. Shall I cancel the trip to Brighton altogether? Or perhaps you would wish to be married by special licence before we leave?'

'We leave the day after tomorrow,' Elizabeth said, giving him a severe look. 'You know that is impossible to arrange everything before that—and Dora is looking forward to the visit to Brighton. We shall not deny her that, Daniel.'

'Shall we marry there, then?'

'Everyone here is looking forward to the wedding. Mr Browning sent word that he would have enough flowers for the church, house—and my posy, which he wishes to make up himself.'

'I think I grow a little jealous of your admirers,' Daniel said, a flicker of humour at his lips. 'But I would not wish to deny anyone the pleasure of seeing you wed—so it must be after we return.'

'But why two days?' Elizabeth asked. 'We shall hardly have recovered from the journey.'

'You cannot surely expect me to be patient longer than two days?' he asked, his eyes teasing her. 'I am impatient for my wedding night, Elizabeth. Perhaps then I shall be able to get you alone at last…'

She laughed as she saw the naughty glint in his eyes. 'I am sure that we shall manage that occasionally before then, my dearest. I think you must resign yourself to waiting for at least one week after our return.'

'Five days,' he said, eyes gleaming. 'I shall give no more, Elizabeth. Five days or I shall sweep you into my carriage and we shall elope.'

'Five days?' She gazed into his face and saw the impatience he was trying to conquer. In truth, she was impatient enough herself. 'Very well, five days should be sufficient and I may order my wedding clothes in Brighton.'

Elizabeth was in the garden the next morning. She had been speaking to Mr Browning about the flowers for her wedding and was returning to the house when she saw the young man and woman hesitating in the drive. They were clearly not gentlefolk, but she sensed they were debating whether to go to the front or the back of the house.

'May I help you?' she asked and the girl bobbed a curtsy.

'Oh, miss,' she said. 'Fred says we should go to the

back of the house, but Lord Cavendish told me we was to ask for him particular. He wants to hear what Fred has to say about Sir Montague… only with him being dead, we wasn't sure he would still want to see us…'

'We should go to the back and ask for a job like he said, Mary,' the young man said, looking uncomfortable.

'But his lordship might want to hear what you have to say about that girl what you helped…'

'Mary…' Fred shook his head at her.

'A girl?' Elizabeth looked at him, immediately alert. 'Did you see a girl in distress? Was it on Sir Montague's estate?'

'Aye, miss, it were that,' Fred said. 'More than a year ago it were. They'd been up to their games again and I knew something bad were going on—so when I saw the girl come running from the woods like that—' He stopped and looked at Mary, who encouraged him with a nod of her head. 'Well, he's dead now so he can't thrash me the way he did before when I refused to help him. I saw the girl was terrified, miss, and I heard them shouting and calling out as if they was after a fox…' He paused, looking at Mary again for reassurance. 'Well, I grabbed hold of her and took her to a place I know—hid her until they had gone.'

'Oh, thank God!' Elizabeth cried. 'She didn't drown herself in the lake that night?'

'No, miss—that happened some days later. It were

a village lass, in trouble they say, and turned out of her home by her father. The other one were a lady. I knew that by looking at her, though she didn't say a word. She fainted when I took hold of her. I carried her somewhere safe and…' He glanced at Elizabeth. 'Did I do right, miss?'

'You did very right, Fred,' Elizabeth said. 'Can you tell me where we may find her—the girl you rescued?'

'That's what Fred is worried about,' Mary said. 'He came looking for me after he'd helped the girl to a safe place, miss. But when we went back to the cottage—it belongs to Fred's uncle, miss, but it has been empty for a while—she had gone.'

'She were unconscious when I left her,' Fred said. 'I fetched Mary to help her—but we couldn't find her. We looked for a couple of hours, but she had disappeared.'

Elizabeth felt a surge of disappointment. She had hoped the mystery was about to be solved, but it seemed they were no further forward.

'Then the girl in the lake could have been her…'

'No, miss. I am certain sure that was Emily Little from the village. She were wearing a dress I gave her,' Mary said. 'I knew it were her, miss, but I didn't say because it would have shamed her family.'

'I see,' Elizabeth said with mixed feelings. 'I think you should speak to Lord Cavendish—tell him everything just as you have told me, please.'

'So we were right to come,' Fred said and looked relieved. 'I thought his lordship might not want to see us.'

'He will want to see you,' Elizabeth replied. 'And he will be very glad to have your information. I am sure he will be very glad to give you both a place here.' She smiled at them. 'Come up to the house with me now. Lord Cavendish is in his library.'

It was not until later that day that Elizabeth had time to ask Daniel what he thought of the information brought to him by Fred and Mary.

'It is the best news we've had yet,' Daniel told her. 'It still doesn't mean that Sarah is alive, but I believe I shall tell Charles that the young girl he is preparing to bury in his family's vault is not his sister.'

'It is a pity that we do not have more to tell him,' Elizabeth said. 'If only Sarah had not run away again when Fred tried to help her.'

'If she did…' Daniel looked thoughtful. 'There is still a possibility that Forsythe found her and locked her away in a whorehouse somewhere—but at least I think we can be sure that she did not die in the lake that night.'

'That is something positive,' Elizabeth said and looked up at him. 'I think you should tell Charles, Daniel. He will want to continue his search for her.'

'Yes, I shall tell him tomorrow,' Daniel said. 'It will mean a detour, but I shall meet you and Mama in Brighton. We shall be away for a time, my darling— but there is no reason why Charles and the others should not go on with the search.'

'Oh, they must,' Elizabeth said. She smiled at him. 'I have a good feeling about this, Daniel. It came to me when Fred told me that he had rescued her. I think she is alive and that they will find her eventually.'

'We must pray that it is so,' he said and drew her into his arms, suppressing the little shudder that took him as he put himself in Charles's place. 'It will shock Charles to learn that the girl he was preparing to bury is not his sister—and it may throw him into turmoil again—but I know that if it were you I would rather believe you were still alive and go on searching.'

'Oh, Daniel, my love.' She looked up into his face. 'We shall pray for them both.'

'Yes,' he said and then he bent his head and kissed her. 'If prayers can achieve anything, he will find her.'

Afterword

Elizabeth came out of the church on her husband's arm to the sound of church bells. The Reverend Bell had married them with all their friends to wish them happiness, and the villagers had joined with the people from their estate to greet them as they came out. Elizabeth laughed and ducked her head as she was showered with rose petals, and they paused to receive small gifts and tributes from the villagers before getting into their carriage to be driven to the house.

Daniel had arranged that a large party should be held in the gardens at the same time as the reception in the house, and he had brought down many of the servants from his London home so that they could take it in turns to enjoy themselves.

Lady Isadora's chef had been cooking for days, but Daniel's own chef had prepared much of the fare that was to be offered to the villagers and estate workers, and there had been great rivalry between the two men to see who could outdo the other.

'I am not sure who has the best of the bargain,' Daniel whispered as they went outside to visit their loyal retainers who wished to toast their health, before returning to their guests to cut the magnificent cake, which had been worked on by both chefs. 'Do not tell Mama, but I think my chef has won hands down…that roast beef looked delicious. I was tempted to sit down with them and forget the reception.'

'You must not, dearest,' Elizabeth reproved. 'Think how upset Dora would be if Monsieur Delfarge left. You might have to let her have your own Monsieur Thierry…'

'Do you say so indeed?' he asked with a lift of his brows. 'Now that would be a disaster of the worst kind. I do not know how I should survive without him.' He kept a straight face, but his eyes glinted with mockery.

'You are very wicked,' Elizabeth said. 'If you do not behave yourself, dearest…'

'What shall you do?'

'I shall delay my leave-taking from the reception for at least one hour.'

'Then I am silenced,' he said. 'For I do not think I could survive such a punishment.'

'Do you take nothing seriously?'

Daniel took her hand, holding it to his lips to drop a

kiss within the palm. 'Nothing and everything,' he said. 'I know the world for what it is, my love. But this is my wedding day, Elizabeth. I never imagined I would find a woman I could love as I do you and I have never felt like this—so you must forgive me my faults.'

She touched the magnificent diamond and pearl choker at her throat. 'You are forgiven,' she said, an enchanting sparkle in her eyes. 'I shall thank you for my present later.'

'I look forward to it,' Daniel said. 'But I shall let you go to your guests, my love. My turn will come later…but not too much later, I beg you!'

Elizabeth turned in her husband's arms, snuggling into the warmth of his body. It was morning and she had slept for a long time after the loving that had given them both so much pleasure.

'Are you awake, Elizabeth?'

She opened her eyes and looked up into his face. 'Yes, I think so. I believe I have slept for hours?'

'You looked so beautiful that I did not wish to disturb you.'

She traced the dark shadow of hair on his chest with her fingertip, causing a little shudder to run through him. 'Do you truly think me beautiful, Daniel? I am not, you know. I have never thought it.'

'To me you are and will always be the most beautiful woman in the world,' he said huskily. He took her hand, kissing her fingers one by one. 'You taste of honey and perfume…delicious.'

Elizabeth gurgled with laughter as she snuggled closer. Already desire was stirring deep inside her once more. She teased him, trailing her fingers down over his navel to where the evidence of his desire was beginning to make itself known once more.

'Wicked wench!' he growled at her. 'I think I shall have to teach you more respect for your husband.' He rolled her beneath him in the bed and began to kiss her, flicking at her breasts with his tongue and taking the nipples into his mouth to suck at them delicately.

Elizabeth arched against him, moaning with pleasure as he loved her again, bringing her to a crescendo of sensuous delight. Their bodies moved in an age-old rhythm, perfectly in tune. It was as if they had been made each for the other and fit as two halves of the whole. Afterwards, she lay in his arms, content and satiated, her hand delicately stroking the arch of his back.

'We are so fortunate, Daniel,' she said. 'It frightens me when I think that we might never have met…'

'I believe our paths were destined to cross,' Daniel said. 'Had Mama not invited you to stay with her, I should have sought you out. I suspected that Forsythe had cheated your father and I would have come to you sooner or later.'

A little shudder ran through her. 'Poor Papa—and Mama,' she said. 'Had it not been for that wicked man…' She looked sad for a moment. 'And there is Sarah. We still do not know what has happened to her. Poor Charles will never rest until he finds her.'

'He has renewed hope. John thought that Charles would be at peace if he knew her to be at rest, but I think it has made him realise that nothing else matters if only he can get her back. The disgrace, what has happened to her in all these months, do not weigh with Charles. He is determined to find her and bring her home.'

'I pray that he will find her! That despicable, evil man…' Elizabeth sighed. 'If only I had made him tell me the truth that night!'

'Hush, my love,' Daniel said and held her closer. 'We can never go back, Elizabeth. He has paid the price and that must be an end to it.'

'Yes,' she agreed and smiled up at him. It would be foolish to let her sympathy for others cloud her own happiness. They would do what they could to help Charles, but they had their own lives in front of them. 'I must and shall put the past behind me. But you will allow me to name my first son for Papa, I hope?'

Daniel looked down at her. 'I shall allow you anything you wish, my love,' he said. 'I have waited for you all my life. You are my life, Elizabeth…my sweet general in petticoats. I am yours to command.'

'My only command is that you will always love me.'

'Then you shall be easy to obey,' he said and kissed her.

HISTORICAL ROMANCE™

LARGE PRINT

NOT QUITE A LADY
Louise Allen

Miss Lily France has launched herself upon the Marriage Mart in style! The wealthy and beautiful heiress is determined to honour her much-loved father's last wish – and trade her vulgar new money for marriage to a man with an ancient and respected title. Then she meets untitled, irresistible and very unsuitable Jack Lovell – but he is the one man she cannot buy!

THE DEFIANT DEBUTANTE
Helen Dickson

Eligible, attractive, Alex Montgomery, Earl of Arlington, is adored by society ladies and a string of mistresses warm his bed. He's yet to meet a woman who could refuse him… Then he is introduced to the strikingly unconventional Miss Angelina Hamilton, and Alex makes up his mind to tame this headstrong girl! But Miss Hamilton has plans of her own – and they don't include marriage to a rake!

A NOBLE CAPTIVE
Michelle Styles

Strong, proud and honourable – soldier Marcus Livius Tullio embodied the values of Rome. Captured and brought to the Temple of Kybele, he was drawn towards the woman who gave him refuge. Fierce, beautiful and determined – pagan priestess Helena despised all that Rome stood for. She knew she must not be tempted by this handsome soldier, because to succumb to her desires would be to betray all her people…

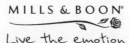

MILLS & BOON®

Live the emotion

HIST0507 LP

HISTORICAL ROMANCE™

LARGE PRINT

THE WANTON BRIDE

Mary Brendan

Mark Hunter managed to vex her at every opportunity! Though to prevent a family scandal Emily Beaumont must turn to him for help. Mark was more than happy to be of service to the delectable Miss Beaumont; with her quick wit and determined spirit she always made deliciously diverting company. But Mark soon discovered that Emily was in danger…

A SCANDALOUS MISTRESS

Juliet Landon

A move to Richmond was the fresh start Lady Amelie Chester needed to escape the rumours surrounding her husband's death. But scandal followed Amelie, and, unwittingly, she falsely confessed to an intimate relationship with Nicholas, Lord Elyot, heir to the Marquess of Sheen! Enchanted and intrigued, Nicholas was quick to take *every* advantage of the situation…

A WEALTHY WIDOW

Anne Herries

Elegant, beautiful and *inordinately* rich, Lady Arabella Marshall is used to fending off fortune-hunters' unwanted flattery – except now such attentions have become deadly! Lady Arabella is quite alone in the world, so she turns to the aloof and enigmatic Charles Hunter for protection. But, for safety's sake, Arabella cannot let her heart rule her head…

MILLS & BOON®

Live the emotion

HIST0607 LP

HISTORICAL ROMANCE™

LARGE PRINT

INNOCENCE AND IMPROPRIETY
Diane Gaston

Jameson Flynn is a man with a mission. Nothing will
knock him off course. Until one summer's evening in
Vauxhall Gardens, when a woman's song reminds him of
the world he left behind. Rose O'Keefe's beautiful voice
and earthy sensuality have made her a sensation. In such
dissolute company, how long can it be before her virtue
is compromised…?

ROGUE'S WIDOW, GENTLEMAN'S WIFE
Helen Dickson

Amanda O'Connell is in a scrape. If she doesn't find a
husband while she is in America, her father will marry her
off against her will. Then Christopher Claybourne – a dark,
mysterious rogue sentenced to death for murder – inspires
a plan. She'll marry him secretly and return home a widow.
But sometimes even the best laid plans fall apart…

HIGH SEAS TO HIGH SOCIETY
Sophia James

Asher Wellingham, Duke of Carisbrook, was captivated
by her! He had happened upon Lady Emma Seaton
swimming naked and, beyond her beauty, had seen the
deep curling scar on her thigh – a wound that could only
be the mark of a sword. Who was this woman? And what
lay behind her refined mask? High-born lady or artful
courtesan, Asher wanted to possess both!

MILLS & BOON®
Live the emotion

HIST0707 LP

HISTORICAL ROMANCE™

LARGE PRINT

A MOST UNCONVENTIONAL COURTSHIP
Louise Allen

Benedict Casper Chancellor, Earl of Blakeney, is the kind
of elegantly conservative English lord that Alessa despises.
The maddening man seems determined to wrest her away
from her life in beautiful Corfu. But the Earl hasn't
anticipated Alessa's propensity to get herself into a scrape.
Now, in order to rescue her, this highly conventional
Englishman will have to turn pirate!

A WORTHY GENTLEMAN
Anne Herries

Miss Sarah Hunter was delighted at the prospect of a season
in London – and at the opportunity to spend time with the
man who'd once saved her life! But Mr Elworthy was much
changed. Rumours and secrets tarnished his honourable
name, and the *ton* had began to wonder where the truth lay.
He found a staunch champion in Sarah – but as she defended
him she was inexorably drawn into the mystery…

SOLD AND SEDUCED
Michelle Styles

Lydia Veratia made one mistake – and now her freedom is
forfeit to the man who all Rome knows as the Sea Wolf. Sold
into marriage, the one thing over which she still has control is
her own desire. So when Fabius Aro offers her a wager – if she
doesn't plead for his kisses in the next seven days, she can have
her independence – Lydia thinks it will be easily won. But Aro
is a dangerously attractive man…

MILLS & BOON®

Live the emotion

HIST0807 LP

HISTORICAL ROMANCE™

LARGE PRINT

THE WICKED EARL
Margaret McPhee

The very proper Miss Langley does not know what she has done to encourage the attentions of a lord, only that they are most unwanted and very improper! So when a handsome stranger saves her from his clutches, Madeline is too relieved to suspect that her tall, dark defender may have a less than reputable reputation...

WORKING MAN, SOCIETY BRIDE
Mary Nichols

Well over six feet tall, with broad shoulders, he was the most good-looking man Lady Lucinda Vernley had ever seen. But with her family expecting her to make a good marriage, it wouldn't do to be fantasising about a man she had seen working on her father's estate... Myles Moorcroft certainly didn't dress like a gentleman, but by his manner there was something about him that had Lucy intrigued...

TRAITOR OR TEMPTRESS
Helen Dickson

Lorne McBryde can't abide the savage violence of the Highlands, and desperately seeks a means to escape. Her wilful streak is countered by her instinctive kindness – yet for Iain Monroe, Earl of Norwood, she will be marked forever by her family's betrayal. Kidnapped in the dead of night, Lorne is now in Iain's hands. She protests her innocence – but does her tempting beauty hide a treacherous spirit?

MILLS & BOON®

Live the emotion

HIST0907 LP